MW00626391

REDEMPTION

A DARK ROMANCE

Fragile Ties – Book Three

Jennifer Bene

Text copyright © 2020 Jennifer Bene

All Rights Reserved

No part of this book may be reproduced in any form or by any
electronic or mechanical means including information storage and
retrieval systems, without permission in writing from the author. The
only exception is by a reviewer, who may quote short excerpts in a
review.

This book is a work of fiction. Names, characters, places, and incidents
either are products of the author's imagination or are used fictitiously.
Any resemblance to actual persons, living or dead, events, or locales is
entirely coincidental.

ISBN (e-book): 978-1-946722-58-4

ISBN (paperback): 978-1-946722-59-1

Cover design by Laura Hidalgo. https://www.spellbindingdesign.com/

❀ Created with Vellum

This book is dedicated to two people who helped carry me through every difficult word to write in this series. Katie, who loved David from the first moment she saw past his rough exterior and who has always been Lianna and David's biggest cheerleader. And Livia, who quite literally held my hand from across the country and helped make this final book happen when I wasn't sure how to get out of bed. Without you both, David and Lianna would have never found their happily ever after, and their story would have never ended so beautifully.

Thank you for loving me… and my crazy characters.

For everyone who has followed the journey of Fragile Ties, thank you for your patience. I hope you enjoy the end. It's a wild ride.

ONE

Lianna

The chain rattled as David pulled it taut, stretching her arms before he locked the links together. It wasn't really uncomfortable, not *yet*, but the leather cuffs were already digging into her ankles, and now her wrists were feeling the strain too. In a matter of minutes, she'd pull on them no matter what logic said, and then they'd start to hurt despite the soft lining.

"How many times do I have to remind you to do what I tell you?" David asked, tracing a finger lightly up her side, gentle until he grabbed her nipple between thumb and forefinger and pinched hard. She bucked, angling her head back as she whined and bit down on her lip. "Answer me, Lianna."

"I don't know," she whimpered, the pain amplifying as he twisted the trapped bud, sending scattered shocks through her nerve endings. "Fuck, please, David…"

He released her nipple to grab hold of her face, hand cupped under her jaw so his fingers could dig into her cheeks. Tawny brown eyes stared down at her as he tilted his head. "Is it complicated to obey me? You're a smart girl, so... I don't think it should be this hard."

"I'm not a puppet," she ground out, glaring at him.

"Oh, but you *are* mine. Pretty strings or not." He smirked, a lopsided smile that made him too damn tempting. "Of course, I much prefer you in chains. Don't I, angel?"

Pushing her face to the side, he let go and plucked at the chain holding one of her wrists. She didn't say anything in response, just balled her hands into fists as she turned to look at him again. David was still looming over her, the smirk lingering he was enjoying this — which he definitely was.

"I'll ask again, since you seem to be having trouble listening today." David stood, moving to the dresser to grab the crop, his perfectly carved chest and abs taunting her as he slapped the crop against his palm. "How many times do I need to remind you to obey?"

"This isn't going to get you what you want, David. It never works and—" She yelped as the crop landed sharply on her thigh, a stunning streak of pain that made her clench her teeth to bite back the cry.

"Oh, I think it works quite well." He chuckled low, trailing the crop over the fresh welt on her thigh, up over her hip, her stomach, and then he rested the little tip on her breast. "Want to try and answer me again?"

"Fuck off," she growled, trying to prepare for the pain, but as the leather popped against her nipple she still whined through her teeth, jerking against the cuffs, making the chains rattle. A second snap landed on her other breast, and she arched off the bed. "David, please——"

"God... you know how much I love the way you look in chains." The crop slid down, between her thighs, and he shifted his hold to stroke the leather through her folds. "And the fucking sounds you make..."

She stiffened, thighs straining to pull together, to protect herself, but it was impossible with how wide the chains held her apart. At his mercy, vulnerable again.

"And look at that"—a quiet, dark laugh interrupted him as he stared between her thighs—"you're already wet."

"That's not me," she snapped, but she couldn't take her eyes off the sight of the leather moving back and forth between her legs. The texture of it sliding through the damning wetness, rubbing against her clit with each shift of his hand as he played her all too well.

"Oh, I know that. This is all me, angel." David grinned and removed the crop, landing it hard across both thighs. She cried out, unable to bite it back with the way her body jolted from the teasing pleasure into the bright strike of pain. "Is that it? Do you do this shit just to push me? Just so you can get punished, make me hurt you? Because I can see you like it, Lianna. You've already soaked my crop."

There was no way to answer that. No *good* way to answer that, so she just pressed her lips together, felt that delirious hum buzzing through her veins as the pain faded into a dull ache and left behind a dizzying rush.

This was fucked up.

They were fucked up.

And the fact that she was chained down again, spread wide for him to torment, was just further evidence of it.

David didn't bother pushing her to answer, he just landed another stripe of the crop below the first. Both thighs. She yanked against the cuffs, hating herself for enjoying the way the leather dug in as she pulled, for the way her pussy squeezed around nothing as the buzz amplified inside her. Another strike, and then another and another until she was whimpering, arching off the bed as brilliant lines of pain marked her thighs from hip to knee.

"Fuck!" she cried out as he suddenly shoved two fingers inside her, immediately adding a third as he leaned over her and groaned.

"So wet." He pumped his fingers in and out, teasing her as she gasped for air and twisted as much as she could, but there was nowhere to go as he stretched her with each push of his fingers. "You can't lie to me, angel. I know you like this. You want it. You want more, don't you?"

"Stop," she whispered, clenching her eyes tight as he slid his fingers free to focus on her clit in damning swirls that pulled a moan past her lips despite her best efforts to stay silent.

"Mmm, I love it when you say that," he growled, forcing his fingers back in as she whined, hips rocking with the rough rhythm he set. "Beg me."

"No," she growled, opening her eyes to find his face just above hers, and then he kissed her. Hard. Teeth nipping her lips before he parted them to dip his tongue in and taste her, taking control with his fist in her hair so she couldn't turn away. Couldn't argue. Couldn't fight. All she could do was accept it, melting under him as he continued to move his fingers back and forth, occasionally slipping them free to rub her clit until she was moaning against his mouth. Desperate and needy, because he knew her body too well. He knew every inch of her. She nipped his lip back and he growled, nipping her back a little harder, a flicker of pain before he soothed it with another shattering kiss.

"Such a naughty girl," he whispered against her lips. "Taste."

His fingers were in her mouth before she could even react, the sweet tang of her pussy coating her tongue as he forced them to the back of her throat. She choked, gagged, but he didn't stop. He only eased back for a second before thrusting them again, smearing saliva and her own wetness on her chin — and all she could do was take it.

"Suck," he demanded, holding his fingers still so she could seal her lips around them and trace them with her tongue. A low groan rumbled in his chest as he stared down at her, eyes so much darker as his pupils dilated. "Fuck... I'm going to make it hurt, angel."

She nodded, breathless as he yanked his fingers free and dropped his pants. Then he was on top of her, capturing her mouth in one more brutal kiss before he broke it to look between her thighs.

"Go on, tell me you don't want it," he taunted, meeting her eyes with that small smirk tilting his lips.

"Please don't?" It was barely a whisper, and it didn't mean anything as he groaned and lined up, stroking the head of his cock through her folds, brushing her clit, which only made her arch.

"Again," he growled, bracing one arm beside her ribs as he stared down into her eyes. Close enough to feel him exhale.

"Don't," she repeated, and he thrust hard, filling her in an instant, and there was no chance she could have bit back the moan. He stretched her perfectly, slammed deep on the next thrust and sent her head spinning as she yanked on the cuffs. Trying to reach for him, to hold on as he started to move. No easing in, no gentle caresses, he just growled and grabbed a fistful of her hair before he drove inside again.

"Fuck, yes," he groaned as he claimed her. "You're mine, angel. All mine."

It was pointless to fight it. She nodded, gasped as he drove deep again. "Yesss..."

"That's right… and you love it when I make you take it." His words were pushing her to the edge faster than the delirious friction he was building between her thighs. All she could do was nod, accept it as he caught her lips in another kiss, sealed together as his strokes brought her to the edge and shoved her off without warning.

The orgasm crashed over her like a tidal wave, the riptide dragging her under as she moaned and broke the kiss, delirious with that first obliterating rush of ecstasy. Everything flashed bright, wicked and perfect, and then he bit down on her shoulder. Yanking her back to earth with a sharp ache that turned her cries into agonized pleasure.

"God, yes, again," he urged as he bit down, overlapping the marks he'd already left behind as he fucked her into the mattress. The chains rattled with each thrust, the bed rocking as a sweet ache took up residence between her thighs and she whined. "You're so perfect," he mumbled against her shoulder as he kissed a path over the painful spot he'd left behind, moving up her throat, and he tightened his hold in her hair to bend her head back sharply. He continued to kiss his way up so he could nip just under her jaw.

"Not perfect," she panted, unable to do anything as she stared at the headboard, caught in his control and powerless.

Just how she liked it.

"Don't argue with me, angel," he growled and released her hair, pushing himself up as he stared down at her. Circling his hips, he teased her by barely moving. Letting his hard cock stroke every inch of her pussy, but without the bone-melting impact of his thrusts. "I can drag this out. I can get you to the edge again"—he pinched her nipple, instantly twisting it to send a sharp pain sparkling out—"and just hold you there. I can wait until you're begging me to make you come."

"No!" Pulling on the cuffs, she lifted her hips to meet him, and he tightened his hold on her tortured bud, drawing a keening whine past her teeth as she lifted from the bed. "Please, please, please…"

"You beg so well, angel. Think you can be a good girl for me?"

"That depends," she said, barely able to focus as he released her nipple, only to take hold of the other and send a fresh spike of pain buzzing through her nerves.

"On what?" he asked, and she opened her eyes to see him grinning as she squirmed on his cock. David thrust deep, holding still, pressed skin to skin, and she could only whimper as he let go of her nipple and sent her head swimming once more. "Come on, angel," he purred. "Tell me why you won't just be a good girl for me… Tell me, and I'll make you come over and over."

Lianna grinned, unable to fight it as she rolled her hips against him. "It depends."

"That's it," he said, almost laughing as he leaned back to release the cuff on her right ankle, and then he twisted to repeat it on the other side. She just bit down on her lip, watching as his hard muscles moved under his skin, and then she moaned as he grabbed her thighs and bent her knees toward her shoulders, spreading her just a little wider. "This what you want?"

"Yes, please," she begged, whimpering as he thrust back in and circled his hips against her.

Hooking her legs over his shoulders, David leaned forward, forcing her to bend as he pulled back and pushed in slowly. "I'm going to make it so you feel me all day tomorrow, angel."

"Yes, please." She was nodding, pulling at the cuffs still around her wrists, trying to shift her hips against him to bring back that delirious friction, but he only gave her a shallow, gentle thrust. "Please," she begged again, and he groaned.

"Not fair, angel. You know how much I love to hear you beg." He strained her farther, knees touching her shoulders as he rocked against her. "I like to hear you scream, and cry, and fall apart under me… You want that? You want me to make it hurt?"

"Yes!" she shouted, whining as she squeezed his cock inside her, desperate and needy.

"Say it," he growled, jaw tensing as she lifted her hips to take him in again.

"I want you to hurt me," she whispered, a blush burning her cheeks as she said it, but it was worth it when he drove in deep, hard.

Muttering curses, he planted his hands on the bed and forced her to take every brutal thrust, every deliciously ruthless plunge that had her aching deep inside in the best of ways.

"David!" she cried out, moaning along with him as he fucked her mercilessly. Hard, fast, he spiraled her back to the edge in a breath, leaving her teetering on that vicious cusp between the perfect ache of his cock hitting the place inside that took her breath away, and the mind-blowing, glittery horizon that felt so close.

"Come on, angel," he panted. "You're gonna fucking take it and come for me."

Pain blurred into pleasure, the ache between her thighs fading into a buzzing hum under her skin as she stole little gasps of air on quiet moans. Reveling in the way he groaned, losing control above her as their skin came together in fierce claps, she whined and pulled on the cuffs as everything inside her tensed. Taut and shivering as he thrust hard again and again and again, she cried out something — his name, or a plea, or a random mumble of letters — it didn't matter as the golden strand inside her snapped and she came.

Fierce bliss raced through her, a chaotic wash of pure pleasure that shattered all of the tension in a glorious *crash*. It was perfect, wiping out everything except for the incredible feeling of him surging inside her again and again until he locked up and she felt every twitch of his cock, each pulse as he came within her.

"Fuck, Lianna…" he groaned, choked on the words, hips pressing her hard into the bed as she tried to remember how to breathe.

Everything was floating, a perfect hum that seemed to vibrate every cell from the top of her head to the tips of her toes, and she weakly pulled at the cuffs because she'd forgotten they were there until she'd tried to wrap her arms around him. It made her smile, a soft laugh escaping past her lips, and David looked down at her with a sly smile.

"What's so funny, angel?"

"Forgot about the cuffs," she answered, almost breathless as he chuckled. Keeping himself buried inside her, he moved her legs off his shoulders and leaned forward to release her wrists. Her hips ached in a fantastic way, a perfect hurt to match the almost bruised feeling inside. As soon as she was free, she reached up, sliding her hands up his chest to rest on either side of his head. "You weren't kidding, baby. I'm going to feel that tomorrow for sure."

"That's right," he growled and leaned down to capture her mouth, another fierce kiss as he kept them linked, rocking his hips against hers as they both came down. Exhaustion teased at her, and she knew he had to be even more tired. Nipping his lip, she smiled when he did it right back.

"I love you," she whispered against his mouth, and he let his weight settle over her as he wrapped his arms under her shoulders. Surrounded by him, she wanted to freeze this moment and live in it forever. Away from the rest of the world and the chaos of their lives.

It was perfect, and only made more so when he kissed her again and said, "I love you too, angel."

After another long kiss, he slowly slid from her, and she whined because she didn't want the moment to end. Didn't want reality to come back, but as soon as he dropped to the bed beside her, he had her in his arms again. Yanked tight against his hard chest as he buried his face in her hair and breathed deep.

"You okay?" he asked, barely a whisper, and she smiled as she wrapped her arms over his and hugged him as much as she could.

"I'm amazing, or did you miss the orgasms?" She laughed, turning her head so she could see him. That shadow was back in his expression, the one that kept popping up whenever the real world reared its ugly head. Then it disappeared, wiped away with a wicked grin before he kissed her.

"Oh, I noticed. Hard to miss it when you're squeezing my cock like a vise." Another kiss and a nip, and then he chuckled. "So, you got what you wanted after being such a naughty girl, didn't—"

"Oh my God, David. I was going to come help you, *you* were just impatient." She laughed when he hugged her hard.

"When I tell you to come help me, I mean right then, angel." A sinful growl buzzed against her ear, and she squeezed her thighs together, reveling in the dull ache he'd left behind. "You should listen."

"Hate to break it to you, but *this* isn't exactly a deterrent," she said through another laugh, but it was cut short when he forced his hand between her thighs, cupping her pussy and sending a shiver through her.

"You like it when I fuck you hard, don't you? When I make your cunt hurt for days and use you again when I want to anyway." He nipped her neck, sliding three fingers into the soaked mess they'd made.

"Yes," she purred, arching and spreading her legs to make it easier for him. It hurt in a good way, especially as he hooked his fingers inside her and held on. "Fuck…"

"Next time I tell you to come and help me hang pictures, I want you to remember that I mean *now*. Not when you decide it's convenient," he rumbled, and she shifted her hips, twitching in his grip.

"Or what?" she taunted, and he mashed the heel of his hand against her clit, rough and way too tempting as tired as she knew they both were.

"Or next time I'll chain you face down and whip your ass before I fuck it." He bit down on her shoulder, the one he hadn't marked already, waiting until she wriggled and whined before he released her. "And remember, angel. Lube is a gift… I don't have to use it."

"Fuck," she whispered, tensing in his arms as she imagined the pain, but her body still squeezed his fingers inside as he chuckled against her ear.

"That's right." He kissed the bite marks he'd just made then slid his fingers out of her to bring them to her lips.

She sucked them in, tasting the mix of them as he groaned behind her. "So, be a good girl for me."

Lianna nodded with his fingers still stroking over her tongue, little murmurs escaping past her lips as she tried to fight the dark temptation he'd laid out for her. It would hurt, she knew that, but more than a little part of her wanted it.

Finally, he pulled his fingers free and reached back to turn off the light. As soon as the covers were pulled up, he wrapped his arm over her again, tugging her tight to his front. "Time to sleep, angel."

"Okay," she whispered, still wound up from the visual he'd planted in her head. Idly, she reached up and toyed with the chain, listening to it clatter softly before she smiled and settled into the warmth of his body.

They were fucked up, but they were perfect.

She just had to hope he'd remember that when they landed in France.

TWO

David
___

Thirty thousand feet in the air, it seemed like everyone was more comfortable in the first-class cabin than him. The lights were dimmed, and although he couldn't see anyone except Lianna, he figured all the other passengers were still sleeping on the long fucking flight to France.

Nine hours on a plane to hell, but at least it was nine hours in luxury.

The seats were incredibly comfortable, and they converted into a flat bed at the push of a button. David had tried it, and he'd even finished off a few of glasses of wine with their first meal to try and sleep... but he'd barely napped. Lianna had told him that with the time change they'd arrive in the morning in France, and it would be best if he slept while they flew, which made sense.

He just couldn't do it.

Everything about the first-class cabin made him uncomfortable. The obvious luxury of it, the other passengers, the over-the-top service from the flight attendants, all of it screamed one thing — *you don't belong here.* And he didn't. His dad had been blue collar even before everything went to shit, and after that, he'd only done odd jobs to try and make ends meet. David had never even dreamed of flying first class anywhere, much less to Europe.

If this was a vacation, simply him and Lianna escaping somewhere together… maybe he'd be enjoying it. Maybe he wouldn't feel like he'd swallowed a lead ball that was just sitting in his stomach, weighing him down, reminding him of exactly how different he was to everyone around him.

Including Lianna.

Glancing over the little wall that separated their seats, he saw she was still asleep. Perfectly relaxed. It would be a dick move to wake her just because he was bored. Sighing, he reached forward to fidget with his backpack again. Pulling it into his lap, David unzipped the front pouch and checked for the hundredth time that his surprise was still there.

"Early bird?" the flight attendant asked quietly, smiling at him as she paused near his seat.

"Flying isn't really my thing," he answered.

"Ah, well, first class isn't so bad." Glancing across the cabin at the other passengers, she eventually turned her gaze back to him. "Would you like some coffee? We've got almost an hour until we begin our descent."

"That would be great. Thanks." Offering a polite smile, he dropped his bag to the floor and waited for her to walk away before he checked on Lianna again. They were in the center of the plane, the only place the first-class seats were side by side, and he was grateful for that, but he would have preferred being right next to her. Able to touch her, to talk to her more easily.

Hell, for the last week he'd had an ongoing fantasy at work that he'd join Lianna in the mile-high club… but that wasn't possible. There weren't enough passengers in first class to sneak away unnoticed, and the lavatory was right by the flight attendants.

No plane sex for him.

Just random movies on the little screen, drinks, snacks, and boredom.

Grabbing the headphones, David tried again to focus on the movie he'd chosen, but his mind kept drifting back to Lianna. The night before the flight, she'd told him to do whatever he wanted with her. That wicked little smile of hers had been all challenge, and he'd been hard before he even had her naked — but he knew why she'd done it. Neither of them knew what the Faure estate would be like, or if they'd get to have any fun at all while they were there, they just knew he was going to hate it.

But when he'd carried her to their bedroom, he'd pushed all thoughts of Jean-Luc and the other bastards out of his head, because he'd known exactly what he wanted.

And thinking about it on the goddamn airplane wasn't helping.

Shifting in his seat, he tried to ignore the growing erection that was doing its best to make his next interaction with the flight attendant awkward as fuck. He should just focus on the movie, wait for Lianna to wake up, and enjoy the coffee.

Which would be easier if he could get the damn images of her out of his head. The sight of her spread out and chained down, just like she'd been in the cell, but on a real bed instead of a cheap mattress and concrete. On *their* bed. It was worse than a wet dream because he'd had her in both places. Heard the chains clatter with each thrust of his cock slamming into her, and the fact that this time she'd wanted it — *craved* it, even as she played their little game of 'no' — only made the distraction that much worse.

She was perfect, absolutely perfect, and every breath he took felt like walking a tightrope of just when he'd finally fuck it up. Probably today.

Definitely this week.

Groaning, he grabbed the blanket off the floor and piled it in his lap, covering the hard-on just before the flight attendant appeared in the narrow doorway with his coffee.

"Thanks," he said, pulling the table out so she could set it down.

"I brought some creamer and a few sugars, but if you need more just ask. Okay?" She smiled, and he nodded at her as she went to check on the other passengers.

After he'd prepped the coffee the way he liked it, it was still boiling hot when he took the first sip, and so he set it down and checked on Lianna again. She'd shifted, her face angled toward him like she knew he was thinking about her, about her soft lips and exactly how they'd feel wrapped around his—

Fuck. Stop it.

Adjusting himself under the blanket, he gritted his teeth and stared at the little screen, willing himself to stop fantasizing about her. The last thing he needed was to be off his game when they landed. As soon as they arrived at the Faure Estate, he had to be perfect. He had to keep her safe… while staying out of her way.

He'd promised Lianna that he wouldn't stand between her and her family, and he'd keep that promise, but he wouldn't leave her alone. He wouldn't leave her vulnerable.

As he finished his coffee, it was a good thing that his mind flipped back to focusing on Jean-Luc's bullshit because it killed the erection in his pants and gave him time to mentally prepare to face the man again. Sure, his stomach was in knots, and he was tense as fuck, but at least he wasn't lost in fantasy anymore.

The lights in the cabin slowly brightened and David pulled off his headphones, looking around to see the flight attendants getting ready for breakfast. *Finally.* Reaching over the wall dividing them, he shook Lianna gently by the shoulder.

"Hey, angel, it's time to wake up," he said softly, loving the way her face scrunched up just before she hid it against the thin little pillow. "I've got a surprise for you if you wake up."

"Surprise?" she asked, her voice stained with sleep, but her beautiful eyes opened as she smiled up at him. "What kind of surprise?"

"Sit up and I'll give it to you," he replied, leaning down to grab his backpack and remove the item.

Lianna yawned, stretching as she sat up and adjusted the seat into the right position. She was in a navy sweater that hugged her curves as she twisted, and he immediately pictured Jean-Luc's face instead of her body to shut down any urges.

"You know, baby," she whispered, looking over at him with a devious grin that was *not* helping his self-control. "I don't think the flight attendants will be okay with your kind of surprises."

"Naughty girl." Shaking his head, he turned the gift over in his hands and then met her eyes again. "It's not that kind of surprise, no matter how much I'd like to join the mile-high club with you."

Laughing quietly, Lianna rolled her eyes. "Not happening."

"Trust me, I know." Sighing, he leaned closer to her. "Look, I didn't want to wake you up earlier, but we're going to land soon, and I wanted to give you this while it was still just you and me. Before we get around all of them. And since midnight happened sometime while we were flying, it's officially October fourth, so... happy birthday." He passed the long, narrow box over the dividing wall, a little frustrated that the ribbon was bent, and the wrapping paper scuffed, from being in his bag, but the excited look on her face showed him she didn't care.

"Oh my God, David. Seriously?" Taking the little gift, she pulled the ribbon free and tore the paper.

"It's not much, but I just wanted to be the first one to tell you happy birthday."

"I can't believe you remembered with everything going on."

"You really think I'd forget your birthday, Lianna? I know everything about you." He grinned when she looked over at him with a slight shake of her head, but then she was shoving the paper into her lap and working the top half of the box free.

"It's beautiful!" she said, a little too loudly in the quiet plane, just before she leaned over the wall and pulled him into a kiss. He wanted to grab her, to take control of the kiss and make sure she remembered exactly what drew them to each other, but other passengers were already watching them, so he just nipped her lip before he leaned back with a smile.

"I'm glad you like it, angel. I know it isn't—"

"Oh, shut up, I love it!" Lifting the necklace out of the box, she dangled it in front of her face, catching the small charm on the end so it would stop spinning.

"Celebrating something?" the flight attendant asked, smiling at them as she put his breakfast on his tray.

"It's my birthday," Lianna answered, still grinning like he'd given her diamonds or something much nicer than a simple silver necklace.

"And he remembered!" the woman replied, laughing a little. "And you're going to France together. What a good guy! My husband never remembers my birthday, and we've been married twelve years."

"He is a good guy," Lianna replied, looking over at him, and even though he should have probably corrected that statement, he let it go.

"Well, happy birthday, and I hope you both enjoy your vacation!" Waving a little, the flight attendant returned to delivering more meals, and David went back to watching Lianna study the necklace.

"You put 'I love you' on it," she said softly, flipping over the small silver heart.

"I do love you," he said, clearing his throat as he sat up straighter. "Just wanted you to remember that if I happen to fuck up this week."

Sighing, she stared at him like he was an idiot — which wasn't exactly wrong. He'd almost lost her by being a complete and utter idiot when it came to her family.

"I'm going to do my best not to fuck up," David added, and she rolled her eyes.

"I'm sure you will." Unclasping the necklace, Lianna leaned forward, her blonde hair tumbling over her shoulder as she reached behind her neck to hook it back together. A second later, she sat up and pulled her hair free, letting the little heart charm rest above the neckline of her sweater. It looked beautiful against her skin, and watching her reach up to play with it, flipping it over to see the words he'd had the store engrave, made him feel a little better about everything.

"I mean it, Lianna. I told you that you're all I care about. I don't like them, and I'm not going to lie to you and say that I think I could learn to like them… but I'm not going to get in the way this week."

Lianna looked over at him, her brows furrowing just a little, and he knew it was doubt. She didn't believe he was going to be able to handle being around her family. Hell, she'd tried several times during the past week to convince him to just stay in New York and keep working on Harry's latest project — and he didn't blame her. It wasn't like he had a good track record when it came to dealing with the Faure family. Actually… it was pretty fucking terrible, but he'd do anything for her. He would go through anything for her.

Even walk into Hell.

"I really love this necklace, baby," she said, and he sighed. Slapping a smile on his face, he watched her touching his gift as her breakfast arrived. As long as she wore that, she'd remember him, remember what they had together.

And if it also served as a way to mark her as his around that fucking family… well, that was just a bonus.

"I'm glad. I know it's not much, but—"

"You really think I care about that?" she asked, sounding a little edgy. "I love it because *you* gave it to me. Because you remembered my birthday and obviously snuck it into your bag so you could surprise me." The irritation faded from her voice as she smiled, leaning close again. "You really can be incredibly sweet when you try, David."

"Only with you, angel," he answered, closing the gap between them to kiss her, and this time he didn't hesitate to lick at the seam of her lips, parting them so he could taste her. He just needed to feel their connection once more before they landed.

A soft, hummed moan escaped her as he slid his fingers into her hair, only tugging a little, just enough to earn a quiet groan before she broke the kiss and looked at him with heated eyes. "That's not fair."

"Nothing about this is fair, angel," he replied with a grin, and she leaned back from him, blowing out a breath as she looked over her food.

"How much longer until we land?" She glanced over at him as she picked up her fork to poke at the meal.

"The flight attendant said we'd be landing in Nice in about an hour."

Lianna grinned, stifling a laugh. "It's pronounced *Neess*, baby. Not *nice*."

Rolling his eyes, he muttered about the bullshit French language as he sat back in his seat to look at the overly fancy breakfast.

"You'll get it in no time. I promise."

"Not fucking likely," he grumbled, shoving a bite of melon into his mouth to keep from insulting the language, or the country, or the stupid trip. It was good practice though. He had a feeling he'd be biting his tongue more than a few times over the next week.

The process through customs was surprisingly smooth. He'd been expecting inspections, some kind of intense interview, but it had been easy. Showing his passport to the man in the booth, Lianna answered that they were visiting her family, and they were waved through to get their bags.

"Jean-Luc said he would have someone here for us," Lianna said as they followed the line of other passengers heading toward the pick-up area.

"Great," he replied, trying not to sound bitter as he hefted his backpack higher on his shoulder. When they stepped out of the hallway, he'd been looking for a guy in a suit with a sign that said 'Mercier' or something like that… but that wasn't what waited for them.

It was a small crowd, holding up big poster-sized signs that said 'Welcome Lianna!' and 'Happy Birthday!' as they cheered and waved at her from behind the metal railing separating arriving passengers from the people waiting.

"Oh my God!" Lianna shouted, her smile spreading as she let out a laugh. "I can't believe you all came here!"

"Do you really think we'd miss the chance to welcome you properly?" Jean-Luc asked, tilting his head toward the opening in the railing with a broad smile. "Come, everyone wants to meet you."

David followed her as she dragged her suitcase toward them, and as soon as she passed the railing, Lianna was immediately enveloped by the Faure family. They hugged her, cheered her name, everyone talking over each other in a rapid mix of English and French. All smiles, they looked like a normal family welcoming someone home.

Bullshit.

Leaning against the railing, he studied each of them, trying to place them in his mind. He recognized many of their faces from the photographs Jean-Luc had sent to Lianna, but the names of the younger generation were fuzzy. The only one he knew for sure was Rémi, the future head of the family. And, of course, Jean-Luc and his wife Cécile.

All four of Jean-Luc's children were there, as well as Rémi's wife and their twins, and Lianna was instantly drawn to the chubby-cheeked toddlers, cooing and talking to them as she took one of their hands. She blended in with the Faures effortlessly. It was like they'd known each other for years, and he hated how easy it seemed to be for her.

Suck it up, David. You're not going to fuck up this early.

One of Jean-Luc's daughters turned away from the group to look at him. "You're David, right?"

"Yeah," he replied, stiffening when she quickly closed the gap between them to pull him into a hug, pressing a kiss to each of his cheeks as he stood frozen.

"We're so glad you could come!" she cheered. "I'm Emilie."

"Hi." Clearing his throat, he tried to smile a little as the dark-haired woman just stared at him, looking sincerely happy to have him there.

"Yes, we're very glad you could join Lianna this week," Jean-Luc said, but David didn't believe that for a minute. Turning toward his family, he pointed at each of them in turn. "This is my wife, Cécile. Our eldest son, Rémi, and his wife Amanda. Their children Gabriel and Zoé. And my other children Anaelle, Mathieu, and of course, Emilie."

"Nice to meet you," David forced out, holding onto his smile even though a muscle in his jaw twitched from the effort. Lianna stepped back to hook her arm through his, squeezing it, and he felt a tiny bit better with her by his side.

"Well, we can all talk once we're back home!" Cécile said, waving toward the exit. "*Allons y!*"

"Come on, baby," Lianna whispered, pressing a kiss to his shoulder as Jean-Luc took her suitcase in hand. "You're doing great."

"Thanks," he muttered, following the family as they led the way out of the airport. He'd hoped to have some time on the ground to prepare for meeting them, but he should have known Jean-Luc wouldn't allow him even that.

No, the man was already doing his best to woo Lianna into their family, and David was completely outnumbered.

Shifting to take Lianna's hand in his, he squeezed tightly, focusing on her perfect blue eyes and her warm smile as she looked up at him. "I love you," he whispered, needing to say it aloud, to remind himself of why he was doing this.

"I love you, too, baby," she replied, leaning up to kiss his cheek, and he trailed his gaze over the necklace, trying to remind himself that this was just a week.

Just a week in Hell, and then they'd be back home. Alone. Together.

I can do this.

THREE

Lianna

The views of the Cote d'Azur had been tempting as they drove away from the airport, heading toward Provence where Jean-Luc's family lived. Her face must have shown what she was thinking, because Cécile had promised to bring them back to enjoy the shopping in Nice and see the beaches, even though the ocean would likely be too cold for a dip.

In the back row of the SUV, she'd kept David's hand in hers the entire time, squeezing whenever she felt him grow tense. He'd been completely silent since the airport, and she knew he was uncomfortable. This was his personal nightmare, but the fact that he was doing this for her only made her love him more.

He's trying, and that's all I can ask.

Everything would have gone smoother if they'd had the drive to the estate to talk, to spend some time together, but she hadn't known Jean-Luc was going to show up. Having the entire family waiting for them had been a huge surprise, and she'd been so overwhelmed by meeting all of them that it had taken her too long to rescue David from the fringes of the group. It would have been better if Jean-Luc had just sent a driver like she'd expected... but everyone had seemed so excited to meet her. They'd hugged her, wished her a happy birthday, and it was almost like they saw her as family already — which felt both odd and wonderful at the same time.

At least the drive hadn't become awkward. The countryside of France was breathtaking, and she hoped David was enjoying it too. His eyes stayed glued out the window at the rolling hills while she'd talked with Cécile and Jean-Luc. It wasn't like they discussed anything serious. Their conversation was mostly about the flight and the various vineyards and farms they passed on the forty-minute drive to their estate. But when it came into view, even David sat up straight.

The high, stone walls surrounding the ornate gate were impressive, and Cécile turned back to smile at her. "I can't wait to show you our home, Lianna!"

"We live in the main house, but there are a few other buildings on the property," Jean-Luc added as the gate opened and they led the small caravan up the drive. Rémi and his wife and kids were behind them in another SUV, and the rest of her cousins brought up the rear in a third one. Each vehicle had their own driver, and Lianna had no doubt that each man was armed. Their serious expressions had made it clear they were protection of some kind — which only proved David's concerns about her family further.

But they had nothing to worry about on the estate.

"We have a room prepared for you and David in the main house, but if you'd like to be in the guest house, I'm sure—"

"We're happy wherever you put us," Lianna replied, smiling apologetically for cutting Cécile off. "I promise."

"We are all so happy you've come to visit. The children have been looking forward to it since Jean-Luc first mentioned it." Cécile reached over to squeeze her husband's arm, and Jean-Luc looked over at her with a face that only showed love.

They're my family. My aunt and uncle.

The words felt so foreign in her head. Weird. But she was quickly distracted again as the main house came into view. It was huge, a beautiful stone façade that looked so natural in the lush greenery of the Provence countryside.

"Wow," she whispered, leaning between Jean-Luc and Cécile's seats to see better. "This is gorgeous."

"Thank you, Lianna," Jean-Luc replied, turning to smile at her before he faced front again.

The large, circular drive in front of the house had more than enough room for the trio of cars to pull up and stop, and as soon as the car halted, their driver immediately got out, walking around to open Cécile's door instead of Jean-Luc's. It was a small gesture, but Lianna couldn't help but smile as Jean-Luc let himself out of the car, holding it open for her to exit between the seats.

"Come, come, *mon oisillon*," Jean-Luc said, taking her hand to help her down. The house was sprawling, two stories tall, and another smaller house was situated a little behind it to the left.

David's hand slid into hers, pulling her attention back to him, and she squeezed tightly as Jean-Luc approached Cécile.

"It's beautiful, isn't it?" she asked, and David nodded stiffly, eyes moving over the huge home and the others as they gathered at the foot of the steps. His back was rigid, his jaw set firmly, and she leaned up to kiss his cheek again before she whispered in his ear. "I'm right here, baby."

"Just don't let him separate us," David replied, his intense gaze meeting hers, and she squeezed his hand more firmly as he added, "Please."

Lianna couldn't fight the grin that spread over her lips as he actually said *please* to her, but she didn't rub it in. "I promise."

"Good," he said, tilting his head toward the entrance where her family was gathered. "They're waiting for you."

"For *us*," she corrected, but he let out a huff under his breath, and she knew he didn't believe that for a second. Approaching the group, she smiled for both of them, gesturing with her free hand. "This is so beautiful! It must be amazing to live here all the time."

"It's okay," Emilie answered, shrugging. "It would be better if we weren't so *far* from everything."

"Emilie," Rémi chastised, rolling his eyes at his sister as he shifted Gabriel on his hip. "What my sister meant to say is *thank you*, and we love our home also. It's been in the family for generations, and my father has done quite a bit with the land."

"Oh, really?" she asked, glancing at Jean-Luc. "Like what?"

"Nothing much, but all of these are things we can discuss *inside*," Jean-Luc replied, smiling at his family as he waved everyone toward the front door, where another man in a suit was already holding it open. As everyone headed in, speaking in rapid French to each other, David hesitated.

"What is it, baby?" she asked, but David just took a slow breath and shook his head.

"Nothing." Tightening his grip on her hand, he started up the steps with her. When they stepped inside, she looked up at him to find his jaw clenched tight as he looked around.

Jean-Luc's home was immaculate. Tiles worn smooth by time covered the floor, but they were spotless. The large foyer branched off into numerous rooms, with a staircase leading up to the second floor at the far end of it. Everything was a quiet statement of wealth, from the art on the walls to the obviously antique pieces of furniture she could see — and she knew David hated it.

She could almost hear him describing the *blood money* that paid for all of it.

The items inside, the estate surrounding the house, and each of the silent men in suits that lurked at the fringes of the family's bustling conversation were the result of the Faure family's dark past — but Jean-Luc had assured her those days were done. They were moving forward, doing things in a new way, and regardless... this was her family.

The only family she had left, and she wanted to get to know them.

"*Pardon*," one of the guards said as two men came in the door behind them, forcing her and David to shift to the side so they could bring in their luggage before shutting the door.

"*Merci*," Lianna replied, smiling at them, and the man nodded at her before he helped the other one line up their bags to one side, waiting for their next orders like soldiers.

"Lianna, I can't wait to show you the view from the terrace!" Emilie said, stepping away from her siblings to face them.

"We've actually had lunch prepared on the terrace, and the view really is lovely," Cécile added.

"After lunch we can give you a tour. Do you like horses?" Anaelle asked, looking over at her.

"I don't think we're going to have time for her to see the horses today," Rémi said, giving his sister a look.

"How about we let Lianna and David settle into their room, and then they'll come down and join us for lunch." Jean-Luc stepped forward, taking control of the room with an apologetic smile. "I'm sure you're a little overwhelmed and would like to freshen up before we all eat. We'll be out on the terrace when you're ready."

"It's just through there," Cécile said, pointing at the hall that went alongside the wide staircase. "Phillipe and Tomás will help you up to your room. No rush to join us, we'll start lunch on our own so you won't have to hurry."

"Thank you." Lianna gave everyone a quick wave as the large family moved down the hallway, but Jean-Luc stayed back with her and David.

"I apologize. All of my children want to get to know you, and I don't think they realize just how overwhelming they can be." Chuckling, he spread his hands a little. "Cécile and I have been outnumbered by them for years, so we're familiar with the feeling."

"They're very sweet," Lianna said, smiling as she felt David's grip on her hand turn into a vise. "I definitely feel welcome."

"That is all we'd hoped to do, *mon oisillon*." Taking a few steps backward, Jean-Luc gestured at the staircase. "As Cécile said, please take your time upstairs. You can join us at the table when you're ready."

"We appreciate it," she answered, trying to flex her fingers as Jean-Luc turned and disappeared down the hall, but David wouldn't let go.

"Follow, please," one of the guards said, his English somewhat stilted, as he lifted her suitcase with David's backpack over his shoulder and led them upstairs.

David

"How are you doing?" Lianna asked as she hung up clothes in the closet.

"I'm fine," he answered, moving more of their things into the adjoining bathroom. She'd brought several bags of *stuff*. Make-up and products and hair crap, while he only had one small toiletry bag with everything he needed.

"Don't lie to me." She had her arms crossed when he turned around, body braced against the doorframe of the bathroom so he couldn't move past without moving *her*.

"I *am* fine, Lianna. I'm still glad that I came with you." Gesturing out the door, he sighed. "Can I finish moving all your shit in here?"

"You don't have to lie to me, David. I know how you feel about them, and I appreciate—"

"Stop." Catching her arm, he yanked her back against him when she tried to walk away, locking her against his chest. "If I have a problem, I'll tell you. But if you call me a liar again, I'm gonna light your ass up. Got it?"

Wide blue eyes stared up at him for a moment, and he loved the way her breathing picked up. He loved the way she responded to him, the way she melted against him even though she was annoyed. "I got it," she whispered.

"Good girl." Leaning down, he kissed her hard, taking control as he pressed her back against the doorframe.

This is what he'd wanted to do on the plane.

Reaching between her legs, he stroked over her pants, fighting a grin when a quiet moan slipped past her lips as he found her clit. "You still sore, angel?"

"Yes," she panted, kissing him again as her hips pressed forward, urging him on.

"Good. That means this will hurt." Grabbing her thighs, he picked her up, sliding her up the bit of wall beside the bathroom door until he could wrap her legs around his waist. Pulling away from the wall, he walked them over to the bed, dropping her on it, but just as he climbed between her legs, she sat up and pushed at his chest.

"No way. We *cannot* do this right now."

"I'm pretty sure we can." Pointing down at the growing erection tenting the front of his pants, he smiled a little and pushed her back to the bed. "Be a good girl for me, Lianna."

"David…" Groaning, she squirmed under him as he shoved her sweater up, licking and kissing his way up her ribs. "Stop, seriously. We have to go downstairs."

"They told us to take our time," he mumbled against her skin, biting her nipple through the thin covering of her bra. Another sweet whine left her, but then she shoved at his shoulders, scooting back on the bed to sit up.

"Stop, stop, stop. They're waiting for us! Come on, we can do this later." Flipping around, Lianna climbed off the other side of the bed while he rolled onto his back with a sigh.

"I don't think they'd notice if we took another ten minutes to—"

"Since when do you *ever* finish with me in ten minutes?" Lianna laughed, grinning wickedly at him as she adjusted her sweater.

"I could make an exception," he suggested, but she just rolled her eyes and walked into the bathroom.

"Stop trying to drag me into bed, David. I'm not an idiot. You're just trying to distract me from the conversation you're refusing to have." The sound of one of her little bags being unzipped was followed by muttering. "I look like a complete mess."

"You look beautiful," he called out to her as she turned on the water. Groaning, he looked down at his dick pressing at his zipper and willed it to go away.

Was he trying to distract her? Probably. But it wasn't like going downstairs sounded even remotely as fun as making her scream. He'd already spent almost an hour trapped in a car with Jean-Luc and his wife, listening to them make small talk with Lianna as if they weren't the heads of one of the most infamous crime families on the planet. Now they had a lunch planned, *on the terrace.* The entire family was a fucking joke. Crime lords pretending to be aristocrats on their fancy estate.

"Don't you want to change your clothes? Clean up a little?" Lianna asked, stepping out of the bathroom with a toothbrush in hand.

"Fine." Dragging himself off the bed, he stripped down and dug out a pair of jeans and a long-sleeved shirt from his suitcase. Leaving the clean clothes on the bed, he joined her in the bathroom to wash his face and grab deodorant.

"You're not playing fair at all, David," she mumbled, glancing at his reflection in the mirror while she started on her make-up.

"Trust me, angel. I'm playing fair."

"Walking around half-naked with your dick at attention is *not* playing fair," she argued, and he laughed low as he grabbed for his toothbrush.

"If I didn't want to play fair, Lianna, I'd throw you on the bed and fuck you with a hand over your mouth so no one could hear you when you came." Shrugging, he added toothpaste and tilted his head down. "And *that* would take care of the hard-on."

"Tell me how you're feeling about being here, and I'll take you up on that." Lianna turned to face him, and he popped the toothbrush in his mouth so he wouldn't say something stupid about her family. "Well?"

"Now who's not playing fair, angel?" he asked around the toothbrush, and she sighed, returning to her make-up.

"You haven't even given them a chance, and you're already judging them."

Clenching his jaw, David forced a deep breath before he rinsed his mouth out. "I'm not having this conversation."

"You can't do that," she groaned, following him as he walked back into the bedroom. "David, I know you hate Jean-Luc, but you have to admit my cousins seem nice."

"It was nice of them to welcome you at the airport like that," he replied with the only truth his stomach could tolerate as he pulled the clean shirt over his head.

"You don't think they seem nice?" she asked, hand propped on her hip, and the only benefit to this interrogation was that discussing the Faure family was steadily killing his erection. Again.

"I thought we needed to get downstairs," he replied, grabbing his jeans. "You almost ready?"

"God, you can be such an asshole, David."

Shrugging, even though she couldn't see it, he stayed quiet as he pulled on the jeans and put his shoes back on. He deserved to be called a lot more than an asshole for everything he'd done in his life, but in *this* situation, he was choosing the only road available to him. Lianna would have come to the Faure estate with or without him, and there was no way in hell he'd let them sink their claws into her without him here to yank them back out.

So, he'd come with her.

Here.

And no matter how much he hated Jean-Luc Faure and everything their family stood for, he was going to keep his mouth shut and do his best not to ruin her family reunion. The Faures did seem genuinely happy to see her, and her cousins *seemed* nice, but he couldn't let down his guard. No matter how friendly they pretended to be toward him.

"Okay, I'm ready," Lianna said, dropping into the little chair in the corner of the room to pull on her boots, zipping them up her calves. She looked perfect. All that golden hair tumbling over her shoulder, the cream-colored sweater hugging her chest, and the skin-tight jeans that showed every curve. When she stood up, he saw the necklace he'd given her, and he felt a little better. "David?"

"Just waiting on you."

"Jerk." She stomped toward the door, but he caught up to her and pulled her back against him before she opened it.

"I'm doing my best, angel. Just like I promised you on the plane… but that means you can't try and bait me into an argument about them. Okay?" Running his lips over her shoulder, he took a deep breath of her perfume. She'd just refreshed it, and it was too damn tempting.

"I'm not baiting you into an argument, David. I can tell you're uncomfortable, I *already* know how you feel about them, and I just want us to be able to talk about it, so you get it off your chest." Turning around to face him, she looked up into his eyes with a sigh. "Preferably without us arguing."

"If I think of something I can tell you without causing an argument, I'll share it. Deal?" he offered, grinning a little when she groaned.

"You're impossible." Lianna then led the way downstairs, U-turning into the hallway they'd watched the Faures go down. Once they came out the other side, it was easy to see where they'd gone. An entire wall was nothing but floor to ceiling windows, with two doors leading out onto a massive terrace.

Just one more over-the-top display of wealth by the Faure family. As if the huge estate wasn't enough, they had a terrace that he was pretty sure was larger than Lianna's entire apartment back home. The family cheered when they emerged, beckoning them to come sit down.

"Lianna, you look beautiful!" Cécile called out, clapping her hands a little.

"Join us!" Jean-Luc called out, raising a glass of wine in the air from his seat at the head of the table.

The only two seats remaining together were in the center of the table, and he tried to keep his smile polite as he pulled out Lianna's chair for her.

"So, are you exhausted? Were you able to sleep on the plane?" the older daughter asked, leaning forward to smile at Lianna as David took his seat.

"I'm good! I slept almost the whole flight, but David didn't do as well," she replied, nudging him gently with her arm. He shrugged.

"Well, maybe you guys can grab a nap before the—"

"Hold on, Rémi," Jean-Luc interrupted, smiling as he leaned back in his chair. "Let them get some lunch before we start barraging them with questions. Okay?"

"Sorry, please eat!" Rémi gestured to the food before he turned back to his wife.

There were several dishes on the table, including fresh fruit and bread, and David absentmindedly added stuff to his plate while he looked around. The terrace seemed to extend across the entire back of the house, elevated above the ground, which offered wide views of the property. On the far end of the terrace was a large swimming pool, while the side they were on was a large open space.

"I thought the house was only two floors?" Lianna asked after she'd made her plate, pointing over the stone railing, and he couldn't help but smile at her because she was looking at her surroundings like he'd taught her to. "It looks like we're pretty high up?"

"Ah, yes. The front of the house is only two floors, but the ground slopes and so the house was built with an additional floor at the back. It has a couple of bedrooms, and the wine cellar." Jean-Luc picked up his glass again and took a sip. "This terrace sits atop that floor, and it does give one of the best views in Provence — if I'm not too prideful."

"It's incredible," Lianna replied, looking out at the groves of trees, and he followed her gaze. It was a perfectly clear day, and from his angle he could see the edge of some manicured gardens blending into a grove. The property was very nice, but he'd already seen some photos of it. His father had gathered them years before as part of his research on the Faure family, and no matter how beautiful it was… he knew everything the Faures had done to gain all of this wealth.

He just had to hope that Lianna remembered it too.

FOUR

Lianna
_____

She'd just taken a bite of chicken when Emilie leaned forward in her chair from the end of the table and called out to her. "Lianna, tell us something about you! *Papa* didn't tell us much, except that you worked for your dad, and you like art."

Wiping her mouth with the napkin, Lianna smiled at her boisterous cousin. "What would you like to know?"

"What did you study in school?" Anaelle asked from across the table.

"I got my bachelor's in art history, and then I went on to get my MBA," she answered, taking a sip of wine.

"You got the MBA before you started working for your father?" Rémi prompted, and she felt the wine stick in her throat.

"Yes." The answer was probably too curt, too short, but she didn't want to discuss her father. Not here. Not in front of David and the family her father had kept from her.

How much did Jean-Luc know about what happened?

"Did you like working there, or were you still hoping to work with art?" Anaelle grabbed one of the desserts, all casual, but Lianna couldn't figure out what to say.

"That's enough," Jean-Luc said, his voice slightly stern, and his children turned to him. "Alain's death was a tragedy, and I don't think asking Lianna to discuss her father, or working with him, is appropriate lunch conversation."

David huffed under his breath, and she wanted to jab him with an elbow no matter how much she agreed that her father's death was anything but a tragedy. If the universe was fair, he would have suffered a lot more than a single gunshot to the head.

"I'm sorry, Lianna," Anaelle said, followed quickly by Rémi's, "I apologize."

"It's okay," she tried to answer, but her voice cracked, and she soothed it with a larger drink of wine.

"What about you, David? What do you do?" Cécile asked in an attempt to rescue the awkwardness that had settled over the table. Everyone focused on David, and she reached over to squeeze his leg, trying to offer him support as he swallowed the bite in his mouth and leaned back in the chair.

"I work in construction. Mostly installing and programming integrated security systems." He spoke evenly, but she was still worried. If he'd just *talk* to her about what he was thinking or how he felt, she'd feel better, but he was keeping everything locked down. He'd refused to even tell her what his initial reaction to the family was.

"What kind of systems?" Mathieu asked, and she was surprised to hear him speak up. He'd been incredibly quiet compared to his siblings, but he seemed sincerely interested.

"Office buildings, usually." David shrugged, looking across the table where Mathieu sat near the end. "A family friend owns a construction company, and he brought me on to offer the security stuff as part of the build. Most of his customers take him up on it."

"That sounds like a great idea. I was here when they upgraded the security system last time, and I found it fascinating. Probably asked them too many questions about it, but I've always liked finding out how things work." Mathieu stared down at his plate again for a second before glancing around at his family. "I know they're not as interested."

"That's not true. It definitely sounds interesting," Rémi said, and his wife nodded next to him.

"Keeping people safe is a very important job," Amanda added.

"David is very good at it." Smiling, Lianna nudged him a little, but David just took another drink of his wine, and she tried to pull the attention off him again. "So, what else would you like to know?"

"I want to know how you two met!" Emilie cheered, grinning from the other side of David, and Lianna felt the blood drain out of her face.

Fuck.

They definitely should have talked about this, come up with a story. How could they *not* have realized someone would ask that question? Panic began to buzz in her veins as a hundred potential stories spun through her head, but then David took her hand in his and squeezed, and she met his steady gaze as a smirk spread over his lips.

"Well, that was all me. I saw Lianna on TV one day, and I thought she was the most beautiful woman I'd ever seen. Then I got lucky and saw her on the street and… basically stalked her until I had the chance to meet her." Lifting her hand, he placed a kiss on her knuckles, a wicked grin spreading as his tawny brown eyes met hers. "And once I had her in my life, I wasn't going to let her go."

Oh God.

A nervous laugh bubbled up from her chest, heat flushing her cheeks, but a chorus of *aww* and *how sweet* resounded from her cousins, several of them chuckling softly. When she glanced at Jean-Luc, she saw him wiping his mouth, and then he cleared his throat as he raised his wine glass.

"I'd like to make a toast. To Lianna, for joining us here at our home so that we could finally meet her and return the missing piece of our family."

"To Lianna!" her family echoed, lifting their glasses, and she released David's hand so she could lift hers in thanks. Then Jean-Luc waved his hand to hush everyone a bit.

"*And* as we all know, today is Lianna's twenty-seventh birthday, and we've planned a little party for this evening." Smiling, Jean-Luc bowed his head a little. "I apologize. I'm sure you're already a bit overwhelmed, but the rest of the family wants to meet you as well."

"A birthday party?" she repeated, remembering the photos he'd sent her. The intense longing she'd felt when she'd stared at those pictures of crowded rooms filled with smiling faces. A real birthday cake with candles, instead of a single cupcake in the kitchen. A birthday spent with actual family instead of a nanny, surrounded by people who cared instead of wondering when her father would have time for her.

"It's nothing too fancy, but we have quite a bit of family here in France, and many of them knew your father when he was young and are looking forward to meeting you." Jean-Luc reached over to hold Cécile's hand. "It has been a very long time since our family was reunited, and this is something we truly wanted to do for you. To make up for all the birthdays we have missed."

"Thank you so much, this is… I just didn't expect you guys to do anything like that. Thank you." Feeling emotion swelling in her chest, she glanced at David to see his eyes glued on the wine glass in his hand, and she reined herself in. "What kind of party is it? Do we need to dress up?"

"No, no. Honestly, a regular suit is more than enough for David, and any dress you brought will be perfect." Cécile smiled at them both.

"Well, I don't have a suit," David replied, his voice deadpan.

Fortunately, Jean-Luc didn't seem to notice as he rescued him. "Rémi has plenty of suits! I'm sure we can find one that will fit reasonably well. You might be a bit broader in the shoulders, but you're about the same height."

"I'll be happy to help you find one," Rémi confirmed, and Lianna squeezed David's hand tight, pleading with him silently to accept the offer.

The pause was too long, but, eventually, David managed to grind out a "Thank you" that didn't seem *too* forced.

"We really appreciate it, and honestly, I didn't expect any kind of party. This is very kind of you." Glancing around the table, she tried to shift the focus off of them. "Please, tell me about all of you. I want to know everything! What did you study? What do you do for fun? Let me get to know my cousins."

Anaelle was the first to reply, talking about how she loved art as well, but she'd studied literature instead, and the conversation seemed to flow easily after that. From discussing specific artists, to the other interests her cousins had pursued, to stories of them as children. The siblings made playful jabs at each other, and Jean-Luc and Cécile added their own comments, but it was clear they cared about one another — and they'd all been involved in each other's lives.

Not just related, but a real family, with a real history.

It drew such a sharp contrast between her life, and the life she could have had. A life where she could have grown up knowing these people, where her name might have been interwoven with the stories they shared.

A life where birthday parties wouldn't be such a surprise.

FIVE

David
_____

Adjusting the suit jacket again, David tried not to pull his shoulders too far forward as he headed back toward their room. The pants were a little shorter than they should have been, but overall they looked fine. It was the jacket and shirt that were the problem.

He felt like he might hulk out of Rémi's clothes if he moved wrong — and there was no way in hell he wanted to know how much they would cost to replace. Based on the price tags for some of Lianna's clothes, he was pretty confident he was wearing a few thousand dollars' worth of fabric, but Rémi hadn't been an asshole about letting him borrow the clothes. Surprisingly, the man had seemed more than happy to find a suit that fit him.

Rémi had even cracked a joke that he should hit the gym more often, so he'd look more like him.

But, just because Rémi wasn't an asshole about his wealth, looking down on the lower classes and all that shit, didn't mean he was actually a good guy. Plenty of people were good actors, capable of pretending to like someone.

Hell, politicians did it all the time.

And no matter how nice he'd been, Rémi was still next in line to head up the Faure family, and despite the bullshit Jean-Luc told Lianna about the family's future, David knew better. No one walked away from that kind of money, especially when they had people to support and an estate like this to pay the bills on.

Rolling his neck, David tapped on the door to their room just before he cracked it open, calling out, "It's me."

"Hey, baby, were you able to find a suit to wear?" Lianna's voice came from the bathroom, and he rounded the bed so he could see her.

Gorgeous.

Of course, Lianna had packed a nice dress. It was a dark blue, and the fabric hugged her waist before it flared out around her hips, falling to mid-knee. In the chaos of their months together, he'd forgotten just how incredibly beautiful she looked when she got the opportunity to really dress up. "Wow, angel."

Her eyes lifted to him in the mirror, Lianna's smile flashed bright just before she turned around. "Oh my God, David. You look great!"

"I was just about to tell you the same thing," he replied, grinning as she walked over to run her hands over the suit jacket.

"Jean-Luc was right, it's a little tight in the shoulders, but you make this look *good*." Tightening her grip on the lapels of the jacket, she tugged him closer, and he dipped his head so he could kiss her. Capturing her lips, he was about to make a move when a little whine escaped her, and she pulled back. "You're going to make me mess up my make-up."

"I'm okay with that," he replied, but she immediately stepped back into the bathroom to check her lipstick. With her preoccupied, he pulled the tie off his shoulder and popped his collar, winding it around his neck. Bringing the two end pieces together, he tried to remember how the fuck to do the knot. It had a name — that he couldn't fucking remember — and on his third attempt, he stepped into the bathroom to look at it in the mirror, but he was distracted watching Lianna put on earrings.

Every movement she made was so damn graceful, and he made a mental note to find time for a real date when they got home. Some place where she could dress up like this... because she clearly loved it. She was practically glowing.

"Any chance we can just blame jet lag and skip this?" he asked, grinning at her when she turned toward him sharply.

"Not a chance." Rolling her eyes, she shook her head and messed with her hair some more.

"It was worth a shot," he added, leaning on the counter to watch her, and her baby blues landed on him, that sympathetic expression passing over her face again.

"I know this sounds like torture, but you look too good not to show off, baby." Leaning close, she placed a chaste kiss on his lips, and he sighed, because that seemed like the only action he'd be getting until after the party. Then

Lianna reached up, tugging at his tie until it was loose. "Let me just fix this, and you'll be perfect."

Fuck. He'd screwed it up that badly?

"I'm not exactly the suit-and-tie type, angel," he said, feeling more than a little defensive.

She laughed softly. "I'm well aware of that, and I don't care if you never wear a suit and tie... even if you do look spectacular in it." Lianna's hands moved confidently, adjusting the fabric, and he hated that she was having to do it for him. It just wasn't something he'd ever learned how to do, and it wasn't as if he'd ever worked the kind of jobs that required one.

"I don't think I've even worn a tie since my dad died." *And I'm pretty sure Harry tied it that time.*

"It's okay, I've got practice. I used to do this for—" Lianna cut herself short, clearing her throat as she tweaked the tie one more time before she stood back. "There you go. Perfect."

She was avoiding his gaze, and he knew why, but he let it go. Lianna was nothing like her father, and that man had burned whatever connection they had the day he pointed a gun at her. Leaning forward, he kissed her forehead and winked. "Thanks, angel."

"Think you can survive tonight?" She smiled up at him as she toyed with his suit jacket again.

"Depends. What do I get as a reward?"

"Reward?" Lianna's brows drew together as she laughed. "You want a reward for coming to my birthday party?"

"In this house? Absolutely." Grinning, he grabbed her by the hips and yanked her against his front. "Tell me what I get if I survive the night."

"If you're not an asshole?" she clarified.

"Right."

"I think we could come up with a few ways to keep me quiet while you get a reward." Lianna's voice was a low, teasing whisper that went straight to his balls. All he got out in response was a groan as she slipped away from him, grinning like a temptress as she braced one hand on the bed to put on her heels.

The visual of her on her knees, her make-up smearing as he made her gag and choke on his cock... that was all he needed.

Do not fuck this up.

"Ready?" she asked, that seductive glint in her pretty blue eyes as she walked backward around the bed.

"The sooner we go, the sooner we can get back up here, right?" Stalking her toward the bedroom door, all he wanted to do was pin her against it, but he held back. *Behave.*

"Just try and have fun. Okay, baby?"

"I'll try," he promised, gesturing to the door. "Let's go celebrate your birthday."

"I love you," she said, leaning back against the door for a second, and his eyes fell to the necklace she was wearing. *His* necklace.

"I love you too, and if *you* are a good girl tonight, maybe I'll give you some birthday spankings."

"David!" Laughing, Lianna pulled open the door, shaking her head. "Absolutely not."

"You know that's my favorite game."

"David." She looked back at him as he shut their bedroom door.

Grinning, he couldn't resist messing with her a little more. "Go on, angel. Tell me no again."

"Oh my God, please don't talk like this downstairs." Groaning, Lianna headed toward the stairs and he chuckled as he followed her.

It was always fun to see the pink rise in her cheeks, to get her all wound up, but he wouldn't embarrass her like that. If the night went the way he planned, he wouldn't speak much at all. It was safer that way, easier to avoid voicing how he really felt about the Faures.

One of the armed guards who lurked around the house was waiting at the bottom of the steps, and he gestured to the side of the stairs as Lianna approached him. "This way, Ms. Mercier."

Pausing at the edge the stairs, Lianna turned toward David, extending her hand and he took it as he caught up. She was his lifeline in this place, the only reason he was here, and he loved her just a little more for wanting him at her side.

Through the windows he could already see that the terrace was lit up brightly, Christmas lights in the trees, and David wondered if they'd been there during lunch or if the Faures had somehow added them in the hours since.

"It's beautiful," Lianna whispered, and he tightened his grip on her hand as the guard opened the door for them.

As soon as Lianna stepped outside, people turned toward her, and then they were cheering, clapping, and the sheer numbers stunned him. *Were there really this many Faures?*

Heat washed up his back, making him feel like he was sweating through Rémi's expensive shirt, but Lianna didn't falter. She waved, smiling brightly, and he recognized the movements from every press event she'd ever done with her father.

Looks like Rémi isn't the only one skilled at acting.

The crowd surged forward, surrounding them, speaking in rapid French and bits of English. He heard a few 'happy birthday's and several people saying how beautiful she was, but most of it was lost in a rush of noise and fancy clothes. Everyone looked like they were ready to walk the red carpet, and there he was wearing a tie that Lianna had to put on him, in a borrowed suit that was at least a size too small.

"*Lui donner de l'air!*" Jean-Luc appeared in the crowd, gesturing people to move back, and when he saw Lianna the man laid his hand over his heart. "*Mon oisillon,* you look beautiful! Happy birthday, Lianna."

"Thank you," she replied, still smiling, and Jean-Luc stepped forward to hug her, which meant her hand left his. Jean-Luc whispered something to her, and she nodded as he leaned back. "Okay."

"*Génial!* Come this way." The crowd parted for Jean-Luc as he moved forward, but David was relieved when Lianna reached back to take his hand again before she followed. Jean-Luc led them through the various people who smiled or waved at Lianna, occasionally saying something to her that she tried to reply to as she trailed after him.

Eventually, David realized Jean-Luc was moving toward a small, raised platform where his son, Mathieu, was standing behind DJ equipment. The music was quiet for now, but it seemed the Faures had not wasted any time putting together a party for Lianna.

Just one more reason I had to be here.

Tightening his grip on Lianna's hand, she squeezed back as Jean-Luc gestured for her to wait where she was. Lifting a microphone, Jean-Luc waved an arm to get the attention of the people crowded onto the terrace, and the noise slowly subsided.

The first words out of his mouth were in French, and David leaned down to whisper against her ear, "What the hell is he saying?"

"He's saying something about how he wants to welcome me in English, but that if anyone doesn't speak English, he still wants them to know they're welcome to his home and my party." Lianna turned to smile at him for a second before she returned her gaze to Jean-Luc.

"Now, Lianna, my beautiful niece. I want to welcome you, and David, to my home. Our family has wanted to meet you for so many years, and we are glad to have you home."

This isn't her home.

David felt himself tense, but he forced a long, slow breath as Jean-Luc continued.

"We are here today to celebrate Lianna's twenty-seventh birthday in true Faure style. Many of our extended family members have traveled from across France and parts of Europe to be here today, and although I know you all want to speak to her, I will ask everyone *not* to overwhelm our dear Lianna. It is her birthday, after all!" The crowd laughed a little, and Jean-Luc smiled down at her again, but all David wanted to do was pull her closer. "One more thing before I let my son, Mathieu, share his music talents. Please try to speak English this evening, as much as possible, although I must admit Lianna's French is quite impressive!"

"Better than mine?" someone called out from the crowd, and David turned to find Rémi's wife waving to Jean-Luc.

Chuckling, Jean-Luc shook his head. "I will refuse to answer that."

Another round of laughs followed from the gathered Faure clan, but he didn't have the urge to laugh. Rémi's wife may not speak much French, but David didn't know any. It sounded like a bunch of drunk people slurring, and how anyone was supposed to tell where one word ended and the next began... he had no fucking idea. Lianna had seemed confident that he'd pick it up, but beyond the random shit he'd learned from television — he was useless.

"Happy birthday, Lianna! Everyone, enjoy the evening!" Jean-Luc waved, returning the microphone to Mathieu, who was focused on the laptop propped in front of him. The volume rose gradually, just loud enough to hear over the buzz of the crowd, and David was surprised to hear normal music. He'd expected some pretentious violins or piano, but this reminded him of going to bars and clubs in New York with Vincent.

"Thank you so much, Jean-Luc. This is definitely the biggest birthday party I've ever had," Lianna said, hugging the man with one arm after he came down from the platform. Her grip on his hand tightened as she embraced Jean-Luc, like she was anchoring herself from the impossible pull of everything the man represented. David knew Lianna wanted to get to know her family, wanted to dive in with both feet… and he'd let her.

He'd just also be there to pull her back out before she drowned.

"Oh, this is nothing! You should have seen Emilie's twentieth birthday party. All of her friends from university came, and the house was overrun with girls. I believe Cécile and I hid in our bedroom the entire weekend." Chuckling, Jean-Luc gestured toward someone behind them. "Ah, look who Anaelle brought tonight!"

"This is Quentin," Anaelle said, tilting her head toward the dark-haired young man at her side as she spoke in quick French to him.

"Hello, I— I feel good to meet you," Quentin replied, nodding at Lianna as he made an apologetic face over his broken English. Lianna answered him in fluent French, and although he hated these people and their language… it sounded good coming from Lianna's lips.

"Your French is so good, Lianna!" Anaelle cheered, smiling broadly as she leaned over to kiss Quentin on the cheek before tugging him away. "We'll let you meet everyone now, we just wanted to say hi!"

"Thank you, Anaelle! *Au revoir*, Quentin!" Lianna leaned into his side, her arm folded over the crook of his, and it felt nice — but Jean-Luc was still hovering at her other side.

"Ah, I see someone else. This way, *mon oisillon*," Jean-Luc said, guiding Lianna through the crowd. For the next half hour there was a blur of names and introductions, some in English, some in French, and David was just grateful they'd made a stop at the bar. The alcohol made all the false smiles easier to tolerate.

Lianna's smile wasn't fake, though.

She was excited to meet each random family member, and she let go of him more and more often as they moved through the party, led by Jean-Luc from person to person. Still, she always reached back for his hand, her blue eyes focusing on him as he stood back to let her get to know all the strangers. An entire goddamn family tree of Faures and their significant others, their children.

David was just about to excuse himself from the monotony to grab another drink when Jean-Luc raised an arm to wave at someone.

"Natalie! Where is my brother?" Jean-Luc called out, a laugh in his voice as a dark-haired woman waved back before heading toward them. "Where is Marc hiding?"

Marc Faure.

Clearing his throat, David stepped a little closer to Lianna. He may not have known most of the names that had flitted past them, but he knew this one. Marc Faure was Jean-Luc's younger brother, the middle child who had stayed behind in France when Lianna's father had run off to the US.

"Oh, we just arrived. He said he needed to check on something, but he should be here soon." Natalie smiled broadly, extending a hand. "And you must be Lianna!"

"I am, it's nice to meet you," Lianna replied, shaking her hand as the woman turned toward the two people beside her.

"These are your cousins, Madeline and Gregory. They've been looking forward to meeting you since Emilie first texted them that you were coming to visit!" Nicole reached forward to touch the ends of Lianna's hair with a sigh. "Look at this, the Faure blonde. You look so much like your grandmother, and Alain even named you after her!"

"I do?" Lianna asked, and Jean-Luc readily agreed.

"Absolutely! *Maman* was beautiful, and I like to think that Alain saw her beauty and grace in you the day you were born." Jean-Luc reached over, resting a hand on Lianna's shoulder, and David had the urge to shove it off. They were just pulling Lianna in deeper with random genetics. Everyone resembled their family in one way or another, it was just DNA at work, not some divine intervention or sign that she was destined for this place.

Fighting the urge to comment, David drank the remnants in his glass, which was mostly melted ice, and scanned the party to see where the bar was as the cousins introduced themselves, switching between French and English with ease as they talked about their lives.

Such bullshit.

Not all of us went to private schools or traveled the world for fun.

It had never been more painfully clear just how much he didn't belong in her world. Everyone seemed to be educated, wealthy, and then there was him. He stood out, and his silence was probably making things awkward for Lianna... but he didn't have anything to say to these people. The conversations they had were outside his experiences, and even when they politely smiled at him — he knew they were only speaking to him out of obligation, some abstract social requirement to include him as Lianna's guest.

But he wouldn't have ever let her come here on her own.

He would have lost her to this place. To Jean-Luc.

"There he is!" Jean-Luc said, interrupting Madeline in the middle of a discussion about some area of London both she and Lianna liked. Raising an arm, Jean-Luc beckoned someone closer, and David followed his line of sight until he saw the blond man moving through the crowd.

"I told you he'd join us soon," Natalie replied, turning to accept a quick kiss from Marc Faure as he approached them with a polite expression.

"This is a nice party, Jean-Luc," Marc said, and his brother laughed.

"It is! So, where have you been hiding? We've been keeping Natalie company in your absence." Jean-Luc moved forward to embrace his brother, and the other man returned it, shrugging as they separated.

"I'm sorry to keep you waiting," he replied, turning his gaze to Lianna. "I'm your *Oncle Marc*, Lianna, and I'm so glad to finally meet you." He offered her his hand, but for the first time that evening, Lianna seemed stiff. Her smile wasn't as bright as it had been, and when they released each other's hands, she had a sip of her wine, a small furrow appearing between her brows.

He wanted to ask her what was wrong, but it would have to wait.

Tonight. I'll ask her tonight.

SIX

Lianna
_____

Swallowing her wine, Lianna couldn't take her eyes off the man who was apparently her uncle.

"Have we met before?" she asked, trying to figure out why Marc's face seemed so familiar.

"Oh no, my dear," Marc replied, smiling as he glanced at his wife. "But everyone always used to say how much I looked like Alain."

"Maybe you recognize him from all the family photos Cécile gave you?" Jean-Luc suggested as Cécile joined them, and he wrapped an arm around his wife's waist. "I'm sure Marc was in many of them."

"Right, that's probably it," Lianna conceded, but something nagged at her. Like a lyric in a song she couldn't quite remember. She'd seen photos of so many members of the family, her cousins included, but no one she'd met that day had brought the sense of familiarity like Marc had.

He does kind of look like Dad. With his blond hair… and around the eyes.

"How long are you staying?" Madeline asked, and Lianna glanced up at her.

"A week or so," she answered, reaching back for David to squeeze his hand. "We're already overwhelmed by how kind everyone has been."

"Of course! You're family!" Madeline replied with a laugh. "We'll have to go into Nice together. It's not far, and Anaelle, Emilie, and I know all the best spots. We go all the time."

"That's true," Natalie added with a chuckle as she leaned against Marc.

"I'm sure our girls could find plenty to do," Cécile confirmed, laughing softly, and Lianna smiled at her. The woman was so warm, so kind, and everyone had been so welcoming. She wasn't lying when she called it overwhelming though, her head was a sea of names and faces while she tried desperately to remember them.

After a few more minutes of conversation, Jean-Luc touched her elbow and tilted his head toward a new spot in the crowd. "Come, come, there are more people that want to meet you, *mon oisillon*! You are the woman of the hour."

"Okay!" Lianna said, summoning her energy reserves to keep looking cheerful and repeating the same conversation again and again. The older members of the family all wanted to talk about her father, *Alain*, or about how she resembled the grandmother she'd never met — but who she'd clearly been named after. The younger ones just wanted to chat about travel or school or her hobbies, and after a while she stopped introducing David to them. She knew he hated it, could read it in every line of his body, and he wasn't very good at hiding his discomfort. It radiated off of him in the tense handshakes, the sharp line of his jaw when he forced a smile, and she wished that Jean-Luc would stop the endless merry-go-round of introductions for just a little while... but it would be rude to ask.

The Faures, her *family*, had gone to so much effort to organize the party for her birthday. Many of them had traveled a long way just to see her, and so she kept smiling through every introduction, every conversation, even when it started to feel like a press event.

"Give her a minute to breathe, *Papa*," Mathieu said when Jean-Luc saw another face in the crowd he wanted her to meet.

"I'm wearing you out, I apologize," Jean-Luc said, reaching over to hug her around the shoulders. "I'm just so excited to have you here, *mon oisillon*. Everyone has wanted to meet you since I returned from the States, and when you decided to join us so quickly... it was wonderful."

"I really am enjoying meeting everyone, but maybe we can take a short break?" she asked gently, and Jean-Luc just laughed as he raised his hands.

"Of course, we have plenty of time," he replied, stepping back. "I will go find Cécile."

"Thank you, Jean-Luc."

"Sorry about him, he really is just excited to have you here," Mathieu explained as Jean-Luc disappeared into the crowd. After taking a deep breath, Lianna looked over her shoulder to reach for David's hand… but he wasn't there.

Fuck.

"I'm very excited to be here, and I am enjoying meeting everyone. Really," she insisted, turning to search for David's tall profile. "But I seem to have lost David at some point."

Mathieu chuckled, lifting the glass in his hand. "I'm sure he just stepped away to grab a drink like I did. I do have to get back to the music, if I leave Emilie in charge it'll be nothing but Kesha."

"Thanks, Mathieu. You're doing a great job as the DJ," Lianna added, waving at him as she slipped through the crowd, acknowledging the various comments from the guests while she searched for him.

The sun had disappeared completely at some point, and the fringes of the terrace were lit only by the Christmas lights wound around the stone railing — which, of course, was where she found David. As far away from the rest of the party as he could get, his drink resting on the stone in front of him, David was simply staring out at the darkened estate.

"Why are you all the way over here?" she asked as soon as she was close enough, and he turned to glance at her, shrugging a little.

"You know why."

"No, I don't. It's just a party, David." Glancing back at the small crowd milling around, eating snacks, drinking, swaying to the music and chatting, she had to admit it was a *little* intimidating. There were so many people she didn't know, but they knew her name. Knew her father, possibly better than she ever had. But no one had made it uncomfortable. "Come on. It's my birthday party."

"And I don't belong here," he replied, his voice almost too low to hear over the music floating across the terrace.

Stepping closer, she set her wine glass beside his drink and wrapped her arms around him from behind, leaning her cheek against his back. "You belong here because you belong with me… right?"

He sighed heavily, and she felt the expansion of his ribs, the subtle shifting of his muscles. "That's manipulative as fuck, angel."

"True," she admitted with a grin, pressing a kiss to his back before he turned to face her. "But Jean-Luc is taking a break from the endless introductions, so we can just enjoy the music and the food."

"Have you eaten anything yet?" he asked, pulling her hips against him.

"Nope." Lianna looked up at him, grinning when she heard him grumble. David could be unpredictable, and completely sadistic — but he was also strangely protective. Especially when it came to her eating.

"How many glasses of wine have you had?"

"I think this is number three?" she guessed, because she wasn't actually sure, but she did feel buzzed, which meant it was more than two. David rolled his eyes, letting out a huff under his breath as he shook his head at her.

"Come on," he finally said, letting go of her so they could get their drinks, but then he caught her hand, holding tight as they returned to the party. "No more wine until you eat something."

"Yes, sir," she whispered, and he glanced down at her.

"Don't be a tease unless you want me to throw you over my shoulder and carry you out of your own party." He spoke softly so that no one around them might hear it, but she couldn't hold back the laugh.

"You wouldn't dare." Her laugh turned into an open-mouthed stare when he just raised his eyebrows at her. "David, no."

"Better eat something then," he commanded, stopping them by the table filled with snacks of all kinds. Small sandwiches, fruit, cheese and crackers, and other hors d'oeuvres. They both filled a plate and found a spot against the railing that was a little closer to the party without being in the middle of it.

"Thank you for coming with me," Lianna said, looking over at him as he popped an entire *something* into his mouth. She chuckled, taking a bite of a small sandwich while he chewed.

"I told you I wouldn't let you come here by yourself," he eventually replied, shrugging a shoulder as he sipped the punch he'd grabbed.

"You still think I'm in danger?"

"Not physically," he muttered, poking at the various things he'd piled on his plate before choosing one.

"David…" She thought about pushing him, clarifying what he meant, but she already knew. He wasn't worried the Faures would hurt her. No, he was still worried that Jean-

Luc and the rest of the family would try and make her stay.

That they would take her away from *him*.

So, she leaned up and kissed him on the cheek, whispering the only thing she needed to say in that moment. "I love you, baby."

"I love you too, angel. Happy birthday." Turning his head, he caught her lips in a kiss, but David kept it surprisingly chaste. It was a warm press of his mouth to hers, drawing her attention to the chill in the air now that night had fallen. When he pulled back, she bit down on her lip, smiling a little at the heat in his gaze.

"Thank you."

David merely gave a slight nod, his eyes lingering on her for a moment before he looked back at the food. "You need to eat."

"I know," she replied, grinning again as she finished the little sandwich. David could be so wonderful when he wanted to be, and *that* was really what she'd wanted to thank him for. Not just for wishing her a happy birthday or caring enough to make sure she always ate something… but for all of it. For setting aside his hatred of the Faure family to come with her to their home, for *wanting* to protect her even when she didn't need it. For pushing past all the bullshit in his history, and hers, to become the kind of man she wanted to stand beside.

Their connection had started in the darkest of places, fueled by pain and rage, but they'd both changed. Become someone new. Evolved, together, and she hoped that continued even though the Faures had a place in her life now.

Because as messed up as their story was… she didn't want anyone else at her side.

They got maybe half an hour of peace before the music faded and Jean-Luc's voice came over the speakers again. "How is everyone enjoying the party?"

Cheers went up, and Lianna joined in just before he repeated a similar question in French, before reminding everyone that he'd be speaking in English for their guests. Leaning over to David, she said, "He's going to speak in English for everyone."

"You mean for me," he grumbled, and she rolled her eyes.

"Amanda doesn't speak French well either."

"I don't speak French *at all*," David said, reaching for the drink they'd just got from the bar as he glared at Jean-Luc across the crowd.

Sighing, she turned her attention back to the man as he called out her name.

"Lianna? Did we scare you away?" he asked with a chuckle.

Raising her glass of wine in the air, she took David's hand as she called out, "I'm here, Jean-Luc!"

"*Magnifique!*" he replied, his voice amplified by the microphone as he waved his hand toward the doors. "It is time to celebrate your birthday, *mon oisillon!*"

Lianna could see a glow from inside the glass doors to the terrace just before two of the guards opened them, holding them wide for someone to push a trolley through. It held a massive cake covered in candles and real flowers in shades of blue and purple, and her heart tripped over itself as Jean-Luc began to sing *bon anniversaire*, and everyone joined in.

Pulling David with her, she approached the cake as everyone sang 'happy birthday' in French. It didn't have the same tune, but she was sure that David understood without any explanation from her. Cécile, Rémi, Anaelle, and Emilie were all standing near the cake, singing along, and Lianna stopped next to it, feeling tears burning the corners of her eyes as she tried to swallow down the lump of emotion in her chest.

Looking around at all the smiling faces singing happy birthday to her, she had to tighten her grip on David's hand so she wouldn't cry and confuse them all, but it was hard. All she could think of were the litany of lonely birthdays she'd had when she was young. And then she remembered the family photos Cécile had sent her, the beautiful pictures of everyone crowded around the dining table celebrating birthdays just like this. Singing to each other like this.

And now they were doing it for her.

The song came to an end and Emilie clapped her hands, gesturing toward the cake. "Go on! Make a wish!"

Closing her eyes, Lianna fumbled through her thoughts, pushing past the confusing emotions to think of something she wanted.

I just want everything to turn out okay.

It was simple, more a plea to the universe than a wish, but she took a deep breath and blew out as many candles as she could. There were too many to take out in one breath though, and so she laughed as she moved around the cake, blowing the rest out as everyone clapped and called out "*Bon anniversaire!*" and "Happy birthday!"

When the last candle finally puffed out, she turned and waved at everyone, raising her voice to make herself heard over the noise. "Thank you all so much! I appreciate this more than you know."

After another swallow to quell the lingering urge to cry, she repeated it again in French, to the best of her ability, and people clapped and cheered again. It was such a surprising outpouring of love, and she moved back to David's side to squeeze his hand, hoping that he could feel it too.

"We have a present for you," Cécile said, coming up to her with a small box, a bright blue ribbon tied around it. Jean-Luc was at her side, smiling as Cécile held it out toward her.

"You didn't have to do that! This party was already too much," Lianna replied, letting go of David to accept the box.

"It's sort of a tradition in our family," Jean-Luc added, shrugging a shoulder. "Normally, we'd give a gift like this when you turned twenty-five, but we're only two years late."

"Open it!" Emilie shouted, her excitement clear.

"We hope you'll like it," Anaelle added, and Rémi nodded next to her as Amanda joined him at his side.

"We helped *Maman* pick it out," he said, and Lianna's curiosity got the best of her.

As she pulled at the silken ribbon, the bow came undone, falling away easily in her hand so that she could lift the lid free. There was a smaller, wooden box inside, and she turned to David so he could help her. He took the lid, and then the outer box as she removed the wooden one. It flipped open on a simple hinge, and she gasped when the lights caught what lay inside.

It was a beautiful bracelet in an old-fashioned style. Intricately woven metal held little sapphires, and what had to be diamonds, in a delicate floral pattern. It wasn't thick, maybe half an inch wide, but the craftsmanship was undeniable.

Raising her eyes to Jean-Luc, she shook her head, speaking softly. "I can't accept this."

"Of course you can, *mon oisillon*," he replied with a warm smile. "You are family, and that bracelet belonged to my mother, Liliane Faure, whom you are named after. Even though she never had the chance to meet you, I know she'd want you to have it as much as we do."

"It's true, Lianna. We all talked about it, and we chose this heirloom for you. That way, even when you're far away, there's always a piece of your family with you." Cécile stepped forward, wrapping her in a warm hug that felt exactly like the kind of hug she had always imagined a mom would give. In that moment, she didn't feel like an outsider... she felt like she was home.

Tears welled in her eyes again, one of them escaping as she managed a soft, "Thank you."

Jean-Luc saved her from having to face everyone when he stepped forward to hug her as well, although his was slightly more restrained. "We are all so glad you came. I hope you've had a wonderful birthday."

"I have." Her voice cracked a little as she sniffled next to his shoulder, trying her hardest to rein in the emotions before she looked at David. He was probably already comparing the bracelet to the necklace he'd given her on the plane, and she didn't need to add on by getting emotional. When Jean-Luc stepped back, she looked down at the bracelet again, trying to wipe under her eyes as casually as possible before she glanced at David.

His expression was blank, but she could read the tension in his shoulders, in the set of his jaw.

"*Maman!* What about the other thing?" Anaelle prompted her mother, tilting her head toward the doors where one of the guards was holding a brightly colored bag.

"Oh!" Cécile hurried over, taking the gift from the guard before she rushed back. "We did have one more little thing for you."

"This is already too much!" Lianna said, her heart racing as Cécile tilted the bag toward her.

"I've got it," David mumbled, taking the jewelry box from her. Snapping it closed, he returned it to the box in his hands, replacing the lid with a stone-like expression.

Shit.

Turning back to Cécile, she couldn't deny the woman's excitement. Lianna took the bag and reached through the tissue paper until she felt fabric and pulled it out, confusion washing over her. "A Christmas stocking?"

"We don't always do stockings here in France, but Cécile is actually quite good at sewing, so she made you this," Jean-Luc explained.

"We were hoping you'd like to come back and celebrate Christmas with us this year. Jean-Luc has always hoped that Alain, and you, would come," Cécile added before she turned to look at David. "Of course, you're welcome as well, David. We'd love to have you both."

Heart pounding in her ears, Lianna glanced at him to find him staring at the present in his hands, his grip on the gift box just a little too tight. Forcing a smile, Lianna turned back to Cécile and Jean-Luc. "That sounds lovely, I think... I think we're just a little overwhelmed by everything. We'll absolutely think about coming back in December."

"No rush, *mon oisillon*." Jean-Luc brushed off the topic with ease, smiling as he stepped to the side to reveal the cake to everyone. "I think it's time for cake!"

Lianna traced her thumb over the hand-stitched letters that formed her name at the top of the stocking. It was thinner than stockings in the States, made out of fabric with a soft pattern, but it was hers, and Cécile had made it by hand. Taking a deep breath, Lianna tucked it away into the gift bag along with any thought of returning in just a couple of months to celebrate Christmas with the Faure family.

I've already asked too much of David.

Stepping closer to him, she held the bag open so he could put the gift box inside, and then she switched the ribbon handles to one hand, sliding an arm around his waist. She wanted to say something to make him feel better, but he clearly didn't want to talk right now. All she could do was lean against his side, resting her head on his shoulder as the staff began to cut the cake into slices.

It was beautiful. Just as beautiful as the terrace, and the gifts, and the entire celebration they'd put together for her. It was more than she'd ever dreamed of in twenty-six years of birthdays.

But that didn't mean it was perfect.

While the party might have been a dream come true for her, it was David's nightmare… and she wouldn't rub it in. She could tell he was miserable, but he was still standing beside her.

A minute later, his arm went around her back, and she smiled a little. He just needed time out of the spotlight again to relax. They could return to their little corner of the party, eat their cake, and everything would be fine.

SEVEN

David

Most of the guests left after the cake, and that meant Lianna was once again surrounded by random people telling her goodbye, or *au revoir*. He'd foolishly hoped that as the number of people dwindled that they'd get to go to bed soon, but the party just continued.

Finally, at almost eleven o'clock, David felt dead on his feet even though he was sitting down. He couldn't stop yawning, but Lianna was still laughing and talking animatedly with Jean-Luc's children. The man and his wife had gone to bed almost half an hour before when the last guests left, yet Lianna didn't seem to be slowing down at all. They'd gathered chairs together, the girls taking their heels off while the men removed their suit jackets, getting comfortable so they could keep talking.

He was definitely more relaxed without Jean-Luc around, but he still felt like he couldn't participate in the conversation. They were telling Lianna about their family, more stupid stories from the past like they'd shared at lunch, and even though some of them were funny... he was too tired to do more than occasionally force a smile for her sake.

"Let's open another bottle of wine!" Anaelle cheered, setting her empty glass down beside her chair, and David had to fight the urge to groan out loud.

"I think I'm going to have to bow out of the next round," Rémi said, standing up to stretch. "The twins will be up early and—"

"Since when do you get up with them?" Emilie asked, laughing when Rémi glared at her. "Amanda says you sleep through them crying."

"That is *not* true."

"Sure," Mathieu added on, chuckling. "We all know you sleep like the dead, Rémi."

"That's because I used to share a room with *you*, and you talk in your sleep!" Rémi retorted, reaching over to smack Mathieu lightly on the back of the head. "But, for your information, I do get up with the twins."

"Every night?" Anaelle asked with a grin, and Rémi snagged his suit jacket from the back of his chair.

"I'm going to bed," he replied, pointing around the little circle of chairs. "And you guys should too. *Maman* and *Papa* will want us all at breakfast, and Lianna and David probably have jetlag."

David wanted to thank the man for being the voice of reason as the rest of them grumbled. A yawn almost cracked his jaw, and laughter broke out just before he was able to open his eyes again. Lianna was grinning at him, and he glanced around the group. "What?"

"I was about to ask you if you're tired, but I think the answer is yes." Slipping her heels on, Lianna turned toward her cousins. "Sorry, everyone. Rémi is right, we should try and get on schedule here."

"That's okay, we can hang out more tomorrow," Emilie said, and David stood up, relieved to be in bed soon.

A second later, he snapped his hand out, instinctively reaching over to catch Lianna when she stumbled to the side as she got out of the chair.

"Guess I'm more tired than I thought!" Laughing, Lianna steadied herself on David's arm before she hugged each of her cousins... but he doubted she was that tired. She'd slept most of the flight, and it was much more likely the multiple glasses of wine that had her off-kilter.

How much had she had to drink?

He'd lost track over the hours of the party, and once the guests had cleared out her cousins had started steadily working their way through the remaining bottles on the makeshift bar. Not that it really mattered, because he could tell she was more drunk than she was letting on.

"This was the best birthday ever," Lianna said, hugging Emilie tightly.

"And the week just started!" Anaelle added.

"Very true. Hope you both sleep well." Rémi nodded, heading inside, and David reached down to grab Lianna's gift bag from beside her chair.

"Night, everyone. We'll see you in the morning!" Lianna was glowing as she released Emilie and turned to look at him.

"Good night," David told the group, wrapping an arm around her waist to guide her inside.

"That was so fun!" she whispered as they passed through the terrace doors, heading down the short hall. "Don't you think that was fun?"

"Mmhmm," he replied, stopping her at the base of the stairs to kneel down. "Step out of your heels."

"What? Why?"

"Because I don't want you breaking an ankle, Lianna." Sighing, he braced one hand on her hip and took her shoes off with the other, tossing them into the gift bag before he stood.

"You're so protective." Lianna grinned at him as he stood up. "I love that about you."

"You're drunk," he muttered, but he couldn't help but smile back as she leaned into him on their way up the stairs.

"I'm not drunk, definitely tipsy though. But it's my birthday! That was my first real birthday party, you know?" Lianna was walking better than he expected as they moved upward, but there was no way in hell he was letting go of her to test her sobriety. "It really was. I mean, I went out with friends and stuff when I was old enough, but that's not a *party*. Going to a bar isn't a *party*. This was a real party, and they threw it for me!"

"Yep," David answered, and he was tempted to point out that she was slurring a little, but it wasn't worth it.

"I'm glad you were at my first birthday party," Lianna whispered, stopping them just fifteen feet from their bedroom door to pull him down into a kiss. She was the one to intensify it, her tongue flicking out to trace his lips before she nipped him, and he was about to pull her against him when he heard voices on the stairs and cut it short.

"We need to get inside, angel." Forcing her to keep walking, he half-dragged her to their room. As soon as the door shut, Lianna leaned away from him and he held on tighter. "Why don't you just lie down, angel?"

"Because I need to use the bathroom," she replied, winking at him as he let go. Lianna wobbled more than he would have liked on the way around the bed, but at least she didn't fall down.

Shaking his head, David quickly took off the suit jacket and shirt, inspecting them to make sure he hadn't damaged them. Fortunately, it seemed like the expensive clothes had held out. Shucking the slacks and shoes, he draped Rémi's clothes over the chair in the corner and waited until the toilet flushed before he followed Lianna into the bathroom.

"I might be a little more than tipsy," she admitted, looking up at him in the mirror as she washed her hands.

"You might be." He shrugged, knowing that he should be happy for her, he just couldn't manage it.

"You see it now, though, right? They're great. Like, really nice people." Lianna sounded so hopeful, but he stayed silent as he stepped closer to unzip her dress. Underneath she was only wearing a bra and a thong, and his cock twitched despite how exhausted he felt. *Not tonight.* Leaning down, he helped her step out of the dress, and she narrowed her eyes at him in the mirror when he stood back up. "Did you hear me?"

"I heard you, angel. We just need to get you in bed." Rubbing a hand over his face, he stepped into the bedroom to hang her dress in the closet. "I don't even know what time it is back home right now."

"Come on, David. Just admit it, they're nice." Lianna was leaning against the doorframe when he shut the closet and he sighed.

"I can tell they care about you a lot," he replied, keeping it to the point before yanking the covers down on the bed to reveal the sheet. "Now, it's time for bed."

"I need to wash my face," she mumbled, turning away from him, and he growled low. He didn't want to have an argument with her. Not here, and definitely not with her half-drunk and half-naked.

Turning off the lights in the bedroom, he went around to the other side of the bed and climbed in. The second he lay down exhaustion slammed into him like a truck. He didn't even know how many hours he'd been awake, but at least he'd get to sleep soon.

The water ran for a few more minutes, but eventually Lianna appeared in the doorway again. "You like Rémi at least, right? I mean, he let you borrow the clothes."

"Angel, would you just come to bed?"

Huffing, she flipped off the bathroom light and climbed into bed, but she'd only lain down for a second before she sat up again to rip off her bra and toss it into the dark. When she settled back down, he noticed that she curled up at the very edge of the bed, as far away from him as possible.

"Pissed at me?" he asked, and she sighed.

"I love you, David, but you're an asshole."

"That's fair," he replied, and she let out another huff.

Lianna shifted for a few minutes, and he tried to get comfortable too, but it wasn't easy without her in his arms — and she definitely wasn't going to let him wrap his arms around her right now. She was always more stubborn with a little alcohol in her bloodstream, and she'd drawn her line in the sand.

He just wasn't going to cross it tonight like he usually would.

David knew exactly what she wanted to hear. Some version of *'Oh, they're so nice! Of course they're not evil criminals running an international empire!'* — but that just wasn't true, and he'd promised her that he'd always tell her the truth. So, that left him with uncomfortable silence and no way to fall asleep even though he felt the exhaustion down to his bones.

Fucking hell.

It wasn't as if he couldn't see her point of view. Rémi did seem like a nice guy. Hell, *all* of her cousins seemed nice. But was it real? Could Jean-Luc's kids really not know about the family's shady dealings, just like Lianna had been blind to her own father's crimes?

Is that what's happening?

Was he painting a whole family with the same brush again? Damning the children based on the actions of the father?

Sighing, he turned over, shoving at the pillow to try and make it comfortable while his brain whirled. It just didn't make sense. Lianna's father had at least had the cover of his company to excuse all his money... what did the Faures have?

Nothing.

The kids were more than old enough to have questions about where the money came from for all of it, and they had to be curious why their home needed armed guards. There was only one logical answer — they knew.

So, were they all just good actors? Was the family routine just a show, or was it real... and they still knew about the criminal side of the Faure name?

The Brady Bunch meets the Godfather — what a weird mix.

David couldn't stop turning over the way the cousins had talked to Lianna, how genuine they all had seemed. Then there was the extravagant gift from Jean-Luc and Cécile, which was clearly meant to buy her loyalty, her affection, and the invitation for Christmas was them just trying to sink their claws in deeper... but the cousins might be real.

Maybe.

Even though he'd never admit it aloud, he was grateful that they had given her a birthday party. It was on a scale he would have never been able to provide, and it had made her so happy, which was all that mattered. He'd chosen his hill to die on, and it was Lianna. If they cared about her, if they treated her well, if it was all sincere, then he'd put up with it for her sake.

Sleep started to slide over him when he remembered the only time all night Lianna had seemed less than happy — the first moment she'd met Marc Faure.

Fuck. He was supposed to ask her about that before they went to bed, but... maybe it was better this way. She'd been drunk and annoyed with him, and the conversation would have probably only irritated her further.

In the morning. I'll ask her then.

He couldn't stop thinking about how strange the man had been, though. Everyone else seemed so excited to see Lianna, but he'd shown up late and had barely spoken to Lianna most of the night. In fact, he was pretty sure the man had only talked to her once Jean-Luc introduced them, and then his family was one of the first to leave — even after the cousins had asked them to stay.

It was strange, but then again, the entire family was strange, and his head was pounding. Turning over, he moved over in the bed until he was closer to Lianna, able to smell the lingering scent of her perfume, which reminded him of home.

Their home, their bed, their life together.

And, eventually, that let him drift off to sleep.

A rapid series of knocks yanked David awake, his heart racing as he sat up. Lianna's arm had been draped across his chest before he jerked upright, so she'd woken too when he moved.

"It's time for breakfast! Come on!" More knocks clattered on the door to pair with the overly chipper voice coming through the wood. "Lianna? David? You can't sleep the day away, we have *plans!*"

"We're up!" Lianna called back, sitting up to lean her head in her hands.

"Yay!" the chipper girl replied. "See you downstairs!"

"Who was that?" David mumbled, and Lianna groaned.

"I think that was Emilie." Rolling her neck, she stretched, her joints popping as David watched her curves moving in the hazy light coming through the curtains. "What time is it?"

Shaking out the watch he'd accidentally slept in, David took it off and rubbed his eyes to get them to focus on it. "Eight thirty. Jesus fucking Christ, why does that feel so much earlier here? And why are they so happy about it?"

"Time zones, and they must be morning people," she replied as she got out of bed.

"Are you sure you're related to them?" he asked, and she turned around to flip him off before going to the bathroom. Chuckling, David lay back down. He'd woken several times during the night, automatically reaching for Lianna, and he was sure he'd only stayed asleep when she finally rolled over and draped her arm over him. But… that meant he had no fucking clue how much sleep he'd actually got.

So fucking tired.

"They'll have coffee downstairs. Good coffee," Lianna tempted him, and he groaned as he made himself get up.

"I'm taking a shower," he said as he entered the bathroom and turned on the water so it would warm.

"Can I go first?" she asked, and he looked at the inside of the shower and back at her.

"Shower together?" he suggested, and she smiled a little.

"We do not have time for you to fuck me. They're obviously all downstairs and sent Emilie to wake us up." Lianna braced a hand on her hip, but since she was naked, the defiant stance wasn't that effective.

Still, she was probably right.

"All right, you go first so you can do all the stuff to your hair."

"Thank you," she answered before blowing him a kiss.

It wasn't long before he was ready, and to be fair, things probably went faster with them showering separately, because seeing her naked was too tempting, and he definitely would have pinned her to the wall for a quickie in the shower if he'd been in there with her.

Don't think about that.

Ignoring the growing hard-on trapped under his jeans, David dug out his phone and turned it on. Lianna was still drying her hair in her underwear, but he was already dressed, so he moved Rémi's clothes aside and sat in the chair to check his phone.

There was an email from Harry asking him if he was alive, and he smiled to himself as he tapped out a quick reply to the old man to confirm he and Lianna had arrived safely. He'd just finished skimming his other emails and switched over to scroll through Reddit when he remembered Lianna's reaction to Marc Faure at the party. Tossing his phone back onto his bag, he moved to the doorway of the bathroom, waiting for Lianna to turn off the hair dryer.

"What is it?" she asked over the roar of it.

"I'll wait. I'm enjoying the view."

Lianna rolled her eyes, but soon enough her hair was dry, and she set the dryer aside to start tugging a hairbrush through all that blonde hair. "Go on. Tell me what you want to tell me."

"I actually have a question, angel."

She glanced at him in the mirror, waiting, but when he didn't immediately speak, she sighed. "Well?"

"It's about something I noticed at the party. When you saw Marc Faure last night… what happened?" he asked, and she paused for a second, the hairbrush halfway through her golden waves, before she continued brushing and shrugged a shoulder.

"I think I just recognized him from the photos Jean-Luc and Cécile sent over," she replied, but he could tell that wasn't true, or at least it wasn't the *whole* truth, and if they were back home he'd spank her ass for it — but who knew who might be hovering outside the damn door.

Instead, he went for the obvious. "I always know when you're lying to me, angel."

"I'm not—" she started, but when he raised his eyebrows at her in the mirror she groaned. "It's nothing, David. Really."

"Tell me."

"Oh my God…" Lianna tossed the brush down and picked up her make-up, leaning closer to the mirror as she used the eyeliner in quick, confident movements. "He just— He—"

"Lianna." He kept his voice calm, but firm, even though he was already tired, sex-deprived, and irritated. "What is it? Just spit it out."

"He just reminds me of my dad," she replied, staring down at her make-up bag as she dug through it. "Something about the way he talks… his mannerisms… and he was just odd. It was like he wasn't even happy to see me."

"Yeah, I think he was the only person who didn't keep pestering you all night."

Lianna looked over her shoulder at him, clearly as irritable this morning as he was. "No one was pestering me."

"Fine," David conceded, crossing his arms as he leaned on the doorframe. "But he did avoid you, and he showed up late. Left early too."

"Maybe his family was busy," she replied as she continued focusing on her face in the mirror.

"You don't think that was weird? As over the top as Jean-Luc has been about how *excited* the family is to meet you?"

"Not everything is a giant conspiracy, David. Just drop it, okay?" Sighing, she turned toward him and nudged him out of the way. "I need to get dressed. They're probably waiting on us for breakfast."

"Another family meal, *yay*," he mumbled, leaning against the wall as she pulled out clothes from the closet.

"What did you think would happen while we're here?" she asked, shutting the door. "We're in their house."

"I thought I'd get at least a little alone time with you."

Pulling a sweater over her head, she smiled at him and moved close to press a quick kiss to his lips. "Later."

"Is that a promise?" he asked, and she sat on the edge of the bed to pull on her jeans and then her boots.

"Sure, but right now I'm starving, and slightly hungover. So, I want breakfast."

"Fine. Back into the fray," he said, saluting her before he gestured toward the door, and Lianna laughed.

EIGHT

Lianna

"I can't wait to show you around," Emilie said, almost bouncing in her seat as she finished the last of her juice.

"There really is a lot to see here," Anaelle added. "Nothing compared to going into Nice, but we'll still have fun."

"I'm just desperate for some girl time." Amanda laughed a little, raising her hands. "And some more kid-free time."

"Girl time sounds great, and everything looked so beautiful on the way in yesterday, I can't wait to see it all." Lianna took another sip of coffee, grateful she'd popped a few pain relievers in the bathroom to help her headache. That, combined with the caffeine and the food, might be enough to handle it.

"If you don't want to hang out with the girls all day, David, why don't you come with me and Mathieu? We can show you around the property the fun way," Rémi said, chuckling as David looked up at him from his plate. "On the four-wheelers."

"The most fun part of it might be seeing just how bad Rémi is at driving one," Mathieu snarked, grinning at his brother when Rémi glared at him.

"I'm pretty sure only one of us broke his arm riding the four-wheelers."

"I was *twelve*," Mathieu retorted, shaking his head. "You're just annoyed that I outpaced you so quickly."

"We'll see." Rémi laughed again before he turned back to David. "What do you say? Come with us, or hang out with the girls all day?"

"You should go have fun," Lianna whispered, leaning closer to him. "Let me have some girl time."

David glanced at her, and she could tell he didn't like the idea of being separated from her, but there really was no reason to refuse their offer. After a long moment, he lifted a shoulder in a slight shrug and turned back to Rémi. "Okay, I'll go."

"Maybe I can pester you about some of the security stuff while we're out there," Mathieu said, and David nodded.

"Sure."

"Why don't you head out now? The views from the eastern grove should be beautiful right now," Jean-Luc suggested, and Rémi and Mathieu looked at each other for a second before they both stood up.

"I get the black one!" Mathieu called out, pushing his chair back in as he hurried toward the door.

"That's not how it works, Mathieu! You're an adult now, you should act like it!" Rémi called, but his brother was already gone. Sighing, the man looked at David again. "Come on, I'll show you where he went."

David got up from the table as well, pushing his chair in, and she leaned back to grab his arm. "Have fun, okay? I love you."

"Love you too," he replied quietly, squeezing her hand before he nodded at Rémi and followed him out.

"He's so *quiet*," Emilie said as soon as David left the room.

"But sweet," Amanda replied, laughing. "My husband was too concerned with racing his brother to even tell me goodbye!"

"I think David is just a little overwhelmed by everything, you know?" Lianna tilted her mug up and finished the last of her coffee. "He's never been out of the country before, so all of this is… a lot."

"Well, you guys seem to really love each other." Emilie sighed, leaning back in her chair. "All the guys I meet are such jerks."

"What guys are you meeting?" Jean-Luc asked, and Emilie blushed as she suddenly sat up straight.

"No one in particular," she answered defensively, and Jean-Luc chuckled.

"You're twenty-five, Emilie. I'm under no belief that you aren't dating, I was just curious." Smiling, Jean-Luc glanced at his watch. "Okay, girls, if you'll give me a few minutes with Lianna, I promise she'll be yours for the rest of the day."

"Thank God," Emilie muttered under her breath, escaping the room, and her father, as quickly as possible. Amanda and Anaelle said their goodbyes and followed after her a moment later, both of them laughing as they walked into the hall.

"I'll go see what boy Emilie is so flustered about." Cécile smiled warmly then leaned over to kiss her husband on the cheek. "See you in the garden."

"I'll be there soon," Jean-Luc replied, watching his wife walk out of the dining room before he turned to look at Lianna again. "I just wanted to check in on you after last night. How are you feeling? Is all of this too overwhelming?"

"A bit, to be honest." Lianna toyed with her water glass. "It feels kind of like when you surprised me in the US. Just… a lot to process at once, but it's not overwhelming in a bad way."

Chuckling, Jean-Luc nodded. "Well, I do hope you feel welcome. That's all we wanted."

"I feel very welcome, I promise." Glancing toward the doorway, she could hear the girls laughing and she wondered what it was about.

"I don't want to keep you, but I wanted to check in and see if you had any questions for me now that you've met everyone." Jean-Luc plucked a grape from the half-eaten bunch on his plate and popped it in his mouth, and she almost declined the offer to ask questions — but then she remembered that there was really only *one* reason she'd been able to come to France at all.

"Actually… there is something I wanted to talk to you about in private."

His eyebrows lifted, but Jean-Luc took a sip of his coffee before he spoke. "All right. What would you like to talk about?"

Just say it.

"Well, I never got to thank you for your generosity in paying for my apartment when my assets were frozen, and, of course, for taking care of my legal issues." Lianna's heart was racing as she laid all her cards on the table.

Jean-Luc stayed silent for a long moment, keeping his gaze on the coffee cup. "I'm not sure what you're talking about, Lia—"

"Don't lie to me," she snapped, raising a hand to cut him off. "I obviously can't make you answer me, but don't *ever* lie to me, Jean-Luc. I had enough of that from my father."

Sighing, he looked up at her, his expression turning pensive as he rotated the cup back and forth on the table. Eventually, he nodded and took a deep breath. "You're right, Lianna. I shouldn't lie to you, and I apologize. Honestly... I had hoped to keep my involvement in your situation confidential because I didn't want it to sway our relationship one way or another. However, you are correct. I did rent the apartment for you."

"Why?"

"It seemed unfair for Alain's actions to take more from you than they already had." Jean-Luc leaned back in his chair, shaking his head slightly. "I handled it through a few companies we own to avoid any easily identifiable links to the Faure name, but I should have known you'd see through that."

"Well, you *had* just arrived in town to meet me for the first time," she reminded him, and he raised one hand from the table, turning his palm up in a half-shrug.

"I admit, it wasn't the most well-hidden ruse, but I assure you I just wanted to help."

"Like you *helped* with the investigation keeping me from leaving the country?"

Jean-Luc's face went blank, and his answer was short. "Family takes care of family. *La famille avant tout.*"

A frisson of anger buzzed through Lianna's veins as she stared at him, waiting for an actual explanation that apparently wasn't going to come without her pushing. "Well, what was it? A bribe? Did you threaten them so they'd drop the investigation?"

"Lianna…"

"We're not in public, Jean-Luc. There's no need to be coy or evasive. I think I deserve an answer, don't you?"

His gaze met hers again, but there wasn't anger there. He didn't seem upset at all. If anything, he looked a little sad.

"You're right. You do, and my answer is similar to why I rented the apartment for you." Jean-Luc sat up in his chair and braced an elbow on the table, cradling his forehead in one hand for a moment. "Everything that Alain did was *his* choice, but as a father he should have thought beyond himself. As parents, it's really all we're here on this earth to do. We are *supposed* to make the world better for our children… and my brother failed you in that."

"Yes, he did."

"Exactly. You didn't deserve to carry the burden of his crimes, Lianna, and so — yes. I used our family's influence to encourage the case against you to be dropped, because there *was* no case against you, *mon oisillon.* They were dragging it out to punish you because Alain was dead, and…" Jean-Luc paused, his hand tightening into a fist atop the table before he moved it to his lap.

"And?" she prompted.

"And I didn't want you to be hurt any more than you already had," he finished, raising his warm brown eyes to hers. "All I want to do is keep you safe, Lianna. And for you to feel loved by your family. If I crossed a line in doing that, I apologize."

The frustration bled out of her as he confirmed her suspicions. She'd been ninety-nine percent sure it was Jean-Luc, but until she heard it from his lips, her mind wouldn't rest. All she'd wanted was honesty, and he'd given her that… and more.

Jean-Luc had talked about carrying the burden of her father's crimes, which she had — in more ways than he knew — but wasn't he asking her to do the same thing? As wonderful as everyone had seemed at the party the night before, the mere fact that he could do something like ending the investigation into her with barely any effort spoke volumes of what the Faures were capable of.

But he'd used all that power to do something good, to help her… so was it still wrong?

She wanted to pretend it wasn't, but she knew in her gut that it was. If they would have eventually dropped the case against her, why not just let it happen in due time? It had sucked to be harassed by the government, to be dragged to interview after interview, but she was innocent and that would have come out eventually.

Innocence doesn't always matter.

Sighing, Lianna shook her head. "I can't pretend that I'm not grateful for everything you've done, Jean-Luc. I didn't want to lose that apartment. I'd worked hard to pay for it myself, and it meant a lot to me. And I was never involved in my father's illegal activities, so I'm glad the investigation is over. But"—Lianna leaned forward, making sure he had his eyes on hers—"I don't want to carry the burden of *your* crimes either. Even if they're for my own sake."

His eyes widened slightly, but then he nodded, his lips pursing together for a moment. "Well said, Lianna. I respect that. As I told you over lunch when I came to see you, I am doing everything I can to change the future for my own children. To move our family away from things that could endanger that future… and I'm doing this so my children never have to bear the burden of my crimes, or any of those done in the name of Faure."

I really hope that's true.

"Thank you for your honesty, Jean-Luc," Lianna said, pushing back from the table to rise from her chair and end the uncomfortable discussion. "That's all I want or need."

"I hope that you feel you can always be honest with me as well, Lianna," he replied, a small smile twitching up the corner of his mouth as another round of raucous laughs came from nearby. He glanced toward the doorway, and once again she could see the clear love he had for his family. "I believe the girls have quite the day planned for you."

"It seems like they do," she agreed.

"Enjoy it. All I want is for you to feel at home here." Standing up, Jean-Luc's smile spread further. "Now, if you don't mind, I have a date in the garden with my wife."

"That sounds like fun," Lianna said, and Jean-Luc laughed a little as he escorted her into the hall.

"Well, my job is to dig the holes and *not* touch the plants. Cécile says I have a black thumb." Waving at her, he pointed into another room as he moved the opposite direction. "I believe the girls are waiting for you in the library. Have fun!"

Lianna stayed in the hall after he disappeared around the corner, letting all of the new information settle inside her. She was glad that David hadn't been present for the conversation, it would have only confirmed all of his negative opinions about Jean-Luc's intentions... but she didn't interpret it in quite the same way he would. Yes, he wanted her to be comfortable in his home, to get to know his family, but none of his actions seemed to be about keeping her in France.

He wouldn't have paid for her apartment if he'd wanted her here.

"*Papa! Nous avons des choses à faire!*" Anaelle shouted as she walked out of the library and almost barreled directly into her. "Oh! I'm sorry, I thought you were still with *Papa*."

"We just finished up," Lianna replied, slapping on a smile as Anaelle waved her back into the library.

"Good, because we've been chatting through our ideas for the day." Anaelle stopped short of the chairs where Emilie and Amanda were sitting. "To start with, I know you studied art history, so I wanted to show you some of the nice pieces our family has here on the property."

"I want to show you the horses. Ours are so sweet, and we can even go for a ride in the grove if you want!" Emilie added.

Amanda held her hands up. "We can do whatever you guys want. I just really want to end the day relaxing around the pool with drinks in our hands. Maybe we can do a tour of Jean-Luc's very well-stocked wine cellar before we relax outside."

"It's too cool to swim right now," Anaelle said.

"I don't need to swim, but sunny and warm with a nice cool breeze is perfect sunbathing weather to me," Amanda replied.

"You only think that because you and Rémi spend all your time in England where there's never any sunshine," Emilie retorted, and Amanda laughed.

"I won't deny that, but it's really up to Lianna what we do today."

Three pairs of eyes swiveled toward her and she shrugged. "Let's do all of it!"

The day flew by faster than Lianna had expected. Between Jean-Luc's incredible collection of art, loving on all the horses, and strolling through the olive grove to take in the sights, she was more than ready to relax by the pool by the time four o'clock rolled around.

Lounging in the sun, there was no chance of getting a tan in her clothes, but it was still the best end to the day. Wine in hand, the sunlight shimmering on the surface of the pool, and getting to know her cousins even more, she felt completely at peace. It was almost like she'd known them for longer than a couple of days. There were no awkward breaks in conversation, no topics that everyone couldn't contribute to in some way, and the weather was perfect for it. A cool breeze meant that even with the clear sky she wasn't too warm, and the views were definitely better here than back in New York.

Turning back to the girls, Lianna smiled as they continued talking.

"You're so right. Netflix is both the best and worst thing ever. I mean, I love that I can always find something to watch, but if I *do* find something it's way too easy to binge watch," Amanda said, shading her eyes to look up at everyone.

"Yes!" Emilie shouted with a groan. "I open my laptop and turn something on and suddenly it's six hours later, and I realize I haven't moved at all."

Laughing, Lianna nodded. "I've done that way more often than I'd like to admit."

The sound of engines getting closer drew all of their attention, and she sat up to look out at the grove of trees. Weaving in and out was a trio of four-wheelers, but what pulled Lianna from her seat was the sound of laughter and male voices shouting over the roar of the engines, which only got louder when the vehicles finally disappeared from view, parking close to the house. Moving to the stone railing, she peeked over the edge and was surprised to see David laughing along with Rémi and Mathieu.

He looked... happy. Comfortable.

Trying to hold herself back from getting too excited by the prospect of him finally getting over his issues with her family, she waved down at them. "Hey guys! We're up here around the pool. Come join us!"

"On our way!" Rémi shouted, and David looked up at her with a wide smile that she hadn't seen in too long.

Turning back to the girls, she spread her arms with a little shrug. "Seems like the boys had fun."

"I never had a doubt. I'm glad David went with them," Amanda said, sitting up on the lounger as the men's voices came up the side stairs to the terrace. "Rémi really wants to help David feel more comfortable here."

"That means a lot," Lianna answered, taking her seat again just before the guys appeared, still laughing. Mathieu nudged David and said something too quiet for the rest of them to hear, but then they laughed even louder. A moment later, their gazes met, and she couldn't help but smile when she saw just how ridiculously handsome he looked with that grin on his face.

"Hello darling," Rémi said, stopping beside Amanda's chair to bend down and kiss her.

David's shirt was clinging to his chest, slightly darker in spots from sweat, but it only made him look better as he approached her. Bracing his hands on either side of her head on the lounger, he leaned close, and she felt that delicious frisson of anticipation run down her spine as his dark eyes met hers. "I missed you today."

"I missed you too," she whispered, and then he closed the gap, capturing her lips in a kiss that was probably a bit more than any of her cousins expected to see — but David managed to keep his hands off her, which kept it rated PG-13 instead of R. Barely. His tongue brushed hers, a low growl rumbling in his chest when he nipped her bottom lip before claiming her mouth again. Finally, he pulled back and sat down on the edge of the lounger, running his hand over her thigh, and Lianna couldn't help but blush, chuckling a bit as she pushed her hair behind her ears. "So... you're in a good mood. Did you have fun today?"

"It wasn't miserable." Shrugging, David turned to glance at the others, a smile hovering on his lips as he watched Mathieu and Anaelle shoving each other on one of the loungers where Mathieu was clearly trying to steal it from his sister.

"It looked a lot better than that," Lianna argued, poking him in the ribs, and he sighed when he looked at her again.

"Rémi and Mathieu are fine," David admitted, which was basically a glowing compliment coming from him. "Mathieu actually taught me a couple of things in exchange for discussing security systems with him."

"Oh really? What did he teach you?"

Leaning close, David's lips brushed her ear as he whispered, "*Tu as été très coquine.*"

You've been a very bad girl.

Lianna's cheeks went crimson, and she couldn't help but laugh in shock at David's rough French saying something so dirty. "Oh my God, please tell me Mathieu didn't teach you that."

"Oh, he did." Chuckling, David squeezed her thigh and kissed his way down her throat. "He taught me another one too."

"Yeah?" she panted, unable to focus on anything but his touch and the low rumble of his voice as he nipped her neck.

"Mon ange, tu vas finir en travers de mes genoux tout à l'heure."

My angel, you're going to end up over my knees later.

"Holy shit," Lianna whispered, her breath catching as he chuckled and sat up straight, his eyes roaming over her.

"I asked him to translate that one." Grinning, David looked over his shoulder at the others, and Lianna realized they were all watching them with big smiles. Mathieu even had the nerve to give them a thumbs up, and she covered her face in embarrassment.

"You did *not*," she whined, but it was clear he had. Bonus points for him making friends with her cousin, but the entire idea of them discussing any of this about *her* was mortifying.

"I did, but you know you're impressed. This stupid language isn't exactly easy."

Rolling her eyes, Lianna dropped her hands into her lap. "It's not a stupid language, but I am impressed. You didn't even butcher it *too* badly."

"That's not very nice, angel." He chuckled as he slid his touch higher on her thigh, his dark eyes intense. "Maybe you need me to teach you a lesson later. Add a few stripes to your sweet ass."

"Oh my God! No!" she whispered harshly, shoving at his hand, but he only tightened his grip.

"What? Are you ashamed of me?" he asked, lifting his brows, but he didn't look upset.

Groaning, she blocked his hand from moving any higher and kept her voice hushed. "Of you? No, of course not. But of the fact that I like getting my ass beat? Um, yes. It's not happening."

"We'll see." David winked at her and then let go, turning to face the others, and she did her best to make the butterflies in her stomach calm down.

Finishing off her wine, she raised the empty glass in the air and stood up. "I need more wine."

"Me too!" Amanda said, laughing, and as they went to the table to refill, she heard everyone pick up conversation again. The woman bumped Lianna with her hip as they looked through the bottles together. "He's completely head over heels for you."

"Thanks," Lianna answered, still fighting the blush burning her cheeks.

"I mean it. Rémi and I used to be like that before the twins. Couldn't keep our hands off each other." Her wistful tone made Amanda seem a little sad, but she was still smiling. "He's softened a lot since they were born, but we still have our fun when we have the energy to stay awake."

Lianna laughed when Amanda winked at her, not sure what to say in reply to the bold confession. "I'm sure it's a lot harder with kids."

"Sometimes. It just takes more effort to make time for each other." Filling her glass, Amanda handed off the bottle. "Remember that when you guys have kids. You've got to make time for each other, so you don't lose that spark."

"Right," Lianna answered, momentarily stunned as Amanda walked back to sit beside Rémi.

Kids?

The idea had actually never even crossed her mind. Well, not with David. She'd thought about kids in general over the years, and she loved being around kids, but everything with David had been so... messy. Ignoring the situation that brought them together, Lianna had still spent the past nine months drowning in legal issues and financial drama. There hadn't been a single moment to think of anything beyond the present.

But, looking at him now, watching him laugh with her cousins as the guys recounted their four-wheeling adventure... it didn't seem impossible.

Just very, very far away.

She didn't even know what David thought about kids or if that was even in his plans for the future, and there was no way in hell she was going to bring that up anytime soon. They just needed to deal with one obstacle at a time, and getting David to accept that the Faures may not be as evil as he believed was the most important thing right now.

NINE

David

Moving up the stairs after dinner, it was impossible to keep his hands off Lianna. For the first time since they'd arrived at the Faure estate, he felt like he could actually breathe. He wasn't sure if it was the fact that he'd spent an entire day away from Jean-Luc, or if it was the effect of the wine that had started flowing on the terrace and continued throughout dinner... but it felt good.

Lianna felt good, and he loved the way she squirmed when he wrapped his arm around her waist, pulling her tight against him as he half-dragged her up the stairs. Much better than last night when she'd been wasted, and he'd had to practically carry her. Tonight, they were both pleasantly buzzed, and she'd been teasing him for the past three hours, so there was no way in hell he wasn't fucking her tonight.

It had been torture waiting for someone else to leave the table first so he could get her upstairs without offending everyone, but Rémi and Amanda had saved the day by leaving to take care of the twins. Claiming lingering jet lag, he'd squeezed her thigh, and then stood to excuse them.

Jean-Luc had even smiled at him as he'd told them goodnight.

Not that David cared about the asshole's opinion of him, but it had let him finally get his hands on her and that's all that mattered. Shoving the door to their room open, it smacked into the wall, and Lianna shushed him. "Oh my God, be quiet!"

"Now is not the time to tell me what to do, angel," he growled, scooping her up to toss her onto the bed before he shut the door with more restraint than he thought he was capable of in the moment. Flipping the lock, he faced her and groaned. Lianna was sitting up on the bed, taking off her shoes, all those golden waves flowing over her shoulder in a cascade that he'd both loved and hated since the first time he laid eyes on her. She was beautiful, but any idiot on the street could see that. What he loved about her was her strength. That iron will that he'd never been able to break, no matter what fucked-up shit he did to her. Lianna might bend for him sometimes, but it was because she could stand up to him that he loved her — and no one else on the planet would ever get to see that side of her. Not like he had.

All mine.

"You need to take those clothes off or I'm going to rip them off you."

Grinning, Lianna looked up at him as she dropped her last shoe to the ground. "Is that a promise?"

"You've been teasing me all afternoon, angel. That's not a promise, it's a fucking warning." Ripping his shirt over his head, he tossed it aside. "Get undressed. Now."

He could tell she was nervous about having sex inside the Faure house, but there was excitement in her eyes too when she finally hopped off the bed to yank her jeans down, followed by her underwear, kicking them aside as she took off her sweater. His cock was already a steel rod before she was naked, and he wrapped his hand around the base and squeezed, forcing a deep breath as he looked her over.

"On the bed," he commanded, stepping over his clothes as she obeyed him, scooting back to give him room, but when he got to the bed, he grabbed her legs and flipped her onto her stomach. "Knees."

"David," she said his name quietly, a breathy, needy edge already taking over her voice. "We have to be quiet."

Landing a spank on her ass, he climbed onto the bed behind her, grinning when she twisted to look over her shoulder at him. "Don't tell me what to do, angel. That's not how this works, and you know it."

"Please?" she begged, and he groaned again, running his hand over the pink handprint he'd left behind on her skin.

"Want me to gag you?"

"No." Groaning, Lianna leaned forward on the bed again, bracing herself on her elbows as he stroked a finger through the wetness between her thighs.

"Seems like I wasn't the only one that got wound up this afternoon."

"After what you whispered to me out on the terrace? How was I supposed to think straight after that?" she asked with more bite to her tone than necessary, and he landed another sharp spank to her other cheek. "David!"

"Keep up with the smart mouth, and I'll get my belt."

Burying her face in the bed, Lianna whined, but the slight wiggle of her hips told the truth. She'd love for him to get his belt, and they both knew it. Lianna wanted the pain as much as the pleasure, and it always made her come harder when he made it hurt — but the snap of a belt would be way too loud. Her family would still be in the halls for a while, and there was no way in hell he was going to wait until they all went to sleep.

"Be a good girl for me." Sliding two fingers inside her, he had to bite down on his lip to fight the urge to replace them with his cock right away. Her tight heat squeezed around his fingers, and he curved them down to focus on her g-spot as he moved closer. "That's right, angel. I want you soaking wet."

"Fuck..." she mumbled into the bed, and he slid his other hand underneath her, seeking her clit. Her hips bucked with the first swirl of his fingers, a sweet little gasp escaping as she pressed back into his touch.

"You want me to fuck you, don't you?" Watching her, he read every twitch of muscle, every hitched breath, as she nodded. Carefully pushing her closer and closer, he sped up the circles on her clit even though his balls ached. He wanted to be able to fuck her hard, to plunge into her cunt without working her up to it, but she had to be wet enough. The wait would be worth it though, and the reward would be her beautiful cries and her pussy clenching him when he made her come again and again. "Answer me."

"Yes. Yes, please." Panting, she lifted her head from the bed, little murmurs of pleasure telling him just how close she was.

"I'm not going to be gentle," he warned, plunging his fingers in hard and holding them deep as he tapped her g-spot, and her hips shifted side to side, seeking oblivion. *Not yet.* Grinning, he leaned down, keeping his voice low. "But you don't want me to be gentle, do you?"

Lianna just shook her head, lost in the search for a climax that he wasn't going to let her have yet. When she started to breathe harder, hushed moans slipping past her clenched teeth, he pulled away and grabbed onto her hip, digging his fingers in as he lined up.

"Beg me for it."

"David... please," she whined, and he barely pressed forward, immediately pulling back when Lianna tried to push herself onto him.

"Tsk, tsk, angel. That's not good enough. I want to hear you beg."

"Fuck..." Grumbling, Lianna lifted her head. "Please fuck me, David. Please. I don't want you to be gentle, I want it to hurt. Just please—"

Thrusting hard, he yanked Lianna's hips back to force himself balls deep in one stroke. Her cunt clamped down around his cock as she gasped, but he wasn't in the mood to drag this out, so he quickly slid back and slammed forward just as hard, biting down on his own groan of pleasure. "God, you feel so good."

"David…" Lianna's back was arched, head high, and he was more than happy to take the offering. Grabbing a fistful of her hair, he used it as leverage to pull her onto his dick again and again, losing track of the rising volume of her cries as he fucked her. Every thrust sent a ripple of sensation up his spine, every squeeze like a skitter of electricity over his skin, and he had to resist the urge to come as she made those little whimpers that always drove him crazy.

"Who owns you, angel?" he asked, releasing her hip to land another sharp spank that was, admittedly, probably too loud. The perfect hand print he left behind was worth the risk though, especially combined with the way her cunt gripped him as he continued to move inside her.

"You," she answered too quietly, and he could tell from the moan that followed that she was close.

"Louder."

"David, please," she pleaded, but he just spanked her again.

"I want to hear it."

"You," she finally said, just loud enough to satisfy him as she moaned even louder. "You own me. I'm yours. Oh God!"

"Good girl," he growled, slamming deep as he released her hair, reaching to the side to grab a pillow and shove it under her. "Now bite the fucking pillow before you come and let the whole house know what a naughty girl you really are."

Lianna moved the pillow, burying her face as she wrapped her arms around it, which made her back curve in the most beautiful way. When he held onto her hips and started to fuck her again, hard and fast, the moans weren't as muffled by the pillow as she probably thought — but he didn't really give a shit. He liked hearing her whimper and moan almost as much as he liked listening to her scream and beg. A second later she tensed, her pussy locking down around him, and he had to clench his jaw to fight the urge to come as she cried out into the pillow, her cunt squeezing him in waves.

"Fuck, yes... come for me." Groaning, he dug his fingers into her hips and yanked her back, driving his cock deeper, fucking her straight through the orgasm. Her muffled pleas and hushed moans just urged him on. Delivering another spank, and another, he growled when she reached back, trying to stop him.

"David! Please, it's too loud, baby. Please," she begged, and he smacked her hand away, landing another spank before he grabbed onto her hips again.

"Put your face back in the pillow. Now." Closing his eyes, he tried to hold back the tension building like an electrical storm in his veins. Everything was narrowing down to the feel of her skin against his, the impossible perfection of her slick heat, the way her body took everything he had to give — and he didn't want it to end.

Not yet.

The clap of their bodies coming together again and again was probably just as loud as the spanks, but he couldn't stop. The only thing that would make it better would be if he could see the desperate need on her face as he pushed her toward another orgasm, but there was no way he was changing positions now. He was close, so fucking close.

Leaning over her, he reached between her legs to find her clit, reveling in the way her hips slammed back into him, trying to avoid his touch.

"Oh God, I can't," she whined, and he shoved her face back into the pillow with a growl.

"I know what you can handle, and I want to feel you come again." Trying to pull his thoughts together was getting harder and harder, but he knew Lianna was just as close as he was, and he wanted to come with her this time. To feel her pull him deeper just as he came. "Be a good girl, angel. Come on."

Her soft murmurs in the pillow were half-bliss and half-torture, and it was exactly what he needed to hear. When she suddenly bucked, gripping his cock like a vise as she shouted into the pillow, he felt fire rush down his spine, and managed to bite down on her shoulder just before he came hard. Muffling his shout against her skin as he thrust deep, filling her as the world whited out in a violent crash of ecstasy.

David couldn't breathe for a second, unaware of everything except the insane beat of his heart crashing against his ribs. Lianna's low whine of pain was the first thing to break through the haze the orgasm left his brain in. Then he felt her back twitch against his chest, and he realized he was still sinking his teeth into her shoulder. Releasing her, he felt Lianna relax under him as he stared at the dark imprint his teeth had left behind.

"Jesus..." she whispered, her head turned to the side as she rested on the pillow. "That was... intense."

"Yeah." That was the only word he could manage for the moment, working to catch his breath as he kissed the mark on her shoulder. Groaning when she squeezed him again as a shudder rolled through her. "Fuck, angel."

"Your fault," Lianna mumbled, and he laughed a little as he pressed another kiss to her skin and then slid from her, dropping to the bed. A second later she was against his side, one leg draped over his, her head finding its place on his shoulder. "I love you so much."

"I love you too," he answered, still breathing hard. Pressing a kiss to her hair, he wrapped his arm around her back, not even caring that they were sideways on the bed, on top of the duvet because *someone* had made their bed during the day. They could move once his brain finished rebooting.

"Needed that." Her voice was barely a whisper, but he caught it, and he hugged her close to his side as a smile took over his face.

"Me too, angel." Having her against him was everything he wanted or needed. It didn't really matter where they were, even in the middle of the Faure compound. As long as she was with him, he was happy. Glancing down at her, he had the urge to say it, but he could tell by her even breaths that she was already asleep.

Stifling a chuckle so he wouldn't wake her, he leaned his cheek against her hair and tried to get comfortable. Eventually she'd get cold and wake him up to get under the covers, until then... he'd just enjoy this.

TEN

Lianna

It was strange how comfortable the Faure estate was beginning to feel. David was even starting to relax, and lunch almost felt... normal.

Like Lianna was always meant to be there.

The large table was more full than usual because Marc's family had joined them, and even though Jean-Luc was upset that Marc hadn't actually shown up, the meal was still wonderful, full of laughter and rapid conversation over delicious food. She was actually starting to recognize their voices, knowing who was speaking even before she saw them, and even when the family talked about things she wasn't present for — she felt included.

Jean-Luc had told her he wanted her to feel welcome, and she did.

More than she'd ever imagined she could.

Lianna may have been denied this side of her family, kept from meeting them her entire life, but she'd never expected to click with them so easily. She wasn't just trying to get to know them better, she actually *liked* them. Her cousins were funny, smart, and nothing like the rich kids she'd known back home. And, despite everything David believed about Jean-Luc, the man had already treated her with more kindness than her father ever had. He didn't treat her like she was different, like some cast-off from the family he'd picked up abroad — even though that's exactly what she was. No, he treated her like family. Jean-Luc had his own history, his own story to tell, and while he wasn't perfect... no one really was.

And he's changing things.

As she took in the grassy space beneath the terrace, a warm, buzzy feeling ran through her when she watched everyone playing, shouting insults at each other in a mix of English and French. Rémi was chasing the soccer ball, knocking into Mathieu to dribble it past him before passing it to Anaelle who narrowly avoided Marc's son, Gregory, to score a goal. Clapping, Lianna cheered for them, and Anaelle pumped her fist in the air, laughing as she waved up at her.

Cécile and Jean-Luc were standing off to the side, his arm around her waist, and they looked like the perfect family. Everything about them seemed to be so wholesome, so full of *love*. He'd told her that he was moving the family away from the darker side of their business, pulling away from their criminal side, and she actually believed him now. There was no faking the way he looked at his family, the way he loved them, cared for them. It was obvious in the photos they'd given her, but seeing it in person was completely different. It was a different kind of family love than she'd ever known. Powerful, earth-shattering, and she wanted to be a part of it. She wanted to have stories with them years from now, to know an inside joke before it was explained.

She wanted to feel less alone in the world.

Swallowing down the sudden swell of emotion in her chest, she headed down the stairs at the edge of the terrace, prepared to rejoin the game, but Natalie's shout distracted her. "Marc! There you are!"

The woman started walking toward him, but when Jean-Luc broke away from Cécile to approach his brother, Natalie stopped short, returning Jean-Luc's wave before she faced the impromptu soccer game once more. Lianna couldn't look away though, everything about their body language was too stiff, almost angry.

Is this about lunch?

Too far away to hear, Lianna could only judge the intense conversation based on their movements, but she felt pretty confident that Jean-Luc was still upset with Marc for missing the big family lunch. He'd stepped out of the room several times to call his brother, and Natalie had texted the man several times, yet lunch had been over for almost half an hour, and he was only just arriving. Unease crept into her stomach, twisting around the food that suddenly felt too heavy as Jean-Luc jerked an arm to the side and Marc crossed his arms, leaning back on his heels.

That gesture... there was something about that gesture. Like a word on the tip of her tongue, she tried to figure out why it made her feel sick and uncomfortable. Then the memory hit her hard, like someone had popped a movie into her brain and clicked play without warning.

She'd come upstairs to the penthouse one afternoon, wanting to swap her shoes for ones that were a little more comfortable, but when she went inside, she'd heard men's voices coming from her father's office. Confused, she inched toward the doorway, but her father had stepped out before she got too close.

"What are you doing up here, princess?" he'd asked, smiling at her, but before she could even answer, another man stepped out from behind him.

"Who's this?" Lianna asked, and the flash of irritation on her dad's face just made her more concerned, but he recovered quickly and introduced him as... something. That part of the memory was fuzzy, but she remembered the way the man stood there with his arms crossed, his brows pulled together as he looked her over in silence. Not even offering his hand to her as an introduction.

After that, she knew her dad had pressed her on why she'd come upstairs in the middle of the afternoon, and when she'd explained the shoes, he'd hugged her and then sent her on her way so he could continue his meeting.

With Marc Faure.

She didn't have a single doubt in her mind that the man from her memory was Marc, no matter what bullshit name her father had made up for him. Marc Faure had been in her home, had met her face to face only a few years ago, and lied about it.

Anger flooded her veins, and she turned away from them, searching out David by the trees where she'd left him. Trying to maintain her composure, she did her best to walk calmly over to him, but she could tell he was already on edge by the time she got close enough for him to whisper, "What happened?"

"Nothing."

"Don't pull that shit with me, Lianna. What happened?" David's voice was gruff, protective, and she knew that the only way he'd calm down was if she answered.

"I remembered where I recognized Marc from," she replied, keeping her voice low so that no one could overhear them.

"And?" he prompted.

"He was at my father's penthouse a few years ago. They were meeting in his office, and I ran into them when I went upstairs to change my shoes. It was during the workday, and he obviously didn't expect me to find them." A bitter laugh bubbled up in her chest as she shook her head. "He gave him some other name. My uncle was standing five feet away from me, and my father wouldn't even tell me who he really was, and now they're all lying about it. Pretending not to recognize me? There's no way in hell Marc didn't know who I was. I look exactly the same."

"I knew there was something wrong with Marc. The way he's been acting, and not showing up for lunch today?" David growled. "He's trying to avoid you so you don't realize they're all a bunch of fucking liars."

"You don't know—"

"Are you really going to keep defending them *now*? You know they've been lying to you, Lianna!" He was being too loud, and she gritted her teeth, trying to stay calm and look calm and happy and like everything was perfectly okay, because the last thing she needed was to get caught in an argument in front of everyone.

"Just drop it, David. I shouldn't have even told you."

"Bullshit. This is what I've been trying to tell you, angel. They don't have any respect for the truth, and this whole show is just—"

"Stop it!" she hissed, taking a deep breath as she looked up at the sky, trying to find some peace in the serene, cornflower blue. "I mean it, David. Drop it right now. I'm not talking about this out here."

"Lianna." He tried to grab her arm as she walked toward the soccer game, but she avoided it, knowing he wouldn't risk causing a scene in front of everyone. It was her own fault, though. She never should have mentioned it to him. Or, at the very least, she should have waited until they were alone.

Silently praying that he would let it go, Lianna waved at Mathieu and rejoined his team. "I'm back in!"

"Now you're toast!" Mathieu shouted, passing her the ball, and she kicked it down their invented field toward Madeline.

An hour later everyone was sufficiently worn out, drinking water in one of the smaller sitting rooms that were flooded with light. Lianna was browsing the pair of bookshelves tucked near one of the windows overlooking the garden, when she saw Marc and Natalie talking in the hall. She looked irritated, but Marc continued speaking insistently until she eventually nodded. A moment later she came back into the room with a smile.

"I'm really sorry, but we need to head back home."

"You're leaving already?" Cécile asked, glancing at Jean-Luc, who was stone-faced for a moment before he summoned a polite expression.

"Marc has some work he wants to finish at home, and—"

"What work is that?" Jean-Luc stood, moving closer as Marc took his place beside Natalie.

"I'm still reviewing last month's shipping manifests," Marc answered casually, but she didn't believe it, and it seemed like Jean-Luc didn't either. The man shook his head a little before looking up at his brother again.

"I do hope you'll come back before Lianna leaves."

"Of course." Nodding, Marc gestured to his children. "Gregory, Madeline?"

"I'm sorry that we're leaving so quickly." Natalie's apology was to Cécile, and the two women embraced as her cousins said goodbye to the others. Lianna met them halfway when they turned toward her, exchanging brief hugs and cheek kisses before they moved toward their parents.

Lianna approached her aunt and uncle, doing her best to make eye contact with Marc, but he avoided it carefully. Still, she spoke directly to him when she said, "I hope to see all of you again before we head home."

"Absolutely," Natalie assured her, and then Marc finally looked at her, offering a short nod of agreement. His smile was a stiff mask, and she wondered how many times her father had worn the same one, but she'd just been too damn naïve to see through it.

After they left, the easy conversation of the room struggled to return. Apparently Lianna wasn't the only one bothered by Marc's behavior, and the reaction of the rest of the Faures told her how unusual it was. Jean-Luc's and Marc's families lived close to each other, the cousins had grown up together, and she was sure that they normally spent hours together when they visited. Hell, she felt confident that they slept at the house sometimes — the estate had plenty of rooms for it.

Her presence was the only difference.

All she'd wanted from her family was honesty, and it seemed that was too high a price.

Lianna's irritation cooled throughout the rest of the afternoon and evening, and by the time everyone was gathered in the comfortable living room after dinner, she'd mostly forgotten her frustration. Mathieu had put on a movie for everyone to watch, but no one was paying attention to it. Spread out around the room, people were having different conversations, enjoying after-dinner drinks, and eventually Mathieu gave up on the movie, sitting on the couch across from her between Anaelle and Emilie.

They'd been talking about Paris, the positives and the negatives of the popular city, when Anaelle suddenly leaned forward and everyone looked at her. "I really love having you here, Lianna. Are you sure you can't stay for longer? Just a couple of weeks, or even longer if you want."

"I'm not sure—"

"Well, you have to come back for Christmas at least. Please? I feel like we've got an entire lifetime to catch up on, and I know I'm not the only one that feels that way." Anaelle nudged Mathieu, and he nodded.

"Definitely, you should come back." Lifting a hand, he gestured at David who was sulking to her right. "Both of you."

"It would be great," Emilie agreed, nodding with a big grin, but David's rough huff made Lianna want to smack him.

"I promise we'll think about it."

"Your French is excellent, Lianna. I don't think you'd have any trouble living here if you wanted to try it," Anaelle pressed, leaning forward. "It would be an adjustment for sure, but I know *Papa* mentioned that you had looked at a job with Sotheby's in Leon?"

"Yeah, I'm sure they'd still have a space for you if you wanted it," Mathieu said, tilting his bourbon side to side. "Why didn't you go for it before? You've got that art history degree."

Lianna lifted her wine glass, taking a hearty drink as she stalled for time. The *real* reason was that David had kidnapped her the same night she'd received the email from Leon, but that wasn't exactly an appropriate answer. Plastering a smile on her face, she shrugged a shoulder. "It just wasn't the right time."

"*Papa* could absolutely get you in with Sotheby's if you wanted it, Lianna. Then you'd be so close!" Anaelle was trying to be encouraging, supportive, and she appreciated it, but there was so much more at play than she could ever explain to them.

"I don't know. It would be amazing for sure," she agreed, keeping her voice upbeat so she wouldn't sound ungrateful. "I'll definitely think about it. Okay?"

"Oh, all right. We'll stop pestering you about it... for tonight." Laughing, Anaelle stood up to get more wine, and Lianna let out a breath she hadn't realized she'd been holding.

"Emilie, what were you saying earlier about working on dress designs?" Lianna asked, trying desperately to change the subject, and it worked. Emilie's eyes lit up, and she scooted forward to the edge of the couch to set down her drink.

"Yes! I've been working on it for a while now, and I love being able to use digital drafting programs. I got an iPad, and it's amazing," she began, and Lianna glanced at David, hating how far he'd withdrawn from everyone. They'd been so close to making this work earlier in the day, and with one stupid comment out of her mouth she'd ruined it. He hadn't spoken more than a dozen words since she'd told him about Marc, and she knew everyone could tell something was wrong.

Please, David. Just let it go.

ELEVEN

David

Of course Lianna wanted to move to France.

She hadn't said it straight out, but that was only because he was sitting two feet away from her. If he'd been in another room, or upstairs, he was sure she would have gushed about how great it would be to take this job with Sotheby's and move to France to live happily ever after with these assholes.

But it wasn't like he was surprised, not really.

The Faure family could give her everything she'd ever wanted in life. Her dream job working with art, a beautiful life where she'd want for nothing, and... what could he offer her?

Jack shit.

Living in New York with him was a life of him basically living off her inheritance like some kind of pathetic leech. He worked, yeah, but he didn't make near enough to cover the kind of life Lianna Mercier was used to. He could buy groceries, cook for her, and fuck her — that was it. What else did he actually bring to the table? A fucked-up history, all the reminders of every terrible thing he did to her?

Clenching his jaw so tight he could feel his teeth creaking, David pushed off the couch and walked directly to the wet bar in the corner. The only advantage to this fucking house was their liquor collection. All top shelf, all expensive, and he was going to get his money's worth before they took her away from him. Dropping a single ice cube into the glass, he almost filled it to the rim with some fancy looking rum. He tilted the glass back, drinking it down to a more reasonable level before he turned toward the couch.

The warm buzz in his brain was small comfort as he listened to Lianna laugh, talking to her cousins like they were her new best friends. He'd tried to explain that they would try to replace him, that they would do everything they could to keep her in France, and he was right — Lianna just couldn't see it. She was blinded by the fancy house, the pretty lies, the wholesome family bullshit that the Faures seemed so committed to portraying every minute of the goddamn day.

Hell, the only asshole that was even partially showing his true face was Marc Faure.

"David?" Lianna nudged him, and he looked over at her, noting the strained smile on her face as she tilted her head toward the opposite couch. "Mathieu was talking to you."

Looking up at the kid, he tried not to be a complete jackass. "What did you say?"

"I was just asking if you'd be open to coming back around Christmas. Maybe stay through New Year's? There's a badass fireworks display down in Nice and—"

"Yeah, right." David couldn't bite back the scoff, shaking his head as he took another long swallow of the rum, barely tasting the flavor of it anymore.

"David," Lianna whispered through clenched teeth, and he brushed off her hand when she tried to grab his arm. "Apologize."

There was a lot he wanted to say, but one glance at the wide-eyed stares of her cousins across from him made him bite it back. Lianna just couldn't let it go, though.

She grabbed onto his arm, tighter this time, and leaned close so she could keep her voice down. "Say you're sorry, and stop being an asshole."

"Fuck this, I'm going to bed," he grumbled, loud enough for them to hear, and when he stood up from the couch, she let go of him. Ignoring everyone's shocked, polite society faces, he stalked out of the living room, heading upstairs. If Lianna wanted to play Faure heiress, she could do that without rubbing it in his fucking face. He didn't need pity invites from her cousins. There was no way in hell he was ever coming back here.

Slamming the door to their room, he sat down in the chair and put his drink on the little table to the side so he could take his shoes off. He'd only just picked his drink back up when Lianna opened the door and shut it much more quietly, but her rage was rolling off her in waves. It was almost like he could see it pulsing around her, and it made him laugh as he took a sip of the rum.

"How could you embarrass me like that?" she snapped, keeping her voice quiet, but the flush in her cheeks told him more than he needed about just how pissed she was.

Waving his drink toward her, he didn't even bother looking at her. "Oh, don't let me interrupt your family reunion. Feel free to go back downstairs."

"What the fuck is your problem, David?"

"My problem?" He chuckled, all the bitterness welling up inside him as he stood, gesturing around the ridiculously appointed guest room that someone probably hadn't seen the inside of in years. "What's *your* problem? Is this what you need to make you happy? All this money? This shit?"

"I don't need money! I don't need any of this shit."

"So, you're not keeping your precious family heirloom that's worth whateverthefuck?" he asked, already shaking his head because he knew the answer.

Stifling a frustrated scream, Lianna balled her fists at her sides. "It was a birthday gift! That doesn't mean I need any of this!"

"*Oh*! So, you weren't seriously thinking about taking the job in Lyon just so you could be closer to your adoring family?"

"I didn't say yes to it!" she argued, and he took a step closer to her.

"But you didn't say no." He pointed at her as he stopped a few feet away. "Admit it. You want it."

"Of course I do!" Lianna shouted, shoving her hands in her hair as she turned away from him for a second before she lowered her voice again. "I went to school for it, David. I studied for this, and that job would be amazing, but even if I looked into it, I would never come alone. You would come with me, and the fact that you—"

"Why the fuck would I come here?" He could barely even process the bullshit coming out of her mouth, and didn't bother to hide his disgust. "You think I want to spend more time with these corrupt assholes? In a country where I can't even speak the goddamn language? How the fuck would I get a job, Lianna?"

"You wouldn't need a fucking job!" she snapped, and he felt a fresh rage burning low in his chest as he stared at her.

His voice was dangerously soft as he finally understood how she saw him. "Oh, so I'm supposed to be your little house boy?"

"I DIDN'T SAY THAT!" she shouted, but he just waved a hand at her as he walked deeper into the room.

"No, but this is what you want," he said, twirling a finger in the air as he took another large drink. "All this shit. The fancy houses, the clothes, the cars, the money. You don't want me. You don't want me to be a part of that, 'cause I'll never be able to give you this."

"That's bullshit, David, and you know it." She moved closer but froze when he turned to stare at her. "How can you even say that to me? Of course I want you in my life. I chose you! Even after all the bullshit you put me through, even after you've fought me every inch of the way to meeting these people! I always choose you, David!"

"And the first chance you had to see the truth about them since you got here, you told me to shut up and sit down." He pointed at her, trying to contain his rage as he clenched his jaw and forced a deep breath. "You told me you recognized Marc. *You* saw that they were lying to you, recognized that he and your fucking father were working

129

together, and your response is to ignore it? Brush it off and tell *me* to shut up and drop it."

"We don't know any of that for sure. It could have been anything."

"What the fuck else were they doing, Lianna?" he asked, laughing as he pushed his hair off his forehead. "He obviously isn't interested in getting to know his niece. Shit, your father didn't even introduce him by his real fucking name!"

"Can you please lower your fucking voice?" Lianna growled, rubbing at the center of her forehead. "You've already made an ass out of yourself tonight, I really don't need them listening to every word of this."

Bowing deeply, David poured every ounce of sarcasm he could into his voice. "Oh, of course, Princess Faure! We're all just here to entertain you. Please tell me what to do next."

"Fuck you, David!" she shouted, and he could see the walls coming down behind her eyes, but his anger was on a roll.

"Shh, I thought we were supposed to be quiet, princess."

Lianna flipped him off, and her glare could have cut him if she hadn't already spat in his face tonight. "I told you never to call me that again."

"What? Princess?" He shook his head. "I'm not the one planning out how to cash in on her daddy's name to take a position in the Faure crime family."

"I'm fucking done," Lianna said, throwing her hands up as she headed toward the door. "I'm going to hang out with Emilie tonight while you sleep it off."

"SLEEP WELL!" he shouted just before she slammed the door shut behind her. Fuming, he emptied the glass in his hand, and wished he'd thought far enough ahead to grab the fucking bottle before he'd stormed out of the room. At least then he could numb the rage and the dull ache hiding underneath it that felt strangely like a knife in his back... or a bullet.

Flipping off the lights, he left the glass in the bathroom and lay down on the bed, trying to slow the constant slam of his heart. He'd given Lianna everything she wanted, he'd even come to this fucking place and played nice with her cousins, and the first opportunity she got to abandon their life in New York... she was basically salivating.

Turning over, he grabbed one of the pillows and punched it until he felt less like breaking every expensive piece of shit in the room. When he finally settled, he couldn't think of anything except how fucking empty his life would be when she chose the Faures over him.

The pounding of a fist on the door ripped him out of sleep, and he sat up too fast, the room spinning slightly as he groaned. Looking down, he realized he'd fallen asleep in his clothes, on top of the covers. Another round of knocks almost took the door off its hinges, and he rubbed at his head as he moved toward it. Expecting Lianna to be back to renew the argument, or come back to bed, but when he opened it there were two men in suits on the other side.

"What do you want?" he asked, his voice rough.

"*Monsieur Faure* wants you downstairs," the goon on the right said, deadpan, and David rubbed his face.

"Tell him I'll talk to him in the morning." David tried to shut the door, but the goon on the left caught it with his hand.

"No. Now."

"I'm guessing this isn't optional?" he asked, but the two men just stared at him, the asshole on the left pushed the door all the way open and stepped forward to keep it there. Sighing, he moved to the chair to put his shoes back on, muttering curses under his breath the entire time.

Jean-Luc had probably heard their argument and wanted to lecture him about it, flexing his power in the process. As if David didn't understand exactly who the fuck the man was. It was Lianna who was confused, not him.

"Come now," the goon on the right said, and he flipped him off, shaking out his watch to check the time.

Two AM? What the actual fuck?

"Now," the other asshole added, taking a step toward him, and David stood up, raising his hands.

"Fine, I'm coming. Just don't touch me."

The walk downstairs was silent, but he wasn't surprised when they took him to a fancy office where Jean-Luc sat behind a massive desk. He was trying to look nonchalant, glancing through papers on his desk as the goons shut the doors behind him and stood guard. *No exit, great.* This was just another power play, and David had no interest in playing into Jean-Luc's bullshit.

"What was so important that you had to get me out of bed at two o'clock in the morning, Jean-Luc?" he asked, and the man looked up at him with a steely gaze.

"You know, David... as long as my niece was happy with you, I was fine to have you in my home, despite your history. But seeing how you treated her this evening?" Jean-Luc spread his hands. "I think we're past that, and it's time for you to go."

"Fuck you! I'm not going anywhere without her!" he shouted, feeling his muscles tense as he realized how trapped he was. No other exit except the one guarded by a pair of assholes who would do whatever Jean-Luc told them. It was his worst fucking nightmare, and he couldn't see an escape route.

"That is not your choice." Jean-Luc's reply was cold, calm, but it only fueled David's rage further.

"If you think I'm leaving her here with your corrupt fucking family, you're fucking crazy."

"*We* are her family. *You* are a monster," Jean-Luc said, standing up to brace his hands on the desk as the first hints of Jean-Luc's anger pierced through. "I've known exactly who you were from the first moment we met. Before you laid eyes on me, I'd already heard about every horrifying thing you did to Lianna... but I had also been informed that you saved her life. For that reason, and that reason alone, I tolerated you."

David's stomach turned, and he felt the blood drain from his face. "H-how?"

"We don't abandon our own, David. The first thing I did when I arrived in New York was visit Joseph Blanc in prison. I believe you know him as Michael Turner? Well, he had so much to tell me." Shaking his head, Jean-Luc tapped the desk for a moment before drawing a deep breath. "If I were not working so hard to change this family, you would be leaving this house the old-fashioned way."

Opening a drawer, Jean-Luc pulled out a gun, setting it on the papers in front of him as a chill ran down David's spine.

"But, since you saved Lianna's life, I will let you leave this house alive. However, I will not allow you to continue to abuse her in my house."

"Abuse her?" he repeated, trying to push through the vague thrum of panic in his veins. "What the fuck are you talking about? I *love* her! Why else would I come here?"

"I saw the mark on her shoulder, David, and I know for a fact that's not the only time you've hurt her." Jean-Luc dropped his gaze, his jaw tight. "And I know that it's nowhere near the worst thing you've ever done to her."

A mark? Head spinning, he tried to figure out what the hell the man could be referring to — and then it clicked. There was a bruise from where he'd bit her. Just high enough on her shoulder to peek out of the neckline of her sweater. Fuck.

"That was consensual, we—"

"Bullshit!" Jean-Luc snapped, his voice finally losing the cool edge as he looked up from the desk. "Joseph told me everything you did to Lianna. You're lucky I don't have them kill you slowly for what you've done to her." Taking a breath, Jean-Luc tugged his suit jacket down and regained control. "Now, I'm aware of how confused my niece is about you, but that is where family steps in to help."

"She's going to hate you if you do this," he whispered, a pit opening in his stomach where all the lingering guilt squatted, just waiting for him to let it in. But it didn't matter if killing him would be right in some ways, he couldn't leave Lianna here. Not with them. Not alone. The only problem was... he had no idea how to stop it.

"She won't hate us. She may have been confused for a while, because she thought she was alone, but she's not anymore. She has a family she can count on now. *La famille avant tout, et tu n'es pas sa famille.*"

"I don't fucking speak French!" David shouted, rage and panic making his hands shake.

The edge of Jean-Luc's mouth twitched upward. "All you need to know is that you're not her family, and while Alain may have failed to protect her, I will not."

"That's bullshit. You pretend to be the good guy, but we both know you're just as corrupt as Alain, and in the end, you'll put everything else before your family, including Lianna. Just like he did."

"You don't know me at all," Jean-Luc replied, the hint of a smile spreading. "And it doesn't matter——"

"I know you, all of you, a hell of a lot better than Lianna does, and as soon as she realizes what you've done... she'll see it too," he spat, taking a step closer to the desk, knowing he had no hope of getting his hands around Jean-Luc's neck, but he wanted the man to hear him, to listen. Unfortunately, the asshole didn't seem concerned at all.

"I think you're the one she's finally seen the true colors of, David." With a snap of his fingers, Jean-Luc sat back down in his chair just as the two goons grabbed his arms. Twisting, David tried to throw them off, but they only dug their fingers in harder.

"Wait!" he shouted as the men tried to pull him toward the door. "I can't leave without telling her goodbye, and I need my bag."

Jean-Luc glanced up at him again like he'd momentarily forgotten he was still in the room, once again calm and in control. "She's sleeping, and I don't think we need to disturb her. It's time for you to go." Waving his fingers, the two goons put their weight into forcing him away from Jean-Luc's desk.

"This is bullshit! You can't just shove me on a plane back to NYC without anything." Before he'd even finished the sentence, one of the goons dug in a pocket and smacked him in the chest with his passport. "NO! You're not going to make me leave her. I won't let you!"

Throwing himself to one side, he knocked one of the assholes off balance and got his arm free. David managed to land a punch on the other goon, but it wasn't hard enough for the man to let him go, and a second later a fist to his stomach took all the air out of his lungs. Choking, he tried to headbutt the idiot who moved in front of him, but the other guy yanked him backward, and then there was nothing but pain.

Gasping for air, he realized he was on the floor and the bastard above him was holding a goddamn taser. "Fuck you," he groaned, pushing himself onto his hands and knees. "I won't leave without Lianna."

"You're already on your way," Jean-Luc said, not even looking up from his papers as the two men grabbed David's arms, lifting him enough to start dragging him into the hall.

A third goon was waiting for them, and as the tiles passed underneath him, David waited until they were in the large foyer by the stairs before he pulled in as much air as he could to shout, "LIANNA!"

Another wave of pain turned his muscles to electric fire, but this time it didn't stop until the darkness swallowed him whole.

When consciousness finally started to return, David could barely breathe. Everything hurt. His joints felt too tight, and his head was pounding, which definitely wasn't a hangover. Someone had hit him, or his head had hit something, and based on the dry mouth it seemed pretty likely he'd been sedated. Twisting, he blinked his eyes a few times, but the metal digging into his wrists told him there was no way he'd have the use of his hands anytime soon.

Lifting his head, he looked around the small space, and for a minute his brain just wouldn't process it. He was on a plane. A fucking private plane.

Someone had dumped him on the floor of the cabin, even though there were plenty of comfortable-looking seats, including what looked like a goddamn couch. Clearing his throat, he shouted toward the front of the plane. "HEY! Let me out of these fucking cuffs!"

"Shut the hell up," someone shouted back, and he growled, leaning his forehead against the floor as the situation slowly settled over him.

He was alive, which wasn't something he would have expected with the kind of knowledge Jean-Luc Faure had about him now... but he'd lost her. The last conversation they'd had was just about the worst one to leave on, and now he wouldn't get the chance to tell her he was sorry for being such a goddamn idiot. *Again.* Jean-Luc could make up any lie he wanted, and he'd be thousands of miles away, unable to defend himself unless he could get her to take his call.

Fuck, he didn't even know if she'd answer, much less believe him.

Getting tossed on a private plane and flown across the Atlantic wasn't exactly something that happened very often. Unless one was the head of an evil crime family. Knocking his head into the floor over and over, he didn't even care that it made the headache throb, he deserved the pain. He'd lost his temper, pushed her away, and just like he'd predicted, Jean-Luc had been waiting in the wings to drive them apart.

He practically handed her over to them on a silver platter, but he wasn't going to give up.

If Jean-Luc wanted to keep him away from Lianna, he should have killed him.

TWELVE

Lianna

"Lianna?" Emilie's voice broke through the hazy remnants of sleep, and she groaned, turning over as her cousin gently nudged her shoulder. "We slept really late. Do you want to go down and have some breakfast?"

"Not really," she mumbled, and Emilie sighed. Lianna felt the bed dip, knowing the girl had sat down next to her.

"How are you feeling this morning?"

"Like hell." Forcing herself to sit up, she rubbed at her eyes, realizing just how swollen they felt from all the crying. Emilie had been incredibly understanding when she'd found her in her bedroom, already crying into a wad of toilet paper. They'd stayed up talking, but Lianna couldn't bring herself to explain exactly what she'd argued with David about. She'd kept it vague, and her cousin had been the perfect friend. She didn't push to learn more, she just called him an idiot, blamed the alcohol, and welcomed her to crash in her bed.

Unfortunately, that meant the whole family probably knew what a mess she and David were. He'd already made an ass of himself in front of them, but this would remove all doubt.

"Okay, how about this. I've got a new toothbrush you can use, and we're almost the same shade, so I think my make-up will work. We'll make sure you look fucking amazing before you go downstairs, and David will have no idea you were ever upset." Emilie grinned, patting her leg through the covers. "Let him think it didn't bother you at all. He'll stew over it all day while we hang out together. Let him suffer for a while."

"I like that idea," she answered, laughing a little as Emilie bounced up to her feet.

"Then let's get it done!"

With Emilie's help, Lianna looked human again in way less time than it would have taken her to do it on her own. Her cousin even let her borrow clothes, and although she was shorter than Lianna — which meant pants were out of the question — the skirt and blouse Emilie picked out looked nice.

She felt *almost* prepared to see David face to face again, but when they walked into the dining room it wasn't even necessary. He wasn't at the table. Not like that should have surprised her as much as he'd complained about attending the family meals. He was probably sulking up in the room, dealing with the hunger just to make a point.

"You guys slept so late!" Amanda said, sounding way too excited.

"I'm sorry, I—"

"It doesn't matter." Waving her hands, Amanda grinned. "We're going into Nice today! Cécile said she can't let you leave without going shopping down there, and I'm so glad because I wanted to make sure I went before we had to head back home too."

"That's right," Cécile added, smiling over her cup of tea. "The weather is lovely today as well, so we'll get to spend some time by the beach. It really is beautiful."

"Yes!" Emilie cheered, running over to hug her mom and press a kiss to her cheek.

Chuckling, Jean-Luc pointed at the dishes on the table. "You two better hurry and eat. Anaelle is upstairs changing, and I believe she threatened to drag you both out of bed so that you didn't take up any more of her time."

Nodding, Lianna started adding a few things to her plate, but she didn't have an appetite. Normally, this was when David would be standing over her shoulder, adding things for her to eat while he watched — but he wasn't beside her, which was the problem.

"Are you okay, sweetheart?" Cécile asked, her brows pulled together in concern.

"I'm fine," she answered, plastering on a smile. "I think I'm still half asleep! As soon as I drink some coffee, I'll feel human again."

"All right." The woman smiled at her, but Lianna could tell she didn't believe her at all. *This* must be what that whole mom intuition thing looked like. Growing up, her friends used to say that their moms could always see through them no matter what, but Lianna had never experienced it.

"You guys are killing me," Amanda said with a groan. "Would you eat already so we can go? It's almost ten o'clock already!"

"Okay, okay!" Laughing a little, Lianna sat down and poured some coffee, focusing on that while she picked at the fruit and croissant.

Anaelle saved her from having to eat in front of everyone when she came down the stairs about five minutes later, shouting that she was going to leave whether everyone was ready or not. Chuckling, Jean-Luc watched her over his coffee cup and tilted his head toward the door. "You can take the plate with you."

"Thanks." She stood, adding more food to the plate that she didn't plan on eating. "I just need to run upstairs real quick. I'll be right back. I promise!"

"You better hurry!" Amanda said as Lianna downed the last of her coffee and picked up the full plate, rushing upstairs to their room.

Taking a deep breath outside the door, she tried to brace herself for whatever mood David might be in, but when she opened the door... the room was empty. Confused, she checked the bathroom just in case, but all the lights were off. Rolling her eyes, she left the plate on the bed for him and grabbed her purse. Once she checked that her phone was charged, she skimmed through her wallet to make sure she had everything she'd need for a day of shopping. Then headed back downstairs to spend a day with her family.

"Finally!" Anaelle groaned, waving everyone toward the door where one of the guards held it open.

Once they were all piled into the SUV, Amanda turned around from one of the captain's chairs to look at her and Emilie in the backseat. "You know what the best part of going on a girls-only shopping trip with Cécile is?"

"Is it the champagne?" Cécile asked from the front seat, lifting up two bottles to the cheers of everyone in the car. Lianna joined in, even though she didn't exactly feel up to partying with them in Nice today. If she'd just been able to talk to David before she left, she would have felt a little better, even if it had just led to another argument. Having him avoid her completely was like a punch to the stomach. It left a hollow feeling behind, and it was hard to focus on anything else.

"Here you go!" Anaelle said, passing back a plastic flute of champagne, followed quickly by another for Emilie. They all raised them, cheering to a great day, and Lianna tried to believe that it would be.

Everyone was talking about what they wanted to do while in the city, and she just kept agreeing to it all. When a lull came in the conversation, she leaned forward and tapped Amanda on the shoulder. "Hey, did you see David at breakfast this morning?"

"No, why? Is everything okay?" she asked, looking concerned, but Lianna smiled and waved it off.

"Never mind, I was just curious when he got up this morning since I slept so late." Looking out the window, she hoped Amanda would drop it, and she felt lucky when the conversation quickly switched back to stores the girls wanted to stop in.

Her mind wasn't on shopping, or champagne, or the Côte d'Azur, though. Instead, she couldn't stop replaying their argument from the night before. Could he really think she was so shallow that she'd choose the Faure family because they had money? Did he think she gave a fuck about having some massive estate in Provence? Sure, it was a beautiful place, and she'd like to come back someday, but it wasn't about the property or the furnishings or the large house. It was her family that she didn't want to lose.

Unfortunately, it seemed that her family was the thing that David couldn't accept, no matter how hard he tried.

He'd said he would always choose her, that he didn't care about anything else as long as they were together... but the first time that promise got put to the test, he'd snapped it in two, grinding it into dust with harsh words before setting the remnants on fire by calling her 'princess' again.

Emptying the glass of champagne, she held the glass between Amanda and Anaelle's seats. "Any chance I can get a refill?"

"Of course!" Amanda took the glass as Anaelle let out a cheer, and soon enough she had a full glass again.

If this was how David wanted to handle their time in France, then she'd let him be miserable. *Let him suffer*, as Emilie had said.

She'd enjoy herself and spend the day getting to know her family even better. By the time she got home that evening, she was sure he'd have cooled off, and sobered up enough, to actually have a productive conversation with her.

THIRTEEN

David

By the time the plane finally started to descend for New York, David felt like he was going to crawl out of his skin. He'd asked the pilots to let him out of the cuffs a few times, he'd even threatened to piss on their floor, but they'd told him to shut up every time. He had managed to get himself upright and into a seat, not that it was comfortable with his hands cuffed behind his back, but at least he wasn't face down on the floor anymore.

Lianna had been alone with the Faures for hours, and they could have told her anything, which meant the first thing he had to do once he got out of the damn cuffs was call her and do everything he could to convince her that Jean-Luc had finally revealed the asshole side of himself and that she needed to leave. He'd probably practiced a thousand ways to phrase it in the silence of the plane, and he still felt like he was gambling.

If he hadn't fucked up so badly, Jean-Luc would have never had the opportunity to throw him out of the house, and Lianna wouldn't have a reason to believe the shit the bastard was probably saying about him.

Glancing out the window, he watched the runway coming closer and rolled his shoulders, easing the ache that seemed like a permanent fixture in them now. Touchdown was smooth, but it still took a while before the plane finally came to a stop.

Eventually, one of the pilots came into the back, lifting a taser in his hands. "This is for if you decide to be an asshole. I'm going to make it very simple for you — you've got two choices right now. Let me take your cuffs off and get off my plane to do whatever the fuck you want to do or fight me and I'll taze you and tell the customs guy that you got violent. You'll get up close and personal with the cops and probably land yourself on the no-fly list. Got it?"

"Yeah," David replied through clenched teeth, but the pilot just raised an eyebrow, so he added, "I want the fuck off the plane."

"All right then." Digging in his pocket, the pilot produced a key and David leaned forward to give him access to the cuffs. As soon as the first one was off, he pulled his arms in front, groaning at how stiff his shoulders were. The pilot chuckled as he took off the other cuff. "Guess I shouldn't have been too worried. Doubt you could land a punch right now anyway."

"Right." Sighing, David rubbed his wrists. "Can I have my phone now?"

"I don't have your phone," the man answered, whistling toward the other pilot, who stepped out a moment later.

"Okay. Can I use yours?" he asked, adding, "Please," when the man chuckled again.

"Not a fucking chance," the first pilot replied as the other one held out his passport, which had a fifty-dollar bill sticking out of it. "Get off my plane."

Forcing a slow breath, David stood up and waited for them to open the door before he went to the exit. He half-expected them to kick him out the door, but they ignored him as soon as he stepped out of the plane. Since he didn't have anything with him, the customs guy didn't have much to talk to him about, and although he refused to let him use his phone, the asshole was nice enough to tell him how the fuck to get to the normal part of the airport.

Just after six AM, he was surprised by how busy the airport already was, but the large number of people in baggage claim didn't seem to be working in his favor. He was exhausted, sore, and he was pretty confident that he looked like shit since no one would talk to him. The fifty bucks was probably meant to give him a cab ride somewhere, but he didn't care about that. He wanted a goddamn phone, but even after he started offering it, every person he tried to stop told him 'no' before he even got the question out.

Finally, he saw a guy in a suit looking at something on an iPhone, and he approached him slowly, holding up the fifty-dollar bill. "Hey man, sorry to bother you, but I lost my phone on vacation, and I just need to borrow one to call a ride. You can have the fifty if you'll just let me use your phone."

"Looks like it was a rough vacation," he mumbled, but it wasn't a straight-up no, so David tried to laugh it off.

"Yeah, that will be the last time I decide to backpack through Eastern Europe." Shrugging, he held out the fifty again, and the man looked him up and down, holding on tight to his phone.

"I guess it's sort of pointless to ask, but if I let you use it, are you going to run off with my phone as soon as I hand it to you? Because, you need my code to change the one on here, so it'd be useless to you as soon as it locks."

"I'm not going to steal your phone," David said, offering his passport as well as the fifty. "Look, you can hold onto this too. I just need to call a ride and call my girlfriend, so she knows I'm alive."

"Okay, fine. Just don't walk off, okay?" The guy handed over his phone, taking the passport and the cash at the same time.

"Thank you. Really." Moving a few steps to the side, he called Lianna's phone first, trying to calm his breathing before she answered. Unfortunately, it went to voicemail after a few rings, which meant he'd have to explain what he could for now. As soon as the beep came across the line, he lowered his voice and hoped no one was eavesdropping. "Lianna, first, I was an absolute asshole. I'm sorry I said all that shit... but I need you to leave there. Jean-Luc had his goons drag me out of our room last night. They fucking tazed me, handcuffed me, and put me on a goddamn plane to New York. I just landed and all I've got is my passport. I'm using some guy's phone to call you right now, but I will call you again as soon as I get to Harry's. I know I've fucked up a hundred times with you, but please believe me. You need to get out of there. I love you."

Hanging up, he tried to ignore the acid etching the back of his throat as he quickly dialed Harry's number. It was early, but the old man had always been an early riser, which was confirmed when his gruff voice came over the line.

"Hello?"

"Harry, it's David, I need you to come get me."

"Uh, where are you? I thought you were in France with—"

"I'm at JFK airport, a lot of shit went down, and I need you to come pick me up. I'm using someone's phone right now, and I don't know how much longer he's going to let me talk to you on it, okay?" He knew he was being an asshole, but Harry was used to it by now.

"Shit, David... I knew you shouldn't have gone." Harry sighed, and he groaned, waving at the guy whose phone he was using when he caught his eye.

"Well, you can bust my balls all you want on the drive home, old man." Scanning the walls, David told him where he'd be waiting, finishing the call with a quick, "Just hurry. Please. I have to give this guy his phone back."

"Please?" Harry chuckled. "Hell, it must have been a rough trip. I'll be there as soon as I can, boy."

"Thanks." Ending the call, he returned the phone to the guy with a nod and took his passport back. "Thanks for letting me use your phone."

"No problem. Hope everything works out."

David nodded at the man and headed toward the bathroom to try and clean himself up.

It took over an hour for Harry's truck to appear, and by then David was rapidly swinging between blinding rage at Jean-Luc, and a bottomless panic that he'd lost Lianna forever — neither of which were particularly helpful.

As he climbed into Harry's truck, the old man let out a low whistle. "Someone try to bash your skull in?" he asked, and David shrugged. He'd seen the bruise near his hairline when he'd stopped by the bathroom, but there was nothing he could do about it.

"No idea. Can I use your phone?"

"Sure." Harry waved a hand at it as he maneuvered the truck back into the flow of traffic. "Code is four, four, four, four."

"Seriously? Do you know anything about security?" Taking it out of the dash mount, David unlocked it and dialed Lianna's number again as Harry chuckled to himself. "What?"

"You think anyone wants the info on my phone?" Harry shook his head a little. "I'm not exactly a prime target, and that thing is a few years old. If they want to steal it that bad, they can have it."

"Fine," David muttered, blocking out Harry's voice as the phone rang, and rang, until her voicemail picked up again. *Dammit.* "Lianna, Harry just picked me up at JFK, and I'm calling from his phone. When you get this, just call me back on this number, and please get out of that house. Come home. I just— Fuck. I need to know you're safe. I love you."

Hanging up, he fought the urge to throw Harry's phone against the windshield. It took a few deep breaths, but the wave of rage slowly passed again, and he managed to put it back on the dash mount without destroying anything. When Harry glanced at him, but didn't say anything, David sighed.

"Go on and get it over with."

"Well, before I decide how much of an idiot you've been, why don't you tell me what happened?" Harry said, pointing at all the traffic. "We've got time."

The last thing David wanted to do was revisit the trip, but he did his best to give a slightly sanitized version of his argument with Lianna and the conversation with Jean-Luc. Harry didn't need to know all the details, and he'd made it clear several times that he didn't *want* to know everything that went on between him and Lianna.

If David were honest with himself, he was glad the old man didn't know all of it. There was no way Harry would have ever been able to look at him the same way again, and he definitely wouldn't be picking him up at the airport.

By the time he'd explained waking up on the airplane and the shit that went down when he landed, he felt even more tired than before.

"I'm not sure what you expected to happen, David. I tried to warn you, but you just went ahead and marched right into the lion's den." Shaking his head, Harry blew out a breath. "You can't fix what you've already screwed up, so... what are you gonna do next?"

"I'm going to get her back."

Harry chuckled. "Yeah? And what are you gonna do if she doesn't want to come home?"

Groaning, he leaned back against the seat, running through his minimal options. He could always try to kidnap her again... from a heavily guarded compound in another country... but that idea was stupid for more reasons than just that. Rubbing at his forehead, he flinched when he pressed on the spot where he was fairly confident someone pistol-whipped him. "Honestly, Harry... I don't have the first fucking idea."

"Maybe you're capable of learning after all, boy," Harry said, reaching over to slap him on the shoulder, squeezing for a second before he returned his hands to the wheel. "We'll do this one step at a time. Get you back to our place, cleaned up, and then we can have a real talk over some food."

FOURTEEN

Lianna

When they finally got back to the house, Lianna had almost forgotten about the drama from the night before. The day had been even better than she could have imagined, and she was still laughing at Emilie's impression of the strange man they'd encountered inside one of the stores as they walked inside.

"Oh my God, I think he almost died when you answered him in French, Lianna!" Anaelle said, fighting to talk through her own laughter as they piled their bags inside the foyer. She'd been grinning and laughing for so long her jaw hurt, and she rubbed at it as Cécile wiped her eyes.

"He deserved it for insulting Amanda and me like that," Lianna replied, shaking out her hands as she heard Rémi call to his wife from the front parlor.

"I didn't even catch the full insult, but his face was worth taking a million insults." Amanda threw an arm around her, giving her a side-hug as they both headed toward the guys. "You're the best, Lianna."

"So are you. I had such a great day today, and I really needed it." Hugging Amanda back, Lianna smiled at her as she approached her husband. Looking around the room, she caught Mathieu's eye when she realized David wasn't with them. "Hey Mathieu, have you seen David?"

"No," he answered, sitting up to look at her over the back of the couch. "I haven't seen him all day. We thought he went with you guys."

"Lianna," Jean-Luc called her over in a hushed voice, and she waved at Mathieu and the girls as she walked over to meet him in the foyer.

"Have you seen David today?" she asked, and Jean-Luc shook his head.

"I need to talk with you. Can you come to my office?"

"Sure, just give me a few minutes," she said, heading for the stairs as she called back over her shoulder. "I'll come back down after I talk to David."

"He's not here," Jean-Luc called after her, and she froze just a few steps off the foyer to turn and look at him.

"What do you mean he's not here?"

Taking a slow breath, Jean-Luc moved to the base of the stairs, keeping his voice low. "I saw how he treated you, and... that's not acceptable in my house."

"What the fuck are you talking about?" she asked, a strange tendril of confusion and concern winding its way up her back.

"Let's go talk about it." Gesturing toward his office, Jean-Luc tried to get her to follow him, but she didn't move.

"No. Let's talk about it right here." Facing him completely, she crossed her arms and asked a question that made her more than a little nauseous. "Where is David?"

"I know you're confused, *mon oisillon*, but after what he did to you… you can't truly want to be with him." Moving onto the bottom step of the stairs, Jean-Luc kept his gaze on hers. "You don't have to be with him, you're not alone anymore."

"How— I'm not confused, Jean-Luc!" she snapped, knowing she was being too loud, but she couldn't stop it as the floor seemed to be slowly sliding out from under her. *How could he know? How?* The answer clicked, but it only brought more anger to the surface. Uncle Mike. Tightening her hands into fists, she pressed her nails into her palms in an effort to stay calm. "Tell me where David is."

"He's gone home, because that's where he needs to be," Jean-Luc answered, his voice carrying that unique edge like he was both talking to a small child and a frightened animal. "But your home is here, with us."

"You don't get to tell me where my home is." Turning away from him, she started up the stairs again, digging in her purse until she found her phone. With a few quick taps, she called his number, but it went directly to voicemail. Muttering under her breath, she looked down at the phone to see two voicemails waiting for her. Clicking the first one as she rounded the top of the stairs, heading for her room, she stopped in place when she realized it was David's voice.

Jean-Luc was still following her, calling out to her to wait and talk to him, but she shut him out to concentrate on the insane shit David was saying. Handcuffs and tasers and a plane to New York. Turning to face him, she held out her hand as the first voicemail ended with David urging her to leave and telling her he loved her.

"What the fuck, Jean-Luc?" she yelled, not even giving a shit that her voice was echoing across the foyer now. As soon as he tried to talk, she held up a hand again and tapped the second voicemail. There was a moment of relief as it confirmed he was safely with Harry, but nothing could hold back the rage she suddenly felt. "You beat him up and threw him on a plane? You're insane! I can't believe you'd do this, you— You're a liar! You're all a bunch of fucking liars. You, Marc, my father, *all of you!*"

"I've never lied to you!" Jean-Luc said, his voice pleading, but when he took a step toward her, she took several back.

"Stay away from me. I won't believe a word you have to say, Jean-Luc." Shaking her head, she felt the betrayal down to her core. "All you do is lie. All of you. You told me you didn't help my father with his business, but I remember Marc. He was at my father's penthouse a few years ago, and you know what? They lied to me then too. They didn't tell me who he really was, they made up some bullshit name — just more lies. That's all you do, you fucking lie! David was right!"

"That's not true! Did David tell you that?" Jean-Luc raised his voice. "He's the liar, Lianna. Not me. Marc and I have never been involved in your father's business. He wouldn't *allow* us to be. He barely helped out the family by moving money around!"

"I saw him!" she shouted, pointing at him. "You're a fucking liar!"

"*Mon oisillon*, please, listen to me. It's not true. I tried to come see you after you were born, and your father turned me away." He was almost begging, but she didn't care. "All I've ever wanted was to know you, to reconnect with my brother and you, and I would never lie to you. All I want is what's best for you. I want to keep you safe, and David is not good for you."

"YOU DON'T KNOW ME!" she roared, and he stopped moving closer, looking lost for a moment as he stared at her.

"But... we want to," he whispered, his voice growing a little stronger as he continued. "We want you to stay here, to be happy, to spend time with your family—"

"I'm going home! I don't need a family if this is what you're like, and I'm not staying where I can't trust anyone." Throwing open the door to her room, she couldn't tell if she wanted to scream or cry, but she knew she didn't want to do any of it in this house. Grabbing the first suitcase she could reach, she tossed it onto the bed and flipped it open, realizing too late that it was David's.

"Lianna, please," Jean-Luc pleaded at the door, but she ignored him, moving as quickly as she could around the room to pack everything away. She didn't care what suitcase things went in, she just wanted to leave as quickly as possible. "Please stay, just talk to me."

"No." Refusing to look at him, she found the jewelry box and the stocking in the gift bag and tossed it at his feet before moving into the bathroom to gather all of her toiletries.

"You should at least keep the bracelet." Jean-Luc picked up the bag, holding it in his hands as he watched her. "It was a gift. Your grandmother would have—"

"I don't want anything from you," she snapped, searching the room for anything she might have missed. The suitcases were a fucking mess, but it didn't matter. David was in New York, and Jean-Luc and the Faures had betrayed her. Just like he'd always told her they would. Tears burned her eyes as she started to line the luggage up at the end of the bed.

"At least... at least let me drive you to the airport," Jean-Luc pleaded, and she could hear the emotion in his voice. The man was on the edge of tears as well, but she didn't care.

"Anyone but you. I don't want to ever see you again." Keeping her gaze on the floor, she grabbed two of the suitcases and wheeled them past him, leaving him standing at the door of what had been her room until about ten minutes before.

FIFTEEN

David
———

"Would you sit down already? You need to eat." Harry sounded more than a little irritated, but David didn't have the capacity to focus on him *and* the whirlwind of shit spinning around in his own head.

"Has she called back yet?" he asked, and the old man sighed.

"Don't you think I would've told you that, boy?" Smacking the table, Harry pointed at the chair. "Pacing a hole in my floor isn't going to make her call you back any faster, so sit down and eat. Now."

"Fine." David dropped into the chair, jabbed the fork into the re-heated leftovers, and took a bite. Shannon's turkey casserole was even better than he remembered, and even though he'd never admit it aloud, it was more than a little comforting to taste something so familiar when the whole world felt like it was collapsing. If he were less of an asshole, he'd figure out how to be thankful without somehow making it sound sarcastic to the old man. David was eating homemade food, he was clean, and wearing Liam's clothes, which seemed to be what always happened when he ended up on Harry's doorstep after he fucked up.

"It's good, isn't it?" Harry said, taking a bite as well, but he seemed to accept David's nod as enough of a response for them both to continue eating.

Unfortunately, by the time their plates were empty, Harry's phone still hadn't rung, and the tension was starting to get to him. Groaning, David put his head in his hands. "This is all their fault. They tried so fucking hard to convince her that life was just so goddamn grand over there. They throw her this ridiculous birthday party the night we get there, give her this over-the-top bracelet covered in jewels, and just shove it in everybody's faces how much money they have."

Shoving away from the table, he stood up to start pacing again. His head was still pounding, and he was sure it had a lot to do with the bruise on his skull, and a bit to do with the lack of sleep. He couldn't even figure out how many hours it had been since he'd actually been asleep instead of knocked out by drugs. As he paced, Harry was just watching him, leaned back in his chair, and he grumbled.

"What?"

"Just waiting to see what else they did that was so terrible," the old man said, his voice deadpan, but that just irritated David even more.

"You weren't there, Harry. They acted like the perfect little family. Straight out of Stepford. Everyone so fucking happy, everyone telling each other they love them." Growling, he shoved a hand into his hair and gripped it. "It was like they had a meeting and planned out how to make sure Lianna would want to stay. All these family meals where everyone sits together and talks as if their stupid lives are actually interesting, laughing and shit like the world is just so fucking grand."

"You could have had that, David," Harry said, shaking his head as he tapped his water on the table.

"No, I couldn't!" he snapped. "How in the hell would I have ever got that fancy house, with all their nice cars and swimming pools and a bunch of fucking rooms that no one even uses most of the year?"

"That's not what I meant, boy. You're describing a family, which is exactly what you've been rejecting all these years."

Confused by the defeat in Harry's voice, David stopped beside the table to stare at him. "What the hell are you talking about, old man?"

"Do you know how many times Shannon has tried to get you over here for your birthday?" He glared at David through narrowed eyes as he gestured toward the stairs. "Hell, the boys try to take you out drinking every year, but you're too busy being miserable."

"I've never—"

"Don't do that. You know we've always tried to include you, we *wanted* you in this family, and it's my own damn fault that I didn't drag you here when I had the chance."

Letting out a barking laugh, David stepped closer to the table, bracing his hands on the back of a chair. "What were you supposed to do? Kidnap me and lock me up here?"

"Well... I wouldn't be the first person to do something like that," he mumbled, and David let out a groan, pushing the chair back in with more force than necessary.

"Really? You wanna talk about that?"

"No," Harry replied, shaking his head as he looked down at the table for a moment. "But I think we both know that if I'd made you come here and grow up with my boys, you would've never got yourself wrapped up in this shit."

Swallowing, David hesitated on how to respond, because when the old man looked at him, he knew it was true. Growing up in this house would have led to a very different life. "But I would have resented you for taking me away from Dad," he answered quietly.

Shrugging, Harry's gaze drifted away for a moment before he looked David in the eye. "I think I could have lived with that if it meant you got a life, boy."

"My life is fine..." he growled. "Or it *will* be as soon as I get Lianna back."

Harry stood and walked over to the fridge to pull out a pair of beers. He popped off the caps before he set them on the table and took his seat again. "Well, what did she think of them?"

"You really wanna know?" he asked, and when Harry nodded and pointed at the chair, David pulled it out took his seat with a sigh. Taking a swig of the beer, he remembered how Lianna had smiled and hugged them in the airport. "She totally fell for their shit, Harry. Right off the bat. Everyone was pretending to be all nice and friendly, so excited to have her in the fold, and—"

"You really think none of those people were excited to meet Lianna?"

"Maybe they were," David admitted, but he quickly shook his head. "It doesn't fucking matter, though. It's all bullshit. They're a bunch of liars. I mean… the first chance Jean-Luc had to alienate her, he tazed me and threw me handcuffed on a fucking airplane."

"I asked you about *her*, not the Faures. Did you change your mind on which hill you plan to die on, boy?"

"No!" he shouted, groaning as he leaned forward on the table, cradling the beer between his hands. "I'm just trying to keep her safe, and she's not safe there. Even you have to see that."

"I don't have to see anything. From my point of view, you're the only one he threw out, and I have a feeling you didn't make the best impression."

"What does that mean?" he asked, his voice low as he tried to stay calm and not take his rage out on Harry.

"You've never been good at hiding your true feelings, David." Gesturing toward him, Harry took a swig of beer. "Like right now, I can tell you're itching to take my head off because I'm not telling you what you want to hear. And I'm sure every one of them could tell how much you disliked them — Jean-Luc included."

"Well, I was right. They're evil."

"And you're in love with one of them," Harry retorted, and David cursed under his breath, shaking his head.

"She isn't like them…"

"They're her family, David, and that's not going to change." Sitting up in his chair, Harry braced his elbows on the table in a mirror of how David was already sitting. "We don't always get to choose our family, and that means there's some things we can't escape. But if you still want her in your life, you're going to have to accept that part of her at some point."

"Pretty hard to do that when I'm half a world away thanks to her goddamn uncle."

"Other than kicking you out, what happened that was so evil?" Harry asked.

"He…" Grumbling, David tried to find the right words to encompass the Faures and what being on their estate had been like. "They're just— His kids aren't all bad, at least not yet, but Jean-Luc was just waiting to take her away from me. To isolate her."

"Because you were an asshole?"

"Fuck off," David snapped, pouring more beer down his throat.

"Exactly." Chuckling, the old man lifted his beer, tilting it toward David. "Whatever you did, I'm pretty sure if you took a minute, you'd see he was just trying to protect her. He'll come around eventually when he sees how much you care about her."

"Yeah, I don't think that's going to happen, since Jean-Luc knows what happened between me and Lianna."

"I'm sure he doesn't know…" Harry's voice trailed off.

David kept his gaze on the table, that empty pit in his stomach opening wider. "He knows. Everything." Lifting a hand, he slammed it back onto the table in a fist. "All the shit you've refused to hear about."

"And I still don't wanna know, but... that makes it pretty clear why Jean-Luc sent you packing."

"I'm aware," he whispered, knowing Harry was right. "But I don't want her there."

"She's with her family, and they obviously don't want to hurt her. As much as you don't want her with them, you have to know that she's safe."

"I don't care!" David shouted, groaning as he wiped a hand over his face.

"I know that, boy." Nodding, Harry tapped his beer against David's and they both tilted them up. "And until she comes back, we'll keep you busy and try and keep your head out of your ass."

"You mean *if* she comes back," he corrected, and Harry sighed.

"Well, whether you get Lianna back or not, you've always got a family here, David. We've always been your family." The old man looked at him for a long moment, his voice serious when he continued. "Always will be, whether you like it or not."

Family.

It felt like a dirty word after spending so many days around the Faures, but when he looked around the kitchen, he had to admit that this shabby little house was the only constant in a childhood filled with evictions, motels, and nights sleeping in his dad's truck. But he'd chosen his dad over

Harry a long time ago, and he'd kept making that choice even after his father died.

All he'd wanted was to finish his dad's work, to not have all those years together wasted — and he'd done it. He'd ruined Robert Mercier, destroyed the company, and Michael Turner had ended up in prison, although the state didn't know even a tenth of the crimes the bastard had really committed. Still, when he'd needed him, Harry had shown up. He'd always been there when shit got hard, and even though he hadn't thought about the future at all, those years were starting to rack up in his head. The more he thought about a life without Lianna in it, the longer those years felt, and having people to lean on wasn't exactly a bad idea.

"Did you hear me, boy?" Harry asked, and David lifted his head to look the man in the eye.

"I heard you, old man… and thanks."

"You're welcome, now finish your damn beer and then lay down on the couch before you pass out on my table." Harry's gruff voice was a relief. The man had never been one to get too emotional about anything, and David was grateful for it at the moment.

It wasn't like he didn't care about Harry and Shannon and their boys. He did. It was part of the reason he'd pushed them away for so long. When the end game of his life was basically a kamikaze mission against his family's mortal enemy, it wasn't exactly responsible to have anyone close when the timer on the bomb was ticking down. But… he'd always appreciated the way Shannon made sure she set aside some of the boys' clothes for him. That, even long after Harry and his dad fell out, the man would still come by with food, claiming they'd made too much. Whenever things got really dark, Harry's family always seemed to show up. Liam or Tommy would suddenly want him to sleep over, to go on a camping trip, and his dad always let him go. But the older he got, the less help he needed, and there was no way in hell he was having a sleepover with the boys once he was a teenager. There was work to do, and whenever he left his dad alone too long, he'd come back to find him passed out drunk.

David had made the only choice he could — take the lead on bringing down Mercier — and that meant Harry's family got pushed away. He didn't regret it, couldn't regret it, because those years with his dad were all he had left of him. But... if he were really honest with himself, he couldn't deny that Harry had always been more of a father than his actual dad ever was after his mom died.

As he sat at the table, thinking over everything Harry and his family had done for him, and everything the man was offering now, he finished the first beer and nodded at Harry when he replaced it without another mention of the couch. Being able to sit in silence with Harry had always been the most comforting thing about being in the house. Shannon had always treated him like just another one of her kids, and Tommy and Liam had harassed him just as much as each other, and they'd all picked on Sean for years because he was always following them around the neighborhood. But late at night, when David couldn't sleep, Harry would get him something to drink, let him eat another plate of food if he was still hungry, and they would sit just like this. In silence, sometimes only by the light from the kitchen window, and Harry never pushed him. Never asked him what was wrong.

He was just always there.

The realization felt both freeing and heavy at once. It gave him a tiny bit of breathing room inside the chaos of possibly losing Lianna to the Faures, but it also meant that he had to do better with the McConnells. He couldn't keep using Harry to save his ass again and again without being there for the family in return. From showing up to work, to actually spending time with Liam, Tommy, and even Sean. That was a heavy responsibility to accept when he was still trying to figure out how to live a normal life, or if a normal life would ever be possible with Lianna Mercier, heiress to the Faure crime family, prior focus of all his hate and stalking obsession, and current focus of his... everything.

Then again, he kept saying he wanted to be a better man, and his dad wasn't exactly the right example to follow. If he wanted to actually do that, he didn't have to look any further than the other side of the kitchen table. Harry McConnell who was still married to his first wife, who had raised three functional human beings who didn't kidnap and torture women — as far as he knew anyway — and who had done what he could to take care of a boy who had never really showed him any kind of gratitude.

Just a fuck of a lot of rage.

He was trying to figure out how to say any of the shit in his head to Harry when the phone buzzed, rattling against the wood, and he lunged for it. Harry snapped it up from the table though, looking at him steadily. "I know what you're waiting on, boy, but this is still my phone."

Answering it, Harry put the cellphone to his ear, and David had to physically hold onto the edge of the table to keep from ripping it out of his hands.

"Hello?" The old man paused, smiling a little as he nodded. "Well, we're glad to hear from you. David's right here."

"Lianna?" he half-shouted into the phone as soon as Harry handed it over, relief warring with the renewed panic that everything could be falling apart.

"Are you okay?" she asked, and her absolutely perfect fucking voice made his lungs seize for a moment. Lianna was actually asking about him. She still cared whether he was okay even after he'd been such an asshole.

"I'm fine." He finally managed to force the words out, swallowing in a suddenly dry throat. "I'm at Harry's. Are *you* okay?"

"I'm pissed. I'm on my way to the airport now, and I'm coming home."

Standing up from the table, he was almost too shocked to ask, "You are?"

"Of course I am!" she snapped, but he could tell her anger wasn't directed at him. A frustrated groan came across the line just before she launched into a loud rant. "I can't fucking believe Jean-Luc kicked you out! Had his thugs throw you out, as if he has any fucking right to make decisions for me. And then he put you on a fucking airplane in handcuffs? It's fucking ridiculous!"

Back to pacing across the linoleum floor, he nodded as she carried on. "I told you, that family is evil!"

Harry cleared his throat loudly, eyeing him, and David rolled his eyes.

"But none of that matters as long as you're coming home, and I know you're safe, angel," he added, and Harry lifted his beer in a silent salute as he leaned back in his chair.

"He had no right to do that!" Lianna continued. "I don't give a fuck what he thinks he knows."

"What did he tell you?" he asked, and she stayed silent for a long moment. "Lianna?"

Lianna

Looking at the guard in the driver's seat, Lianna couldn't help but second-guess the rant she'd just gone on about Jean-Luc, but she doubted that he would allow any of his men to hurt her. He'd still been begging her to stay and talk to him when she was getting in the SUV to head into Nice.

However, it probably wasn't a great idea to share all of her dirty secrets within earshot of someone who was definitely loyal to the Faures.

"Lianna?" David sounded worried, and she took a deep breath.

"Apparently he knows about…. us," she finally answered, trying to stay vague. "All the shit from before, but he absolutely doesn't know me, and he doesn't have any right to dictate who is in my life."

"God, I love you," he said, and she couldn't help but smile.

"I love you too, and I'm getting on the first plane I can to New York." Shaking her head, she leaned against the window, gazing at the remnants of the sunset over Provence. It was breathtaking, one of the most beautiful sights she could remember... but she couldn't even enjoy it. Rubbing her eyes, she lowered her voice. "I still can't believe he would do this."

"It doesn't matter, angel," David replied, taking control just as she started to feel weak, and she loved that about him. "Just tell me when your plane is landing so I can be there to get you."

"It's going to be really early. I haven't got a flight yet, but I'm going to try and book on my phone as soon as we hang up. I've saved Harry's number so I can call you when I have the info. Where's your phone anyway?"

"He kept it. Along with the rest of my shit," he growled, the anger a rumbling undertone to his voice, but she couldn't blame him this time. Hell, she was pissed too.

"Well, I packed up everything in our room, but I'm pretty sure your wallet and phone weren't there. Unless you had them tucked away in your backpack already?"

"That sonuvabitch..." David continued cursing under his breath, and she took that as a 'no.'

"It's fine, we can replace all of that. It's annoying, but I'd rather do that than have to deal with them again." Her rage spiked as she realized how incredibly petty keeping his stuff was. It was just to fuck with David. It didn't have anything to do with her safety, or whatever bullshit Jean-Luc told himself. It was pure manipulation. Clenching her first, she dug her nails into her palm as she kept her voice low, hoping the driver couldn't hear her. "I just should have known he'd try to control me, just like my father. Paying for the apartment, getting the FBI to drop the charges... it was all just a tactic. Just Jean-Luc trying to get me to trust him, to come *here*."

An awkward silence followed her hushed rant, and she knew David was biting his tongue, she just couldn't stand to hear the words right now.

"Don't say it."

"I wasn't going to say anything," he replied, but she let the lie slide because he was just avoiding another argument.

"Right... Anyway, I'm going to hang up so I can try and grab a seat on the next flight out," she said, talking at normal volume again as she pulled her phone away to check the time. Seven o'clock already. "And I need to hurry. I'll text Harry's phone as soon as I have the flight number."

"Okay, angel. I'm just... I'm so glad you're coming home."

"I am too, baby," she whispered. "I love you. See you soon."

"Love you, too," he said, and she ended the call before she hesitated any longer. She was already cutting it close on a flight, and they were still thirty minutes outside of Nice. Slumping back in the seat, she swiped to an app to start looking for flights, glancing up at the driver in the rear-view mirror. She was sure the man would tell Jean-Luc everything he'd heard, but she didn't give a shit. The man deserved to hear just how badly he'd fucked up. He deserved to know that he'd burned a bridge that they hadn't even finished building yet.

But it served her right too. She had been naïve to trust a Faure. Her father should have been warning enough, but she'd wanted to believe the lie Jean-Luc sold her so badly that she'd ignored every warning sign, ignored every roadblock David tried to put in her way.

And she'd gotten hurt. Again.

At least this time, if Jean-Luc took back his gifts and her life fell apart, she knew what to expect. It would be hell, but she had no doubt that David would stand beside her in the fire. He hadn't blinked once the last time her world crumbled, and if all she had at the end of this nightmare was David Gethen... she'd be okay.

SIXTEEN

Lianna

Lianna had checked everything except their backpacks on the return flight, and while hauling two backpacks through the airport had been a mess, it was nothing compared to trying to find a luggage cart and load it by herself when she landed at JFK. In the past, she'd always had someone there to help her, but she managed to get everything off the carousel and organized on the cart, wheeling it outside to wait for David and Harry.

They weren't far away when she called, one benefit of having plenty of time to warn them about when her plane would be landing, but she still felt incredibly alone waiting on the crowded sidewalk where happy couples and families were getting picked up, chattering about their vacations. The only people she seemed to connect with were the weary business travelers who looked as miserable and exhausted as she felt.

"Lianna!" David's voice caught her attention and she jerked her head up to find him hanging out the window of a truck. Just setting eyes on him lifted some of the heaviness off her soul, and she waved at him so he knew she'd heard.

Before the truck had even pulled to a stop, David jumped out and ran for her, picking her up off the ground and claiming her mouth in a kiss that erased everything else from existence for one perfect moment. For one breath it was just them, his arms locked tight around her as their lips crashed together, and she didn't feel alone at all. David was there for her. Even after their stupid fight, even after he'd been a complete jackass, even after her uncle had him beaten and sent to another goddamn country — he'd been worried about her. Both of his voicemails had ended the same way, with him begging her to leave, to come home, to him. Because he wanted her safe, and as insane as Jean-Luc thought she was, Lianna felt completely safe in David's arms.

"Would you two stop making out and get in the damn truck?" Harry's gruff voice ended their kisses, and David relaxed his hold on her so she slid down his front, but she couldn't take her arms away from his neck yet.

"I missed you," she whispered, and he leaned down to press one more kiss to her lips.

"You have no idea how fucking worried I've been about you, angel." David smacked her ass and grinned before tilting his head toward the truck. "Come on. You get in and we'll get everything loaded in the back.

Blushing, she finally turned to Harry and waved. "Hey, Harry. Thank you for coming to pick me up."

"Not a problem," he said, lifting one of the suitcases to toss it in the bed of the truck. "You two can sit in the back."

"Thanks." Lianna opened the cab's rear door, climbed up, and scooted over to give David room. He joined her a few minutes later, immediately putting an arm around her to squeeze her into his side. Harry shut the doors before walking around to get back into the driver's seat.

As they pulled into the slow river of cars, David leaned closer to breathe in her hair, picking up the little heart necklace she hadn't taken off since he gave it to her. When he hugged her just a bit tighter, she smiled, taking his hand and intertwining their fingers so she could hold on to him. After a couple of minutes, he leaned back enough for her to see him.

"Are you okay? Did you eat?" he asked, and she laughed a little.

"Not really. The food on the plane wasn't exactly... edible?" she finished lamely. Rolling her neck, she tried to get rid of the stiffness, but it wasn't going to happen anytime soon. "Honestly, I forgot how terrible flying in coach is. How the hell do people do that? A transatlantic flight with no leg room, and you can't even lay back?"

"I've never even been to Europe," Harry said from the front seat.

"Most people haven't," David added, and she felt the heat flood her cheeks again.

"Oh... right. Sorry." *Way to be ungrateful, Lianna.* "Well, it wasn't that bad. I mean sleeping at the airport sucked when I couldn't get a flight out last night, and there was no real food on the plane, but it wasn't so bad. I'm just glad I'm home. That being said, I'm definitely starving. Can we pick something up?"

"Sure, what do you want?" Harry asked as he turned around to check his blind spot before changing lanes.

"We can get anything you want." David ran his fingers up and down her arm, pulling her closer as he kissed her hair. "I think if I actually see you eat something, I might be able to think straight."

Laughing a little, she shrugged, trying to think of something close enough to the apartment that wouldn't be impossible to park near. "How about Engelmann's Deli?"

"That works." David kissed her again before he turned toward the front of the truck. "I'll tell you how to get there, Harry."

Traffic in New York was always a nightmare, but it didn't really faze her as she asked David about the bruise on his temple, feeling even angrier when he couldn't tell her exactly how it happened. That meant they'd either hit him when he was still out from the taser, or they'd hit him so hard he couldn't even remember them doing it. Either option was completely ridiculous, and she was sure David was hiding other injuries just so she wouldn't worry — but she'd see them later.

Then she'd decide just how furious she needed to be, and how much she'd need to yell about the bullshit Jean-Luc had pulled.

Unfortunately, by the time they got to the deli, it was a little after noon, and it took so long to get the food that her stomach was growling by the time Harry pulled up to her building, which had David in overprotective mode.

"You need to eat," he grumbled in her ear, and she nodded as he moved to help Harry unload the bed of the truck.

When they'd gathered the suitcases, her doorman was already on the way out with a cart to help.

"Harry, why don't you come up and eat with us?" she offered, smiling at the man. "It's the least I can do since you got me and David from the airport two days in a row."

He pulled off his baseball cap for a second, shaking it out before he tugged it back on. "Nah, you two should catch up."

"Come on, old man," David said, wrapping an arm around her waist again as the doorman loaded their bags. "I thought we were supposed to be family?"

Grumbling for a second, Harry looked over at the doorman. "Where can I park the truck?"

"If you'll leave the keys with me, I'll have it moved to our garage, sir."

"All right. Thank you," he replied with a nod, and even though he didn't look happy about it, he handed over his keys and looked up at the towering building. "Let's go eat then."

When they finally made it upstairs, she unlocked the door and led the way in, holding it open for the doorman to wheel in the cart and remove her bags. Harry followed the man in, glancing around for a few seconds before he looked at her. "This is a nice place."

"Thanks." She smiled as she scanned the apartment that looked a lot more like a home since they'd been living together. "David has actually been helping me redecorate a little."

"David has been decorating?" Harry asked, a slow grin spreading over his lips as turned toward him.

"I hang things that she tells me to hang."

"He's lying," Lianna said as David glared at her with an expression she knew was a warning, but she was so glad to see it again, she didn't stop talking. "He actually helped me pick the color for the new drapes."

"Who knew he was so domesticated?" Harry laughed, and David let out a low groan as he moved toward the doorman.

"It's a good thing I'm at least slightly domestic or Lianna might have starved to death by now," he snapped before opening the door and thanking the man as he took the cart and left.

Lianna started unpacking the bag of food when her stomach growled again. "That's true, he can cook. I'm assuming you taught him that?"

"That would be Shannon, my wife," Harry answered, heading into the kitchen to wash his hands. "I can't take credit for David knowing how to cook since I burn water. Although I do know how to grill."

Laughing a little, Lianna followed him to get the airplane germs off her skin before they started eating. As Harry was drying his hands beside her, she looked over at him and had the overwhelming urge to hug him, but she didn't. "You're a really good guy, Harry, I'm glad you're in David's life."

"I'm in your life too, sweetheart," he corrected, handing her the kitchen towel. "I know you and David are a package deal, and I can see how happy you make him."

The grin wouldn't leave her face as she turned to watch him finish unpacking the food. "You think so?"

"I've known David since he was born, and I knew his parents a long time before that. Jacob was like a brother to me, and I know he'd be happy to see what you've done for David."

"Yeah..." The mention of David's father felt awkward considering the terrible things her father had done, so she grabbed a few of the food containers and escaped toward the dining table as she spoke over her shoulder. "I'm not so sure he'd be happy that it's *me* making David happy."

"He's not here anymore, so that doesn't really matter," David said, shutting that conversation down as he and Harry brought over the rest of the food. They all sat down, and he opened his sandwich then looked up. "Can I have the chips?"

"Sure, baby," she answered, pushing the collection of bags into the middle for everyone to choose from. "I want to hear what else Harry has to say, though."

"What?" David asked, looking across the table at Harry with a doubting expression. "You really think Dad would have been fine with me ending up with Lianna?"

"Listen, Jacob had a lot of issues, and he carried a lot of anger after he lost Elizabeth," Harry explained, arranging his food on the deli paper. "But... just like David has seen you for the woman you are, Lianna, I think Jacob would have done the same."

"You really think so?" she asked, and the man's weathered blue eyes met hers as he nodded.

"Yeah, I do."

Scoffing, David ripped open a bag of chips. "I doubt it," he grumbled, popping a chip in his mouth as she sighed.

"I never thought you'd ever get over your anger, David." Harry tilted his chin towards her. "But you did... for her."

"That's different," David argued, refusing to even look at the man.

"No, it's not, but you're as stubborn as ever. Just like Jacob," Harry sounded completely resigned, not even attempting to get into an argument with David over something that neither seemed willing to budge on.

The conversation died for a few minutes, but no one seemed to mind as they started eating. She probably wasn't the only one hungry, since her plane had landed around eleven o'clock New York time, and they'd probably left Harry's an hour before that. For the first time in memory, David didn't have to nudge her to finish her sandwich. She easily demolished the turkey club, along with the side salad, and almost a whole bag of kettle chips. When he reached over to squeeze her thigh, she knew he was feeling better, but without the hunger distracting her, Lianna couldn't resist the urge to learn more about David's family.

Clearing her throat, she took a sip of her water before she looked up at Harry. "So... you were friends with Jacob when everything went down with my mom and his dad?"

"I was," Harry said, but he was stiff, not meeting her eyes as he gave the clipped answer.

"Can't we just enjoy lunch?" David asked, and she shoved his shoulder lightly.

"I just want to know the truth."

"I've told you everything, angel," he said, grabbing the little box of dessert he'd picked. "There's nothing more to know."

When Lianna looked back across the table though, Harry was just staring at the table, not looking up at them anymore, not eating, not even moving, and she had to trust her instincts. "I want to know what Harry knows."

Harry looked up at her, then at David, but he didn't say anything, and his face was too damn stoic for her to guess at whatever he was hiding.

"He doesn't know anything else," David muttered, obviously irritated by her pushing his friend. "He knows what I know, what my dad knew. And I've shared all of that with you."

Leaning forward on the table, Lianna waited for the older man to make eye contact, and she held onto his gaze for a moment before she prompted him. "Harry?"

Muttering a curse under his breath, Harry ripped his hat off and ran a hand over his thinning hair before pulling the cap back on with a sigh. "It's... it's not important."

"What's not important?" David pushed the little container away from him, leaving his fork impaled in the brownie as his attention zeroed in on Harry. "Do you know something, Harry? What the fuck is it?"

"It doesn't change anything, *won't* change anything that's happened," he said, scrubbing at his face before he finally looked up, gesturing toward them. "And you two are together now, which is all that matters."

"Bullshit," David growled, his voice taking on an edge that seemed both angry and hurt. "Have you seriously kept some secret of Dad's all this time? From me?"

"Hasn't there been enough lying?" she asked, and all she wanted to do was let out her frustration with the world by breaking something, or throwing things, but none of that would solve the issue at hand, and David needed these answers as much as she wanted them. Steadying herself, she tried to sound confident, serious. "If you know something about his dad, you should tell him, Harry."

"It's not just about Jacob, it's about that whole mess he got himself wrapped up in with Vanessa."

It was like the floor dropped out from under her when her mom's name crossed his lips, and all attempts at sounding steady and calm disappeared. "Wait, this is about my mom?" she asked, voice wobbling slightly until she realized Harry wasn't answering her. Raising her voice, she pushed. "What is it? What do you know?"

"Just fucking tell us, old man!"

"Hell… it doesn't matter!" Harry groaned under his breath, resting his head in his hands.

"You keep telling me to put this shit behind me and let it go, but I'm never going to be able to do that knowing you've got some bullshit secret you're still hiding for a dead man." David looked like he was about to rip the older man out of his chair if he didn't start talking, and she wouldn't blame him.

"You know what? Fine." Harry slapped his hands down on the table, lifting one to cut it through the air. "But after this we put it to bed. It's over. And every one of us is moving on."

"Fine! Just tell us what it is!" Lianna snapped, losing her temper, and Harry looked between the two of them, shaking his head as he took a slow breath in and out.

"Shit... I should have known you two would end up crashing into each other one way or another." Rubbing at his forehead, Harry leaned back, looking defeated. "When Jacob saw Vanessa in that damn penthouse — when she asked him to help her — he just wouldn't let it go. I told him to keep his nose out of it, I told him not to get involved, but he ignored me. Just like David does all the damn time."

"I knew that part already," David grumbled.

"Be patient," Harry said, pointing at him, and she was surprised when David leaned back in his chair. "As I was saying, what you didn't know was that he used one of our mutual connections to get Vanessa her way out. They wanted information on Mercier, and the Faures, and she was willing to trade it if they got her and your girl out of that house."

"Mutual connections? What mutual connections?" she asked, looking between them.

David looked just as confused as she was for a few seconds, and then he lifted his gaze to Harry's. "You mean the Corozzos? They were the ones helping my dad get Vanessa and Lianna out of there?"

"Dammit, boy..." Harry groaned.

"I don't care if she knows who they are!" David shouted. "Were they the ones involved or not?"

"They were the ones who had a plan to get her out, but as soon as things went south... they backed off," he explained. "They didn't want a war with the Faure family over nothing."

"Over nothing?" Lianna repeated, her stomach turning as confusion morphed into anger. "She was my mother! She wasn't nothing!"

"I know that, but they weren't going to get any answers after Mercier made her disappear. And you weren't exactly old enough to share anything important," Harry replied, finally meeting her eyes.

"That's bullshit," she said, or at least tried to because her voice broke on the curse. "Those... assholes! They just abandoned my mom? Me?"

"They hung my dad out to dry?" David asked, and he sounded just as hurt and surprised as she was.

Harry just sounded angry as he leaned forward and pointed at David. "How many times have I told you to keep your nose clean, David? How many times have I said you needed to stop going to see them? You act like you're protected, that because you and Vincent are friends that family wouldn't turn on you in a second... but that's incredibly stupid. You're not one of them, and that means you're expendable. You always have been. You *and* Jacob."

"And my mom," David filled in the missing blank, and Harry lifted his hands in the air, shrugging as his tone turned bitter.

"I've always told you they're not good people, boy. No matter how cheap their bar is."

"And Dad knew?" David asked. "Dad knew they abandoned us, left us in the fucking wind while Mercier came after us?"

"After Elizabeth died, your dad didn't care what happened to him… or you, really. He just wanted vengeance, and the Corozzos had the connections and the information to make that possible," Harry explained, his voice softening a bit as he looked at David. "Why do you think I kept telling you to back off? To stop going to them?"

"I just thought you were being an overprotective asshole."

"That may be true, but I wasn't wrong. I'm *not* wrong. And while I don't approve of how you two found each other, I am relieved that having her in your life has meant you've stepped out on your own and stopped following in your father's footsteps. You don't need the Corozzos, David. You never did."

Lianna's head was still spinning, but she didn't miss the meaning hovering between Harry's words. Turning toward David, she hoped she'd misunderstood. "Wait, you were meeting with the Corozzos?"

"Before," he answered, not even looking at her. "When I was digging up information on your family."

"Then who is Vincent?" she asked, and he finally looked at her and she saw the way his eyes widened slightly before he masked it.

"He's a friend," David answered, trying to sound casual. "I've known him since we were kids."

Shaking her head, she shoved his arm. "Oh, so you can be friends with a crime family, but I can't?"

"That's different!" he argued, and she huffed out a laugh.

"How is it different? You don't even have the excuse of being related to them!" she shouted. "You were just friends with them, using them to dig up dirt on me, and my dad, and my fucking family so you could come after us? Yeah, that's *so* much better, David!"

"Maybe I should leave…" Harry said, standing up.

"No way," David growled, and Lianna rounded on the older man, pointing at him.

"Sit down! I'm not done with you."

"You're not dropping this bomb and leaving me here to pick up the pieces," David continued, jabbing a finger down on the table. "Sit."

Sighing, Harry slowly took his seat again, folding his hands in front of him before he looked up at them both. "I told you it doesn't matter, and it doesn't. You two have been mixed up together since you were kids because of the decisions your *parents* made. Jacob was trying to be a good man," Harry said, meeting David's eyes for a moment before he looked at her. "And Vanessa was trying to protect you, Lianna. They both tried to do the right thing, and they both paid a high price. But no matter what shit came after, you two have pulled just about the only good you could from it." Reaching across the table, he shoved the trash from their meal aside and grabbed their hands, laying them roughly on top of each other, squeezing David's hand into hers as his voice grew insistent. "*This* is good. Out of all that tragedy, you two have each other, you *love* each other, and that's all that matters."

Harry looked between them, keeping their hands together for a while longer, but eventually he sat back, and David wove his fingers between hers, squeezing tight. She wasn't sure what she'd expected Harry to tell them, but she hadn't been prepared for *this*. Her blood felt like a curse, like some terrible burden she'd never be able to escape; and hearing the story again from Harry's perspective had only amplified the nagging guilt she still felt over what her family had done to David's... and to Harry too.

How far had her father's decisions rippled out? How many people in the world were suffering because of what he'd done? Because of what the Faures did?

Clinging to David's grip on her hand, she pushed back the urge to cry, refusing to break down about this right now. Not in front of Harry, and not when David was still trying to process everything as well. As if he knew exactly what she needed, David pulled his hand from hers, replacing it with his free hand so he could wrap the arm around her shoulders, pulling her into his side. For a moment he just held her, and then she felt him kiss the top of her head, and it was a little silly just how much it helped.

"Anything else you need to get off your chest, old man?" David asked, not letting go of her.

"That's all I know. I promise," he said, and even though she didn't know him very well, she believed him. But the knowledge was out there now, and it explained more than just how everything fell apart for her mom.

Taking a breath, Lianna squeezed David's hand and sat up straight to look the man in the eye. "At least I finally understand why we've never become friends, Harry."

"What are you talking about?"

Shrugging, she swallowed the swell of emotion down. "You lost your best friend because of my family. I'm sure you were just as angry as David over what happened, so it makes sense I wouldn't be your favorite person either."

"I don't have a problem with you, Lianna. I never did," Harry said, gesturing at David with a huff. "I tried to get this idiot to see that you couldn't be blamed for your father's shit. I lost Jacob because he couldn't let go of his anger... At least you got this dumbass to see the truth."

"Thanks, Harry," David said, his voice dripping with sarcasm.

"You're very welcome, boy," Harry said, a tight smile appearing on his face as he stood up again. "Now, I really do think I'm going to head home. This is two days that I've got my boys at the work site alone, and God only knows what they've fucked up."

"I appreciate all your help, Harry. And everything you've done for David," she added as she and David got out of their seats as well.

"That's what family does for each other," he said, reaching over to hold her hand in both of his, patting it lightly. "You just keep him in line, and make sure he gets his ass back to work soon."

Laughing a little, Lianna nodded. "I think I can do that."

"I'd love to see you try and boss me around, angel," David said, grabbing her by the hips to yank her back against his front. "We both know how that works out."

"David!" she shouted, blushing as she pushed his hands away so she could walk Harry to the door. "Maybe we can see you again soon?"

"I'll see about the boys' schedules. Shannon and I would love to have you two over."

"We'll be there," David confirmed, reaching forward to shake Harry's hand, but the man used the handshake to pull him into a quick hug, slapping David on the back a few times. When they separated, David was smiling. "Thanks again, Harry."

"Just remember what hill you want to die on, son, and make sure she knows you love her," Harry said, smiling at her as he opened the door. "Every single day."

"I'm on it, old man," David answered, waving at Harry as he turned toward the elevator. As soon as he shut the door and flipped the lock, David turned and grabbed her, pulling her against his front. "I finally have you all to myself."

"What are you going to do with me?" she asked, grinning up at him as his hands roamed down to cup her ass and squeeze.

"So many terrible things," he growled, just before he leaned down and threw her over his shoulder. Lianna couldn't bite back the short scream that escaped, but it quickly turned to laughter as David landed a hard spank on her ass. It didn't really matter what David had planned, she loved the wicked things he came up with, and whatever terrible thoughts he'd been cooking up while they were apart... she knew she'd love them too.

Because she loved him, and he loved her, and even though the universe had crashed their lives together in the worst of ways — on more than one occasion — Harry had been right. Out of all the tragedy, all of the violence and chaos and suffering, they'd managed to pull the only good thing they could out of the ashes left behind.

Love.

And they'd fight anyone who tried to take that away from them.

SEVENTEEN

David

Four Days Later

"You're asking for salmonella, you realize that, right?" Lianna asked, and he laughed as she unlocked the door.

"You are going to cook the chicken all the way through *without* drying it out," he replied, following her inside the apartment as soon as she grabbed the bags from the ground, but he could tell she was rolling her eyes even though she wasn't facing him. "I know you don't believe me, angel, but I'm going to teach you how to cook without burning down the kitchen."

"It wasn't my fault that the towel caught on fire."

Chuckling, he grabbed her by the hips, turning her around so he could wrap his arms around her. "So, you're telling me that someone broke in, stole absolutely nothing, but decided to move one of the kitchen towels next to the burner on the stove."

"And then fled the scene," she finished the bullshit story for him, and he grabbed a fistful of her hair and bent her over in the middle of the kitchen, landing a rapid series of spanks across her ass. Lianna had her hand wrapped around his wrist and the other one trying to deflect his swats, but she was wearing jeans, and he knew she could handle a hell of a lot more than this.

"Sticking to that story?" he asked, and she whined through her teeth. "Okay then." He spanked her once more, just a little harder, and then reached for his belt. As soon as she heard the movement, she started squirming and digging her fingers into his wrist.

"Fine!" Lianna shouted through a laugh. "There was no arsonist burglar involved, I just happened to lay it too close to the stove."

Lifting her upright again, he grinned as he let go of her hair, cupping her face in his hands. "Setting fire to the kitchen isn't going to get you out of learning to cook, angel."

"It wasn't on purpose." She said it with such exasperation he knew it was true, but whether Lianna Mercier was actually capable of learning to cook was still up in the air.

"All right then, finish putting the groceries away, but leave the chicken out on the counter," he commanded, and she tucked her hair behind her ears before she crouched to dig through the grocery bags. Heading into the living room, he dropped into the chair to take off his shoes, smiling when he heard Lianna humming in the kitchen.

A week before, he would have rolled his eyes at the term 'domestic bliss,' but if this was what that felt like with Lianna... then he was okay with it. As messed up as their trip to France had been, it seemed to have resolved the last things standing between them. Lianna knew her family, the good and the bad, and he knew that when she had to choose between him and their life of luxury with all of their happy family bullshit... she still chose him.

It wasn't like she hadn't told him that she wanted him again and again, but whoever said 'actions speak louder than words' was a wise motherfucker. He'd loved Lianna, but some part of him still hadn't trusted her. Not completely, anyway. Whether he was fully aware of it or not, he'd been waiting for her to leave him. To find something better, someone better, and jump ship from the complete dumpster fire of a person he was. It could have happened when they finally dropped the charges against her, and it almost happened when Jean-Luc showed up in her life. Those days they spent in France had just fueled his paranoia, built it up, and when she'd talked about moving there... he'd snapped.

Looking back at everything made him feel like a fucking idiot. He knew why he'd acted the way he had, even though it was just his own bullshit driving it. But, more importantly, he could see that during the entire trip, Lianna had never given him a real reason to doubt who she wanted to be with. She'd been choosing him even when she was surrounded by all those two-faced family members who had pulled out all the stops trying to take her away.

He just hadn't been able to see past his hatred of the Faures, or his fear of losing her, to realize that he was the only one fucking it up.

As much as he still hated the asshole, Jean-Luc had done him a favor in trying to come between them. By drawing a line in the sand and forcing Lianna to choose between him and Jean-Luc's family, the bastard had actually managed to make David's relationship with Lianna stronger. That one action had been worth more than anything else Lianna could have said, because when she left the Faure estate that night, she'd *actually* chosen him.

And she was still choosing him.

Jean-Luc kept calling her, but she'd declined them all. He'd warned the man in his office that she'd hate him, but Jean-Luc hadn't believed him because he didn't know Lianna. He hadn't seen her breakdown when she realized who her father actually was, hadn't seen her own father point a gun at her, and he definitely hadn't been there for the fall-out.

David wasn't innocent in any of it — not by a long shot — but at least he'd been there.

He'd seen her strength firsthand. He knew just how much rage and pain hid behind that pretty blonde exterior. But Jean-Luc had made the same mistake his brother had; the same error David had made before he actually spent time around her... he'd underestimated Lianna, assumed she was just a beautiful doll, empty, without any depth, and ready to be molded into whatever Jean-Luc thought his family was missing.

But that wasn't Lianna. She didn't break for anyone.

And he loved her all the more for it.

"Baby, were you serious that I have to flatten the chicken with this? It's going to get everywhere." Lianna was standing at the edge of the kitchen, holding the mallet in one hand and wearing a look of disgust and concern that made him stifle a laugh.

"That's why I said we'd put it between plastic wrap." Standing up, he headed back into the kitchen to see a badly mangled chicken breast on a cutting board. "Okay, angel. I'm going to show you how to do this without shredding the chicken."

Chuckling under his breath, he cleaned up the mess she'd made and pulled out the things they'd need to get started for real this time. How he'd zoned out enough to miss Lianna wielding a mallet in the kitchen, he had no idea, but at least she'd only ruined one of the chicken breasts.

Almost an hour later, they had all of the chicken pounded flat and breaded, ready to go in the cast-iron pan as soon as the oil was hot enough. Lianna was wiping down the counter with cleaner, obsessed with the idea that she'd somehow contract salmonella if she didn't go over it a hundred times.

"I promise that's fine," he said, tugging her away from the counter. "Now, about Sunday—"

"Are they really *all* going to be there?" Lianna asked, cutting him off as her anxiety rose to the surface again.

"Yep. There's a game on Sunday and so Tommy, Liam, and Sean will be there. Tommy and Liam are married, and Tommy has two kids." He shrugged. "Sean is still a fuck-up, so he'll be there alone."

"Is this retaliation for me making you meet my entire family?" she asked, smiling a little, and he wrapped his arms around her, leaning down to kiss her. Gently at first, but when she wound her arms around his neck and pressed herself close, he took control of it. It wasn't until she moved one hand down to his belt that he pulled back.

"Naughty girl. We have to finish dinner first."

Her groan had him chuckling again as he turned them, pinning her against the counter. "I promise I'll make it worth it, even if you fuck it up."

"What happens if I ruin dinner?"

Leaning in, he nipped her throat before he whispered directly into her ear. "Bad girls don't get lube."

"Fuck." The little whine that slipped past her lips had his cock waking up behind his zipper, but he pulled back from her before she tempted him to turn off everything and fuck her first.

"Want to pay attention now?" he asked, and she nodded, that pink flush spreading over her cheeks. No matter how nervous she acted, he knew she'd be soaking wet if he shoved a hand down her pants to check — but *that* line of thinking wasn't going to help the hard-on go away. Rubbing a hand through his hair, he stepped away from her. "What were we talking about?"

"You retaliating against me dragging you to France by making me meet Harry's entire family at once." Lianna grinned at him, and he fought the urge to spank her again.

"Maybe it is, maybe it isn't, but at least the McConnells aren't secretly running a massive criminal empire. They're all in construction."

"And friends with the Corrozzos," Lianna added, and he groaned.

"As Harry pointed out, he's *not* friends with them, but he'll do work for whoever pays him." Turning toward the stove, David hovered a hand over the oil, frustrated that Lianna's stove was taking so long to heat it up. "It's not ready yet, but once the oil is hot enough we'll—"

Her ringtone went off, and she sighed, leaning over the counter to look at where it was charging on the bar before she declined the call. "You were saying?" she asked, but she'd barely finished it when her cellphone rang again. Huffing, Lianna declined again, and crossed her arms as she faced him.

"Jean-Luc?" he asked.

"The call is from France, so I guess he's just decided to try a different number now." Lianna took a step toward him, and the phone rang again. She let out a frustrated groan, spinning around, but he caught her arm.

"Let me handle it." Walking around the bar, David yanked it off the charger and answered the call gruffly. "Leave her alone. I think she's made it pretty damn clear that she doesn't want to talk to you."

"David? Is that you?" The voice threw him for a second, because it definitely wasn't Jean-Luc, but then he recognized it.

"Rémi?"

"I need to speak with Lianna," he replied, his voice flat, and David just laughed.

"If you're calling to plead on behalf of your father, you might as well hang up. She's not talking to him after the shit he pulled, and calling her over—"

"Give her the phone, David. Now," Rémi snapped, and he fought the urge to lay into him. Setting the phone back on the counter, he plugged it into the charger and then tapped the speaker phone icon as Lianna moved closer, her brows pulled together.

"It's Rémi, and he's being an asshole," he explained, and Lianna blew out a breath.

"Hello, Rémi." She didn't sound happy at all, and he loved that she wasn't hiding her irritation with her cousin. "What do you want?"

There was a pause before Rémi's voice came through the phone, rougher than before. "Did you do this?"

"Do what?" Lianna asked, meeting his gaze over the counter as she raised her hands in a silent question. When Rémi didn't answer, she leaned closer to the phone. "Look, if you're pissed at me for leaving, you need to talk to your dad. He knows what he did, and he knows how I feel about it."

"I can't do that, Lianna," Rémi answered, his voice cracking. "He's dead."

"Who's dead?" she asked, and a chill rolled down David's spine, a sinking feeling rapidly ruining his appetite.

"My dad," the man whispered, and David wished more than anything that he'd misheard him, but he knew he hadn't. All the color drained out of Lianna's face as she stared at the phone, her hands braced on the counter in front of her.

When he realized she wasn't going to speak, he asked the important question. "What happened?"

"Are you sure you don't know already?"

"What the fuck is that supposed to mean?" David felt his anger surging forward as he raised his voice. "We're in New York, Rémi, which is exactly where your father sent me."

"But I just saw him," Lianna said, sounding more than a little dazed. "He was fine. He looked healthy."

A harsh sound came across the line before Rémi spoke. "I don't think it matters how healthy you are when someone puts a bullet in your chest."

"Someone *shot* him?" Lianna shouted, and David grabbed onto the bar just to ground himself in reality, because this couldn't be happening. He wasn't upset that Jean-Luc was dead, it was the fact that Rémi had already made it clear that the Faures thought they'd done it.

This is bad. Fuck, this is very, very bad.

"Be honest with me, dammit!" Rémi shouted, and there was no doubt that the man was crying, or close to it. "Did you have anything to do with this? Did you really threaten my father?"

"*Threaten!*" Lianna shouted, and he wanted to cover her mouth so she didn't say the wrong thing, but she was on the other side of the counter, and the flush had returned to her cheeks along with her temper. "I didn't threaten him at all! You were there! You heard me leaving, you heard everything. I'm sure all of you did!"

"Maybe you didn't threaten him then, but what about after? What about David?" Rémi pressed, and he clenched his jaw tight. "Everyone knows how David feels about my father, and he did send him away."

"I didn't do anything to your father!" he growled.

"David has been here, with me, in New York," Lianna said, still pissed, but she sounded a lot calmer than he was capable of at the moment. "How in the hell could we have been involved?"

Rémi scoffed. "Don't pretend like your father didn't have the same kind of connections my family does. It's not like it's hard to find someone willing to kill for money, and my father made sure you had plenty."

"You've met me, Rémi! You really think I'm capable of something like that?" she asked, and he hated that he could hear the pain in her voice when she continued. "I had no fucking idea what my father was doing, and—"

"That's what you keep telling everyone, isn't it?" Rémi snapped, his voice growing angrier. "But my father crosses you, and less than a week later he's dead."

"You're wrong," David said, shaking his head even though the other man couldn't see it. "Lianna has always been innocent in this shit. Her father kept it from her and killed himself when he realized it was going to come out."

"Unless he didn't kill himself," Rémi retorted, and David felt sick.

Had Michael Turner told Jean-Luc that part too? Had Jean-Luc already shared the details of everything that had happened with his son? The heir to his proverbial throne?

"Maybe Lianna wanted all of them out of the way," Rémi continued. "I mean Marc took a bullet too, but he's still alive."

"Someone shot Marc too?" Lianna asked, her eyes searching his for some kind of answer or comfort, but he didn't have any. This was bad.

"In the arm," Rémi answered. "Guess their aim was off."

"Is everyone else okay?" she pressed. "Did anyone else get hurt?"

"None of us are okay, Lianna," Rémi growled, muttering in French for a moment before he returned to the phone. "We're all in hell right now, but no, no one else was shot. My dad went to see Marc to talk about *you*."

"So, who else was with Marc and Jean-Luc?" David asked.

"Why would that matter?"

Rolling his eyes, he remembered the weird way Marc had acted around Lianna, and the argument they'd had during the soccer game. "It's pretty convenient that the only witness is also the only survivor, Rémi. Even you have to admit that."

"I don't have to admit anything. You've hated us from the beginning, David, and you haven't tried to hide that. We all know how you felt about my dad, and now you're just shifting that hate onto my uncle, who has absolutely nothing to gain from betraying us. He doesn't inherit the family, I do."

Leaning forward, Lianna moved the phone closer to her. "I don't care who inherits the family, Rémi. This is insane. I wasn't happy with your dad, but I'd never hurt him. I wouldn't hurt anyone!"

"We'll see," he replied, and there was too much pain and anger in his voice for David to feel anything but dread as the man kept talking. "I want you to know that I won't rest until I find out the truth, and I will figure it out."

"This wasn't me," Lianna said, and he realized she was close to tears when her voice broke, which only made David angrier at the whole bullshit situation.

Grabbing the phone off the counter, he talked directly into it. "She'll be waiting for your apology when you realize the truth, Rémi."

There was no response, and when David looked down at the phone, he realized Rémi had hung up on them. Shoving the phone back onto the counter, he looked up just in time to see Lianna start hyperventilating, the tears turning her blue eyes into that vibrant tone that he loved under almost any other circumstance — but not now. She slid to the floor on the other side of the counter, and he cursed under his breath as he moved around to pick her up.

Then he realized he could smell smoke.

"Fuck!" Rushing to the stove, he turned off the burner and grabbed the handle of the pan before he could stop himself. He bit down on the shout of pain as he ripped his hand back from the burning cast-iron, fumbling for a potholder to pick up the damn thing. Carrying it carefully to the sink, he dropped the smoking mess in and swung the water to the other side so he could run cold water over the burn. It didn't look that bad, and now that the kitchen wasn't going to catch on fire, *again*, he could handle what was actually important.

Lianna had her knees pulled up to her chest, her face buried in her arms, but that was only going to make her breathing worse. She was still hiccupping whenever she tried to take a full breath, and the last thing they needed right now was her passing out.

"Come on, angel." Crouching down, he scooped her off the floor, adjusting her against his chest so he could carry her into the living room.

"H-how is this even possible?" she asked, wiping at her eyes as he settled them on the couch.

"I don't know. I mean, it's not like that family doesn't have plenty of enemies. It's never just been me."

"But *why*?" Lianna looked at him, and it was only because she seemed to be calming down that he even thought about discussing the idea that had been forming in the back of his mind while they were arguing with Rémi on the phone.

Looking down, he ran a hand over her thigh before grabbing her hand and holding it tight. "We both saw Marc acting weird in France, pretending he didn't know you even though you remember seeing him at the penthouse with your father. And... didn't Jean-Luc deny them ever meeting when you argued with him?"

Lianna sniffled, sitting up on his lap before shifting to lean against the armrest, her legs draped over his as her brows pulled together. She was thinking, all those wheels turning behind her perfect eyes, and he started running his fingers up and down her back as she turned over the idea. After a minute or two, she looked up at him again. "You think it was Marc?"

"It makes sense."

"But after all this time? Why?" Shaking her head, Lianna scrubbed at her face, wiping the last tears away. "And

Rémi's right, he doesn't have anything to gain. It's not like he gets to take over. The family passes to Rémi, not Marc."

"Unless he was keeping secrets from Jean-Luc," he said, shrugging a shoulder. "Things he didn't want anyone to know."

"About my father," Lianna finished.

"I don't know, angel. I think it's possible, especially since you saw him yourself." Blowing out a breath, he groaned. "If I still had all my files we could try and find proof, but—"

"Michael!" Lianna jumped up from his lap, walking around the coffee table to pace back and forth. "Michael spoke to Jean-Luc about me, *us*. And if he's always been a loyal little lackey to the Faure family, then do you really think he'd destroy all the evidence against you? All the information you had against my father? Against them?"

The mere idea that Michael Turner still had evidence against him made him sick, but he couldn't deny Lianna's logic. He only had one question. "If he had that all this time… why wouldn't he have used it by now?"

"Because I told him not to," she answered, nodding as she walked back and forth. "But if Jean-Luc had told him to take you down, I think he would have. I think he'd keep whatever he needed to so that he could continue to serve the family, even from prison."

"Oh no. *Hell no*," he said, standing up as he realized where Lianna was headed. "I know exactly what you're thinking, angel, and if you think I'm just going to let you go to Rikers—"

She stopped pacing and faced him, meeting his gaze with all the fire inside her. "You'll what? Tie me up? Beat my ass? Etcetera, etcetera?" Lianna was using his own words against him, and he hated it, but he managed to keep his mouth shut as she started pacing again. "I thought we weren't doing the ultimatum bullshit anymore, David."

"I don't like this," he forced out through clenched teeth, and Lianna turned to look at him, a victorious little smile ticking up the edge of her mouth.

"Good thing you don't have to like it."

EIGHTEEN

Lianna

Lianna had never been to a prison before, and why would she have? It wasn't like the life she had before everything fell apart involved criminals... or, at least, not *known* criminals. Looking at the stark walls, the depressing line of people waiting to register for visitation, she almost felt bad for Michael.

Almost.

Whenever the crushing aura of the place started to make her feel guilty over his presence there, she just had to remember that he'd killed her mother and had almost certainly been involved in the death of David's mother — and probably many others. Michael had chosen his path in life long before she was born, and she had to believe he always knew this was a possibility — ending up in prison because he served the Faure family.

The guards were gruff and unfriendly when she and David finally made it inside the building. They were ordered to remove their shoes and belongings before they could pass through a metal detector where she had to wait on the other side for the guard to empty out her purse and rifle through the random shit she had in the bottom. After she shoved it all back into her purse, they were allowed to wait in another line to speak to a guard who took her ID, and David's passport, to document their visit before they got their visitor passes.

It had already taken forever to get that far, but when she moved to sit down on the chairs against the wall, David caught her elbow. "We're not at the right building."

"Seriously?" Groaning, she followed him out a different door and onto a bus that eventually drove them across the prison grounds, dropping them off at the end of another line. This one seemed to move faster, but the same kind of unfriendly guards were waiting once they were inside. Lianna filled out the form they handed her, but she felt strange filling out Michael's name, knowing he'd changed it. Knowing he'd lied to her about everything. And when she wrote 'friend' into the space asking for their relationship, it was definitely a lie. They'd been as close as family a year ago... now she only felt resentment.

The next line led to a second metal detector, and she felt her patience wearing thin. What could she have possibly grabbed between one metal detector and the next while *inside* a fucking prison?

It was only the silent hope that Michael might have an answer that kept her from commenting as they swabbed her hands for traces of chemicals, and then made them put all their things into a locker. By sheer luck, David still had change in his pocket from grabbing them coffee at the deli that morning, otherwise they wouldn't have been able to pay for the locker at all. When a female guard waved her to the side behind a row of women and children, she wanted to ask what was going on, and why David was in a separate line, but David had made her promise not to draw attention to herself.

He was already uncomfortable coming to the prison, and she knew he didn't want to see Michael face to face again... but what choice did they have? Rémi was convinced they had something to do with Jean-Luc's death, and she didn't need David's confirmation to know just how bad that was. If they couldn't prove otherwise, it wouldn't matter that she was blood. She'd be in danger for the rest of her life, and she wasn't sure how long that would be.

"Shoes and socks off," the female guard ordered her when it was finally her turn to step behind the sectioned-off area. After a quick review of them, the woman was suddenly in her face. "Open your mouth. Lift your sleeves. Bend forward and pull your bra away from your body. Stand up."

Lianna followed every command, even though it felt incredibly awkward, but she wasn't going to stand out from the others. David had even made her dig through her closet for the most average clothes, the ones that didn't look designer, which meant she'd ended up in yoga pants and an old sweater with a camisole underneath. When the guard finally waved her through, she picked up her shoes and stopped on the other side of the private area to put them back on. It was hard to imagine Jean-Luc going through that process. He wouldn't have had a bra to pull away, but she found it difficult to picture him strolling through all the security measures without hesitation.

The government had to know who he was, and a French passport would definitely draw the attention of the guards here... and yet he'd come to see Michael before he'd sought her out. He'd known everything David had done before he'd even knocked on her door, and she'd never had a clue.

If that didn't speak to his acting skills, she didn't know what would.

"Come on, angel," David said, helping her up from the floor as they followed the directions of the guards until they sat down at a table to wait.

Everything was bolted down, from the tables to the chairs. Permanently fixed in place, spaced out, but she had trouble understanding why it would be necessary when the room was mostly mothers with children or older family members. No one here looked dangerous, even if they were coming to visit dangerous people.

"What are you thinking about?" he asked, and Lianna turned toward him.

"Nothing."

"Really?" David's voice was heavy with doubt, but she didn't want to talk about the other visitors or what her thoughts were on the prison industrial complex.

Taking a deep breath, she picked something else on her mind. "Tell me the truth, was Harry mad about us canceling Sunday lunch today?"

"I already told you he was fine with it."

"Yeah, but I don't want to piss him off, or make a bad impression," she explained, venting the anxiety over that concern instead of the other crap floating around in her head.

"Stop focusing on it," David insisted, reaching over to wrap his hand over hers. "I told him we had something urgent we had to handle, and Harry knows when he shouldn't ask questions. We're fine. I need you to focus on why the fuck we're here."

Blowing out a breath, Lianna turned her hand up to squeeze his. "I know he's got answers, David. He has to."

"We'll see…" he mumbled, but she knew he didn't have much hope that Michael would help them out. If he still had David's files, there was no guarantee he'd admit it to them. Especially since she'd brought David with her, but he'd refused to let her go alone — even if that would have given them a better chance at convincing Michael to turn over anything he might have saved.

A little girl started crying near the wall, and Lianna turned to watch as her mom pulled her onto her lap, shushing her, but there was no missing the way the girl said 'daddy' in a heartbroken voice. Feeling a pang in her chest, Lianna shook her head and faced the table again to give them what privacy she could. "This place is so sad."

"Yeah, thanks for not sending me here," he mumbled, and she rolled her eyes, bending the corner of the little guest pass which was the only thing they'd been allowed to bring into the visiting room. David squeezed her hand tight, tugging at her until she looked at him. "Don't roll your eyes at me. It's the truth. I should've been sent here for what I did."

"I think we've had that conversation enough times," she whispered, refusing to revisit the topic, and he didn't get the chance to push it because a guard opened the other door and prisoners began to file in. Sitting up straight, she waited for Michael's face to appear. The minutes stretched as she searched each one, until he finally appeared in the doorway, the second-to-last prisoner.

He looked older, tired as he scanned the room, but those familiar eyes went wide when he saw her. His lips twitched toward a smile — and then he saw David. His gaze had shifted away from her, and the sudden stiffness of his shoulders told her everything she needed to know about how he felt as he slowly approached them. Jaw tight, Michael took the seat next to hers, across from David, without offering a handshake or a hug even though they'd been told they could touch at the beginning and end of their hour-long visitation.

"This is a surprise, Lianna," Michael said, eventually breaking the silence as he raised his eyes from the table to look at her. "I thought you'd decided you were never speaking to me again."

"Circumstances have changed."

"Apparently not *all* circumstances," he replied, narrowing his eyes as he glared at David.

Sighing, she shook her head a little. "No, that hasn't changed, and it's not going to. And, more importantly, it's not why we're here today."

"And why are you here?" Michael asked, shifting his hands into his lap as he looked at her again, leaning back in the seat.

Lianna did her best to keep her voice quiet as she leaned forward and whispered, "Jean-Luc is dead."

Michael looked stunned for a moment, and she wasn't even sure he breathed until he braced his elbows on the table and leaned closer to her. "What?"

"He was killed," she answered, speaking softly. "Shot."

"Where?" Michael asked, a little too loud as he sputtered for a moment, shaking his head. "This isn't possible."

"I felt the same way when Rémi called me. Apparently, it happened on Marc's estate. Jean-Luc was shot in the chest and Marc took a bullet in the arm."

"Rémi told you this?" he asked, locking eyes with her as his brows pulled together, his expression softening. "You've met Rémi?"

"We were just in Provence visiting the family," she explained, her tone taking on an edge as she continued. "Meeting everyone that *you* and my father kept me from."

"You were there when this happened?" Michael looked confused, and she hated having to recount everything that absolutely wasn't important at the moment.

"No, I left a few days before."

"I can't believe this…" he hissed, his hands turning to fists on the table. "Who would dare…"

"Well, Rémi seems to think Lianna had a hand in it," David filled in, and Michael's glare snapped up to him.

"That's ridiculous. Lianna would never do something like that."

"Nice to know you think so highly of me since you made sure to tell Jean-Luc the absolute worst things about me and David," she said, leaning back from the table as Michael swiveled toward her with a blaze in his eyes.

"I told him the fucking truth. This bastard doesn't deserve you. He deserves to be in here with the rest of the dogs."

"I'm the one who took a bullet for her, not you," David replied, waving a hand at him as rage peppered his voice. "You let her father pull the goddamn trigger."

"I'm paying my dues. When are you gonna pay yours?" Michael snarled, and she balled her fist up and banged it on the table as quietly as she could manage.

"This isn't why we're here!"

"Why exactly are you here then?" he asked, leaning back to look between the two of them, his tone bitter and his expression sour. "Just to tell me the news? To rub it in my face that you're still with this monster?"

"No," she forced out through gritted teeth, trying to take deep, slow breaths to calm down before she looked at him again. "I need to know what information you have about Marc and my father."

"What do you mean?"

"What were they doing together?" she asked. "Jean-Luc told me Marc had never worked with my father, or gone to see him, but I saw him myself. In the penthouse a few years ago, in the middle of the day, and he pretended to be someone else. Then, when I saw him again in Provence, he acted like he'd never met me before."

"Maybe you're mistaken," Michael replied, and she tried to swallow down her anger, grabbing onto David's arm when he suddenly leaned forward like he was going to talk again.

"It was only a few years ago, Michael. *Joseph.* Whatever." Shaking her head, she pushed away the litany of lies the man had told her throughout her life. "Regardless of what you and my father clearly thought of me, I'm not an idiot, and I know it was him. I told Jean-Luc about it before I left, and just a few days later he dies on Marc's estate? And Marc just gets a flesh wound? You can't tell me that doesn't sound suspicious."

"And he avoided Lianna the entire time we were there," David added, much calmer than before. "Like he didn't want her to confront him about it in front of the family."

Pointing at David, Michael seethed rage. "*You* don't get to talk to me. She can talk to me. Not you."

Rolling her eyes, Lianna smacked the table in front of her. "Can we get on track? I need answers. Did Marc visit my father a lot?"

Sighing, Michael wiped a hand over his face before staring at the table. "I wasn't aware they were in contact… but that just makes me suspicious of it. If I'd known he came to see Robert, *Alain*, then I probably wouldn't have thought a thing about it. They were family." Wiping at his mouth, he shook his head slowly. "But hiding it from me… that means he wanted to keep it from Jean-Luc."

"Would you have told Jean-Luc if you saw them together?" she asked.

"Probably," Michael admitted, and she was surprised to see how easily he set aside his loyalty to her father. "If Jean-Luc asked about it, absolutely. He leads the family, and even though I worked for your father, we were all ultimately loyal to him."

"Except Mercier wasn't exactly loyal..." David muttered, and Michael gritted his teeth, his hands balling into fists again.

Men.

"I think the more important question here is... how loyal is Marc?" Lianna waited for Michael to look at her again, and she did her best to show him how much she needed answers, because as much as she wished it were anyone else on the planet... he was the only one that could give them hope.

"I don't know Marc well enough to answer that question, Lianna, but if you're right that he was meeting with Robert here in the states... and keeping it from me and Jean-Luc..." He lifted a shoulder in a slight shrug. "Then that doesn't look good."

"It's too bad you went and destroyed all of the evidence my father and I painstakingly put together over a decade, because we'd probably be able to prove it," David said, crossing his arms.

Michael dropped his head into his hands and propped his elbows on the edge of the table, but he didn't answer. She couldn't be sure if that was because David had said it, or if Michael really had destroyed everything like he'd told her, but silence reigned for a long minute.

When he started shaking his head, Lianna leaned closer, keeping her voice quiet. "What are you thinking about, Michael?"

"Could you just call me Uncle Mike? Even once?" he asked, looking up at her with pain in his eyes. "I've known you since the day you were born."

"And you took my mother from me," she whispered. It hurt to see him in pain, she couldn't deny that, but he deserved to hurt.

"Dammit, Lianna..." He groaned, and she could have sworn his voice broke as he stared at the table, dropping his fist onto it. "If you only knew everything I protected you from. I did my fucking *best*."

"You don't want to have this conversation with me, Michael," she warned, feeling the rising tide of rage inside her that she'd never had the opportunity to launch at him or her father. "Are you going to help me or not?"

Michael shook his head, hands pressed to his temples, and she could see the emotion in him. As much as she wanted to erase the memories, seeing him made her remember all the times he'd played with her when she was little, the panic when he'd taught her to drive, and a hundred other memories tainted by the overwhelming one of him admitting that he'd killed her mother.

There was no coming back from that. Not ever.

"Fuck it," she whispered. "Maybe we should just leave."

"No!" Michael said, loud enough to draw the attention of the guards. Muttering under his breath, he finally brought his gaze back to hers. "Look, I'm doing this for you, Lianna. Not for him. *You* are the only person I'd do this for, because... cause I'm hoping it might redeem me a little in your eyes. Hell, I didn't even tell Jean-Luc what I'd kept."

"What did you keep?" Lianna held her breath, trying not to let her hope build too much.

"Copies," he answered, keeping his voice low. "The files this asshole and his father put together. All the shit he did to you."

"You *kept* that?" David asked, shock and anger blending together.

"I swear to God, do not say another word to me," Michael growled, leaning forward like he wanted to wrap his hands around David's throat — which he probably did. "The only reason I didn't make sure you ended up in this shithole, or six feet under, was because *she* told me not to. But I wasn't going to miss my chance if one day she woke up and realized how stupid it was to try and protect you. And, someday, she might still do that, and I hope I'm still here when she does just so I can welcome you properly."

"Michael," she snapped. "Where are the files?"

"In a safe deposit box at First Republic Bank in midtown Manhattan," he answered through clenched teeth, still glaring at David for a moment before he turned toward her and let out a huff of breath. "Number 118. The key is with my ex-girlfriend, Natasha Edmunds. I gave her a lot of money to hold onto it, so I'm sure she still has it."

"You had a girlfriend?" Lianna asked, surprised by the idea. She'd never seen Michael with a woman... ever.

"Before this? Yeah." Nodding, he sat back from the table, running a hand through his hair. "I told her to move on when I took the deal for six years, but she's holding the key for me until I get out, and she doesn't know what it goes to."

"How are we supposed to get her to turn it over? And where is she?" she pressed, and Michael got a look on his face that was somewhere between a smile and stifling a frown.

"She still writes me sometimes," he answered quietly, clearing his throat. "Hasn't changed her number. I think she's trying to wait for me... but it's only been seven months. I don't think she'll be there for me when I get out, but she'll still have the key. I know that much." Looking up at her, Michael chewed on his lip for a moment before nodding once. "She'll give it to you. Just call her and tell her that I want you to have the key. Tell her who you are... and remind her about the date we took to Coney Island where she threw up cotton candy on my shoes."

"Really?" Lianna asked, trying to imagine anyone throwing up on Michael. Other than her anyway... he'd always been the one to try and take care of her when she got sick.

Sighing, Michael nodded. "Yes. She'll know I sent you. You're going to have to memorize her phone number though." Gesturing at the empty table, he smiled a little. "Nothing to write with."

"Okay." Lianna closed her eyes to focus as he rattled off the number, and she repeated it back. When she fucked it up, he did it again, and again, and again, until she could recite it perfectly. David even started whispering the numbers under his breath along with her, just to prove they both knew the woman's phone number.

Natasha Edmunds — their only hope.

Glancing up at the clock on the wall, she knew they were running out of time, but at least they'd got what they came for. They had a chance. Swallowing, she looked at David, noticing how tense he still was, and then she looked back at

Michael to find him already staring at her. "If there's proof in there... this might save my life."

"And where will we be?" he asked softly.

"I don't know yet," she answered, and he sighed, groaning under his breath.

"I just wish you'd believe me," he whispered, speaking a little louder when he looked at her again. "Believe that I always tried to do my best for you. To keep you safe. To protect you from everything your father was involved in."

It was tempting to shove away the pretty words, but she couldn't deny them that easily. In the end, he had chosen her over her father, even though he'd almost been too late. *Would* have been too late if not for David. Still, she had too many memories of him taking care of her, showing up when her father didn't, and she couldn't deny that there were probably a hundred, a thousand times that he'd sheltered her from her father's actions. Licking her lips, Lianna tried to find the right words. "I... I do believe you, Michael. About that anyway. And I know you're only in here because you're still trying to protect me."

"That's... nice to hear." There was a hint of emotion in his words before he swallowed hard.

When she really looked at him, it was surprising what seven months had done to the man who used to always look so professional, so put together. She'd only seen him out of a suit and tie a handful of times in her life, and he'd always seemed larger than life to her. A constant, strong presence... but he'd lost weight in here. There wasn't enough color in his cheeks, and the tired haze in his eyes seemed permanent judging by the bags under them. Lianna knew it would probably irritate the hell out of

David, but Michael had helped them, and she needed to return the favor. "Look, is there anything you need in here?"

"A get out of jail free card?" Michael deadpanned.

"Ha. Ha." Shaking her head, she felt a smile tug at her lips. "What about money for the commissary? Books?"

Michael looked a little surprised, leaning back from the table to stare at her for a second before he nodded. "That would be helpful."

"I can do that," she replied. "They finally unfroze my accounts."

"I'm glad they finally left you alone. And, I'd appreciate whatever you can send."

Glancing at David, she shifted closer to Michael, intent on having his attention so he'd really listen. "I know you hate him, and I even understand why... but I need you to understand that he's not that guy. Not anymore."

"You don't have to defend me to him," David said, his voice low. "He's got his own list of sins, and even if this doesn't pan out, I'm going to keep you safe."

Michael turned toward David, staring at him hard. "I may hate you, but I'm still counting on you protecting her. If there isn't evidence in those files to point at Marc, the target is gonna stay on Lianna's back. So, you better put yourself between her and anyone that tries to hurt her."

"I did last time, didn't I?" David replied seriously, and Michael softened a little as he looked at the table.

"Yes, you did... and it's one of the only reasons you're still alive."

Done with the endless male pissing contest, Lianna pushed to her feet, ready to go even though they had a few minutes left, but Michael's eyes widened as he tore his gaze from David to look up at her. "Do you have to leave so soon?"

"What else is there to talk about?" she asked, and Michael opened his mouth like he was going to say something, but he shut it a second later, a heavy sadness passing over him and pulling his mouth down at the edges as he nodded stiffly. Reluctantly, he stood, and she saw David rise in her peripheral vision, but no one made a move. It was too awkward, because she had no idea how to say goodbye to him.

"It was really great to see you, Lianna," Michael finally whispered, breaking the silence. "It's the best thing that's happened to me in seven months."

A pang of guilt made her chest hurt, and despite everything she knew he was guilty of — for a moment she just wanted to hug him again. Michael had done many things wrong, but he was also the man who'd taken her shopping for her first pair of heels, snuck her out to an ice cream truck when she saw one on TV and begged to go to one. Michael was dangerous, just like all of the Faures, but he'd been her Uncle Mike long before she knew he was Michael Turner, or Joseph Blanc.

Pushing her hair behind her ears, Lianna spoke softly. "Michael... I don't know if we can ever be like we were before. I don't think that's possible, but I am grateful for what you did for me, and for David." Looking over at David, she was glad to see he wasn't broadcasting his irritation for the man anymore. Turning back to Michael, she took a breath. "And I'm sorry I haven't come here to say that before now. It's been a little rough being investigated by the FBI."

It may have been a lie, she wasn't sure whether she meant it or not, but it was the right thing to say. The small smile on Michael's face was all the proof she needed that the words meant more than any care package she may have sent along.

He looked into her eyes for a moment before he tilted his head to the side. "I've understood why you haven't come. I figured your lawyers were telling you to stay away anyway, but I remember the last time I came to your apartment."

"When I told you I never wanted to speak to you again."

"Yeah." He nodded a little, taking a slow breath. "I guess I should feel lucky you came at all. But I want you to know that I'm glad you did. I'm glad I know what's going on, even though now I'm just more worried about you. If they really think you did this, Lianna... there is no forgiveness. They'll come after you."

"It's why we need proof."

"And I hope you find it," he said, stepping forward, arms spread like he planned to hug her, but he stopped almost as soon as he started. When his arms dropped, she closed the gap between them, wrapping her arms around his back in a light hug. He leaned his cheek against the side of her head, his arms coming around her, and she felt a surge of emotion bring tears to the edge of her eyes as she remembered a million hugs just like it. When he was Uncle Mike, wearing a perfectly pressed suit, listening to her complain about school or friends or boys. It was easier to just give in to the comfort, the memories, and she pushed away all the betrayals she still felt like a raw nerve just beneath her skin. She'd needed to hug him more than she'd guessed, even if only to thank him for protecting her during the fallout of her father's corruption.

"I'll send you a care package, okay?" she whispered, and he squeezed her just a little tighter.

"This is better than a care package."

"Break it up," a guard barked, and Michael kissed her hair, holding onto her for a second longer before he stepped back, and she caught the shine in his eyes that likely mirrored her own before he rubbed them with his fingers and cleared his throat.

"Please update me as soon as you can," he said, his voice a little more gravelly than before. "You can get the mailing address from the guards if you really want to send something."

"We will. I promise."

Nodding slightly, Michael clenched his jaw tight and then he looked over at David, intense and serious when he spoke. "Keep her safe. I don't care if you die doing it."

"I think you'd prefer that," David snarked.

Michael shrugged. "No arguments here." He stared at David for a little longer before he looked at her again. "I'll always love you, Lianna. You're family to me. The closest thing I'll ever have to a daughter."

"Thanks, Michael," Lianna mumbled, unable to process what he'd said in the moment. "I... I'll try to come back sometime. If we survive this."

"Then I'll keep my fingers crossed," he whispered, the words almost overwhelmed by the sounds of other visitors and families standing and embracing.

"Time's up." David reached over to take her hand, pulling her toward the exit, but she hesitated, and he looked back at her. She just couldn't take her eyes off Michael, not yet. Good memories warred with horrifying ones, too many thoughts and too much knowledge kept her from feeling the way she had about him once... but it wasn't completely gone. She'd thought it was, she'd thought she hated him, but standing in front of him — she knew it wasn't true.

She didn't hate him, but she didn't love him anymore either.

He wasn't her Uncle Mike, and he never would be again. But even though he'd told Jean-Luc what he knew, he hadn't told him *everything*. He hadn't turned over the files, which would have doomed them both.

"Lianna?" David called for her, squeezing her hand tight as he pulled harder, but she only stumbled a step closer as she kept her eyes on Michael.

"You should go," he whispered, flicking a glance at the guards before he looked at her again.

"I know."

"Then..."

Lianna shook off David's hand to hug Michael again, ignoring the bark of the guard as he hugged her back even tighter.

"I miss you. The old you. How you... how *we* were before," she whispered, trying not to let her voice crack as the tears overflowed.

"I do too, Lianna, and I'm sorry. I'm so sorry." Michael was yanked back from her, and she saw the guard with his hand wrapped around Michael's arm. For a moment the guard looked angry, but when he saw her face, he softened his hold.

"Visitation is over."

"I know, I'm sorry, sir," she answered, and the guard nodded at her, nudging Michael toward the door.

"Go on, inmate." The prison guard led Michael out of the room, but he looked back at her once more before he disappeared into the hall. David ran his hand down her spine, resting it at the small of her back.

"You okay?" he asked, and she shrugged, scrubbing at the tears.

"I can't forgive him... but I can't hate him either."

"I get that," David answered quietly, and she looked at him in surprise. "I don't like him, and I think he's an asshole, but when it came down to you or your father, he did what had to be done. He kept you alive, and even if he hates it, he's protected you *and* me. So, I get it. I'll never forgive him either, but I can't hate him when we're only alive because of what he did."

"Yeah." Lianna nodded, stunned that David had been able to put into words what she couldn't — too overwhelmed by the war still raging inside her.

"Come on, angel. Let's go make a phone call." His mouth tilted in a lopsided smile as he led her to the door where another guard was waiting for them to start the long process back out of Rikers.

NINETEEN

David
_____

They'd called Michael's girlfriend once they'd passed through the exit process for Rikers Island, and Lianna put the phone on speaker so he could hear the conversation, which mostly consisted of the woman pretending she had no idea what they were talking about for about ten minutes. Even after Lianna had introduced herself several times, and explained her connection to Michael, the woman had continued to argue that she didn't know anything about a key — until Lianna remembered the stupid Coney Island story.

The line had gone silent for a minute, and then it was Natasha Edmunds' turn to grill them on what the key went to and why they needed it. Eventually, David had just told the woman that Michael had made them swear to keep the information he shared private, and she'd finally relented. Her address in Queens wasn't in the best neighborhood, but it was clear she took pride in the house and the flowerbeds out front. To both their surprise, she'd handed over the key without any further argument, but once David had it in his pocket, Natasha and Lianna had sat down on her front steps to talk about Michael and how he was doing.

He'd given them space, leaning on the fence in front of her house until they were done. About half an hour later, Lianna hugged her, and David was pretty sure she'd been crying when Natasha finally went back inside and Lianna headed toward him.

"You okay?"

"Fine," she answered, a little stiff as she straightened her sweater. "The bank will be open tomorrow morning. We should go early so we can see how much of your stuff he saved and get started on it."

"Sure, we'll leave early. You... want to talk about what happened with you and Michael?" He didn't look at her, not wanting to pressure her as he pulled up the Uber app to get a car home. "We don't have to."

"Not today. I think I just want to go home and drink."

Nodding, he wrapped an arm around her. "Sounds good to me, angel."

Lianna leaned into him, and he decided that had to be enough for now. If she wanted to talk, she would, but they fell into a comfortable silence as they stood on the sidewalk waiting for the car. Still, he had a feeling that Lianna was just one problem away from a full-blown breakdown. If they didn't find what they needed in Michael's safety deposit box... he didn't know what he'd do. The Faures had a long reach, and they knew who Lianna was now. Worse, they had the money to find her even if they ran. But he'd still do everything in his power to protect her.

Not because Michael Turner had told him to, but because he would have anyway.

He'd been thinking about it since the call with Rémi.

If there was no evidence of Marc's betrayal, or if he couldn't find out who'd really done it before things reached a boiling point... he'd tell Rémi it was him. Lianna would never forgive him for sacrificing himself, and he hated the idea of her being alone, but he'd been damned long before he'd first laid his hands on her. The things he'd done since weren't near enough to balance the scales — but if he could keep her alive, give her a chance at a real life, then maybe whatever came next would take pity on him. And even if it didn't, at least he'd die with the knowledge that Lianna was safe.

Tilting her chin up, David looked into the bright blue of her eyes, still too shiny from the lingering tears, and he knew it was the right decision.

No, it was more than just a choice, it was a promise... and he sealed it with a kiss.

"Are you sure it was number 118?" Lianna whispered, the anxiety rolling off her in waves, and he nodded.

"Yes, angel. I'm sure."

"What if it was 180? Could he have said that instead?" she asked, and he reached over to squeeze the back of her neck, gripping just hard enough to make her breath hitch.

"You need to listen to me. I remember the box number. I'm not wrong. The bank doesn't care who we are, they only care that we have the key — which we do." Leaning down, he put his mouth right beside her ear as he tightened his grip a little more. "If you don't calm down, I'm going to take you home and stripe your ass until you can't sit down without making that pretty little whine I love so much. Do you understand?"

Lianna swallowed then nodded slowly, but when he let go of her, she seemed a lot calmer, if not a little dazed.

He'd been able to get her to drink enough wine the night before to go to sleep, but as soon as their alarm went off that morning she'd been in a constant state of stress. Unable to stop moving, asking a thousand questions, most of them repeats, and although he had a very clear understanding of just how important the contents of Michael's safety deposit box were to them, if she asked him about the damn box number or the process to get it one more time he was going to drag her out of the bank by her hair and make good on his promise to belt her ass.

"Ms. Mercier?" the banker finally called, and David said a silent prayer of thanks as Lianna waved at the man and moved to follow him.

Staying on her heels, the banker led them back into a room filled with boxes, some small and some large. He was trying to find 118 in the larger rows, but when the banker pulled out a long, thin one, David felt his stomach sink.

"If you need any assistance, please just press that button." Nodding, the banker left them alone with it, and Lianna was chewing the fuck out of her lower lip as she stared down at the long, skinny box.

"It's too small, isn't it?" she asked, and he refused to answer. "Is this just some bullshit game Michael is playing with us?"

"I don't know, angel. We just have to open it."

Attacking her lip again, Lianna lifted the top, her lip popping free a second later as her brows pulled together. "What the fuck is this?"

Chuckling, David reached in and lifted out the little black rectangle, turning it over in his fingers. "*This* is an external hard drive. Two terabytes, which is probably enough room for most of the shit I had on my computer and in the cabinets."

"Then why didn't *you* have it all on a hard drive?" she snarked, and he looked up from the device to stare at her.

"Because, angel... my dad wrote over half those files himself."

"Oh... I'm sorry." Stepping close, Lianna pressed a kiss to his shoulder before she leaned her head against the spot. "Does this mean it'll be easier to find what we need?"

"Easier?" he repeated, flipping the drive over in his hand again and again as he thought about the possibilities. "I don't know. If he encrypted it, that will slow me down. And there's no guarantee that he'll have used any kind of organization for all of it. He probably just dumped the data from my computer onto the drive, and when it comes to the paper files... fuck. I won't know what we're dealing with until we get it back home and I get started."

"Let's go home then." Snapping the lid shut on the box, Lianna took the key and held her purse open for him to drop the drive inside. When she closed it and adjusted the straps on her shoulder, she looked up at him with a wicked smile. "Am I still in trouble?"

"Not right now," he answered, but when he saw her deflate a little, he grabbed her hand and pulled her toward the door, grinning as he added, "But we still have the ride home for you to piss me off."

Lianna

Having David's fist in her hair as he kicked the door shut shouldn't have felt so incredibly comforting, but the pinprick rush of tingles over her scalp made the constant whir of her thoughts slow down a little.

"You know, angel, if you want me to hurt you, all you have to do is ask," he growled, shoving her forward with his grip on her hair until she hit the wall, his body caging her in from behind as he ran a hand down her side. "Constantly questioning me about my memory, my ability to find files on a drive I haven't even fucking opened yet, and then calling me an asshole in front of the Uber driver is *not* how you do it."

"It's working, isn't it?" she replied softly, smiling, and he stepped back to deliver a series of burning spanks through the thin fabric of her dress as he kept her cheek pressed to the wall using the fist in her hair. She gasped with the first strike, but she bit down on any further sounds. This was what she needed. Since he'd threatened her with it in the bank, it was all she'd been able to think about. The rush that followed the pain, the blurring of all her complicated thoughts.

David stopped just as quickly as he'd started, and she heard him chuckle behind her. "You're sticking your ass out for me, angel. You want more?"

"Yes, please."

"*What* do you want?" he clarified, yanking her off the wall to crane her neck back so she was looking up at him. "Tell me."

"I... want you to hurt me."

"Why?" he pressed, wrapping his other hand around her throat as he marched her backward toward their bedroom. He wasn't squeezing that hard, just enough for her to feel that buzzing building in her ears as she stumbled in her heels, almost falling when he turned her through the doorway. "Answer me, Lianna, or I tie you down and leave you in here alone while I start looking at the drive."

"You wouldn't." She didn't believe him until he suddenly let go of her hair and shoved her onto the bed. Catching herself on the edge, she expected him to be on top of her a second later, but David stayed by the door, leaning against the frame as he crossed his arms.

"Angel, there's a whole list of things I'd like to do to you right now, but I want an answer first."

"I just— I want a distraction," she answered, groaning when his eyebrows just lifted slightly. "I mean, I want *you*. I want you to do whatever you're thinking of, because..."

"Because?" David echoed, reaching down to pull his shirt over his head, and as she watched his carved abs moving under his skin, she couldn't help but smile.

"Because you're incredibly hot, and while it makes absolutely no sense to me, everything feels better after you hurt me."

"Is that right?" Stepping closer, he undid his belt buckle, and goose bumps rose on her skin at the sound of it, a tingling rush following in their wake that ended directly between her thighs.

"Yes," she whispered, and he grinned at her, pulling his belt free in a swish of leather that made her fist the bedding on either side of her. With that wicked, lopsided grin of his, and his dark eyes focused on her, she could see the dangerous side of him, the half of him that liked to hurt her, to make her scream, and as fucked up as it was... nothing else in the world turned her on more.

"You going to beg me for it?" he asked, folding the belt in half as he toed off his shoes and kicked them aside.

"Maybe." She stood up, slowly closing the gap between them to press herself against his hard chest. Tilting her head up, she brushed her lips across his, not quite a kiss, and he didn't go for one as she popped the button on his jeans. Smiling, she slid his zipper down, brushing her hand over the steadily growing bulge before nudging his jeans out of the way to grip his half-hard shaft through his boxers.

"Lianna..." he groaned in a tone that was closer to a warning than urging her on.

"Is this on that list of terrible things you want to do to me?" she whispered against his lips before trailing kisses down his throat and nipping at his skin so that the rumble of his next groan buzzed against her mouth.

"Nothing about this is terrible." David's breath caught when she moved her hand into his boxers, stroking him slowly as she shoved his jeans down further until they finally dropped to his ankles. Rolling her thumb over the head of his dick, she grinned and turned him slowly so that her back was to the door, continuing to run her hand up and down his length. Watching the play of pleasure on his face as he closed his eyes tight when she squeezed lightly.

"But you want to do terrible things to me, don't you?"

"Always," he whispered, and the look he gave her when he opened his eyes again could have easily combusted her clothes if he had the power. She knew it was true — an honest confession that should have scared her at least a little, but it only amped up the tingly hum in her veins.

"Well then," she said, pulling her hand from his boxers to slide it up the ridges of his stomach, onto the firm muscles of his broad chest. "You're going to have to catch me first."

David barely had the chance to look confused before she shoved him back onto the bed and bolted for the living room. The sound of him hitting the floor had her laughing as she hovered near the end of the hall, waiting for him to get his jeans free of his legs. Tossing her heels toward the front door, she waited, and he appeared a few seconds later with the belt hanging at his side. "Calling me an asshole in the car wasn't enough?"

"Apparently not," Lianna answered with a shrug, and then she ran. The tights were helpful when it came to sliding around the furniture on the tile, but it was a lot harder to get traction for speed.

He almost caught her when she fled from behind the couch and ran for the space behind the fireplace, but he missed her, and then followed her path around the back of it like he always did.

Sprinting across the living room, she leapt over the coffee table, landing on the carpet between the chair and the couch, which meant she had plenty of options for escape. David jogged to a stop on the other side of the coffee table, shaking his head a little as he adjusted his hold on the belt.

"If you come over here and get on your knees right now, I'll use lube when I fuck your ass later. After I add a few dozen stripes to it." David wasn't even breathing that hard as he threatened her, but neither was she. Eventually they'd need to get a bigger place just so she had farther to run. "Going to be a good girl?"

"When have I ever been a good girl?" she asked, laughing as he groaned and rubbed himself through his boxers, gripping his hard shaft.

"Oh, I can *make* you be a good girl. We both know that, angel. You just need to remember that lube is a gift, and it's one you definitely haven't earned today."

"Guess we'll see." Grinning, she went for the gap between the table and chair, faking him out, and when he lunged for it, she got the chance to move to the other side of the coffee table. Running around it, she backpedaled a few steps, watching him as he slipped between the table and chair to take her place. Laughing, she put her hands on her hips. "I can't believe you fell for that again."

"Keep taunting me. It's just a matter of time before I catch you. This game always ends the same way."

"You promise?" she asked, bending forward to brace her hands on the edge of the coffee table, which gave him a perfect view down the top of her dress.

"You want me to hurt you?" David asked, shoving a hand back through his hair as he chuckled, low and dark. "That's good, because trust me, angel. When I get my hands on you, I'm going to make you regret pushing my buttons."

"Have to get your hands on me first," she taunted, shifting her hips side to side, but she was ready when he lunged for her again.

Or, she *thought* she was ready.

Instead of going around the coffee table like he had a hundred times before, David planted a foot on top of it and launched himself right over, catching her by the arm as she tried to run for the kitchen.

"You mean get my hands on you like this?" David's fingers dug in hard, yanking her toward him. He dropped the belt to grab her under the chin, and she knew the game was over, but it was what she'd wanted. *No way in hell he's tying me to the bed and leaving me there now.*

"You cheated," she whispered, unable to talk very easily with his hand cupping her jaw.

"I don't cheat." Leaning close, David kissed her hard, biting her lip sharply enough to make it sting when he pulled back with a grin. "Don't stop fighting now, angel. No more smart-ass comments for me?"

"I'm not cleaning your footprints off the table," she answered, and he let out a low laugh just before he shoved her to the floor. Catching herself, Lianna tried to get back up to run, but he pushed her back down, pressing a knee into her back to hold her there. Slapping at the tile, she tried to twist, but he leaned more weight into her until it was hard to breathe. "Fuck!"

"Don't be too disappointed with yourself, angel. The trick with my jeans was cute." David yanked her dress up around her hips, easing the pressure on her back before she felt him tugging at her tights, quickly followed by the sound of them ripping. "Distracting me with the hand job tease was clever too."

"Thanks." Her breath was still short with him pinning her under his knee, but he wasn't using all his weight... which meant there might be a way to knock him off balance. She was trying to figure it out when she heard the metal of the belt dragging over the tile and then a line of fire landed on her ass. Clenching her teeth on the whine, she yelped when another strike followed it almost instantly. Then another and another and another, until all Lianna could do was try to breathe through the vibrant onslaught of pain. She tried to twist, to push away from him, but when she reached her hand back, he just grabbed onto her wrist.

"Going to tell me to stop?"

"No," she snapped, and he groaned.

"Well, that's good, because I'm just warming up, angel." The whisper of the belt moving through the air wasn't near enough warning for it to crash down onto that impossibly agonizing strip of skin where her ass met her thighs. She cried out, tears burning her eyes as she kicked, digging her toes into the floor to try and move, but she was caught. Each blistering strike only hurt worse than the last, building on top of each other, bleeding together until her ass and thighs throbbed and she couldn't hold back the sobs anymore.

Finally, he stopped, releasing her wrist and removing his knee from her back so he could rip her off the floor by her hair. She only made it to her knees, but he leaned down to look into her eyes.

"God, I love it when you cry for me."

TWENTY

Lianna

Yanking her forward, David claimed her lips in a kiss that seemed to concentrate all the heat in her ass between her thighs, a pulse of need making her moan as he bent her backward to control it completely. Then the world tilted, and she was on the floor, with him on top of her, his knees forcing hers apart as he moved down her throat, nipping and kissing.

"No! You cheated!" she shouted, shoving at his shoulders, but he caught her wrists and pinned them above her head. Glaring up at him, she whispered, "You didn't win, you used the furniture to get to me."

"So, you can jump *over* the coffee table, but I can't step on it?"

"Exactly." Grinning, she tugged at his hold on her wrists. "Let me go and catch me for real."

"Too late for that, angel. I've already got you," he replied, and she pulled hard, managing to get one of her hands free so she could tuck it against her chest. David just grinned, shaking his head at her. "Look at you, being so defiant after you practically begged for this."

Sitting up, David reached over to grab the belt from the floor, and when his weight shifted, she bucked her hips, twisted, and knocked him to the side. As soon as he was off her, Lianna flipped to her stomach, pushed up to her feet, and ran for the fireplace again. She wasn't even halfway there when he slammed into her back, his arms coming around to squeeze her tight, lifting her off the floor as he laughed in her ear. "You know I like it when you struggle, so, feel free."

"Fuck you," she snarled, grabbing onto his arm and dropping her weight to try and get a foot on the ground for leverage, but it didn't work.

"Nervous now, angel?" he asked, carrying her back across the room while she kicked, trying to break his hold or buckle his knee, but she just ended up breathless and coughing when he dropped her over the arm of the chair. A sharp spank woke up all the brilliant welts across her ass, and she whined as she pushed up from the seat.

"Such an asshole," she mumbled, her ribs sore from the impact, still unable to get a full breath, but he just shoved her back down with a hand between her shoulder blades and lit up her ass with another vicious series of lashes from the belt. "Fuck, fuck, fuck!"

"That's the plan," he said on a laugh, pinning her legs to the chair as he pressed himself against her. Leaning forward, his weight made it impossible to get up, and she let out a frustrated scream through gritted teeth.

"You didn't win."

"Seems like I did, angel." Grabbing for her wrists, David fought her to pull them together, but even struggling as hard as she could... she wasn't a match for his strength. Once he got the loop of the belt over her hands and cinched it tight, she knew it was over. Relaxing, she saved her strength while he wove the strap through and tied the end of the belt into a knot, keeping her wrists locked together — but at least they were in front of her instead of behind her back. It meant she could brace her elbows on the cushion to keep her face off it, but she couldn't do much else. The side table wasn't within reach, and he kept his knees firmly against her thighs as he shredded her tights further.

"You didn't need to ruin those," she grumbled, and he swatted her ass.

"I won, so I can do whatever the fuck I want with you. Like ruin these," he said just before she felt him pull her underwear away from her body, the sides burning her hips as he tried to tear them as well. They were lacy, but it still took him a lot longer before she finally heard the tell-tale sound of fabric ripping.

Groaning, Lianna rested her forehead against the seat cushion. "I liked those."

"Too bad. They're gone now."

With him sliding his fingers through her folds, she felt a shiver of anticipation, her hips twitching uselessly as he carefully avoided her clit.

Leaning down, David whispered against her ear, "Go on, tell me no."

"You'd like that too much," she said, glancing over her shoulder at him with a smirk, and the look on his face would've made her wet if she hadn't already soaked her underwear. He didn't reply with words though, instead he thrust three fingers inside her, stretching her suddenly, and she couldn't bite back the gasp as she bucked against the chair.

"Your cunt definitely wants me," he purred, teasing her g-spot with devious taps that had her panting, mouth open as she leaned down, arching her back to give him easier access. "But what about your ass?"

"Wait!" she shouted, lifting herself, but David shoved her back down as he moved his fingers to her ass, pressing one against the tight ring. Groaning, she clenched her teeth, tense until he finally pushed inside, the strange sensation of invasion making her breath catch. "Fuck, stop."

"Nah, we're just getting started. Guess you're lucky your pussy was so wet, huh?" David had a laugh in his voice as he started to work a second finger in, but that was a lot harder. Her ass burned as he pushed, the hand between her shoulder blades stroking her gently. "Relax, angel, or it'll only hurt more."

"I know," she growled, but that was a lot easier said than done. A keening whine slipped through her teeth as he got both of them past the ring of muscle, a slightly painful stretch that she knew was nothing compared to his dick. "Please, don't."

"That's it. You know what I want to hear." Working his fingers in and out, she heard him spit, and then they moved a little easier, but it was taking her too long to adjust without lube to ease the way.

"I'll be good, I promise, just please get the lube," she begged, and he chuckled as he slid his fingers free. The hand on her back moved into her hair, tightening into a fist to pull her head up. "Please."

"I gave you the chance to earn lube. You refused." David ran the head of his cock through her folds, slowly pushing inside her pussy, and she couldn't bite back the moan. For a moment she had hope that he'd changed his mind, but then he ripped it away. "This is the only lube you're going to get today, angel. So, you better squeeze my cock, get me nice and wet."

"David, please don't," she whined, panting as he started to fuck her in long, deep strokes, and she did what he told her to. Squeezing him inside her, trying to focus on the pleasure and not the impending pain so that she could get even wetter. *This feels good, this feels good, think about that. Just that.*

"I do love your cunt," he groaned, slamming into her harder, and she moaned softly, biting down on her lip as that delirious combination of the stinging welts and the friction between her thighs pushed her higher and higher. "And I love the sounds you make... but I can't break a promise."

"No!" she shouted when he pulled out, his cock pressing against her ass a second later. "Don't, don't—"

"You can either relax, or not, but you're going to take it." David wrapped his hand over her hip, fingers digging in hard enough to bruise as he held her still, unable to do more than squirm and whimper as he craned her neck back. The pressure intensified, her tight ring burning as he forced her to open for him, moving steadily forward until the head of his cock finally popped inside and she cried out, tears burning her eyes. "Gotta admit, angel. It's fucked up, but I like these sounds a lot more."

"Please," she begged, her voice wobbling from the pain as he stretched her ass, pushing deeper while her back muscles twitched and spasmed, fighting the intrusion no matter how hard she tried to relax so it would be easier.

"You can do better than that," he growled, slamming his hips forward, and she screamed as the torment spiked, ripping the air from her lungs on a sob as he finally released her hair and she bent forward. "God, yes... scream for me."

"Stop, stop, stop." Digging her nails into her palms, she tried to distract herself from the next wave of pain as he slid back and thrust forward again. Harder. It didn't matter though, she still cried out through clenched teeth, groaning loud and long when he started to move. A steady rhythm that at least meant she could predict the next burning stretch as he gained inches on each drive. When he finally slammed deep, his hips meeting her ass, all she could do was whine.

"Fuck. I'm gonna make you come with my cock in your ass," he promised, but she shook her head.

"No, you won't," she said, gritting her teeth so hard she could feel them creaking.

"We'll see," David replied on a dark laugh, thrusting again and again. It hurt for a while, when all she could do was whimper and beg quietly, until finally... despite the tears still burning her eyes... it didn't hurt as much anymore. There was still a dull ache, a lingering sting when he slammed deep inside her, but she mostly just felt *owned*.

Dominated. Filled. Completely controlled.

"That's it," he groaned, bruising her hips as he tugged her back onto his cock over and over. Then he spat again, and she felt his thumb dragging the saliva down her crack to her ass, easing the next thrust as she swallowed a moan. "You feel so fucking good."

"Please," she begged, but she had no clue what she was begging for anymore. Her head was swimming from the delirious rush that always followed the pain, and she couldn't deny how much she liked him forcing her to take it — but there was only one reason her brain reacted that way.

David didn't just want to hurt her, to make her scream and cry for him... no, he wanted her to *like* it.

When he pulled her further back on the arm of the chair, she had to brace her elbows on the cushion to give her ribs a break, and she was more than happy to do that when one of his hands slid over her hip, moving between her thighs to find her clit. "Oh, God..."

"That's right, angel. You're going to come with my dick buried in your ass, because you don't have a choice with me, do you? You just have to take it, because you're *mine*." David swirled his fingers in tight circles, and she found herself rocking in time with his thrusts, whining and moaning under her breath as he leaned down, his forehead resting against her spine as he groaned low. "Every inch of you is mine."

"David," she whispered, the stretch of his next thrust sending an incredible ripple through her nerves that left her needy for the next as he focused mercilessly on her clit. Pulses of pure pleasure mixing with the memory of pain, blending with each clap of his skin against the welts and bruises on her ass, and the feeling of being completely full, completely possessed by him.

"Come on, Lianna. You know you like this," he growled, nipping at the skin on her back before kissing the spot as he picked up the pace, not holding back as he fucked her hard, the chair shifting on the carpet from the power of it. "You love it when I make you take it, when I make it hurt, when I hold you down and force you to take every inch of my cock. Don't you?"

"God!" she moaned, suddenly so close to that brilliant edge of bliss, and every word he spoke against her skin was only driving her closer. It was the sheer strength of him, the incredible way he took control of her body, her mind, her every breath — and *fuck* he knew her body too well. His fingers sped up, circling over her clit, and she couldn't breathe as the tension inside her built until every stroke, every slam of his hips against her ass, had her crying out for more. It felt good, better than good, and she wanted to hover on that glorious edge of perfection for just a little longer, riding the pleasure for as long as she could, soaking it in. But it was impossible, her body couldn't hold back the rising wave. Ecstasy crashed into her so fast that for a moment she was silent, every muscle tightening as glittering light turned her veins to molten gold. Too hot, too overwhelming as she drowned in bliss, the orgasm finally drawing a shout of release past her lips as all memories of pain and stress and the nightmare they were trapped in disappeared into the flickering lights behind her eyes.

"Fuck, yes..." David growled against her spine, slamming deep inside her, and in the dreamy haze she felt his cock kick, filling her with jet after jet as he groaned, holding her hips tight as he pressed her harder into the arm of the chair. It was hard to breathe, but she didn't have the energy to care. Everything was humming and wonderful, and the symphony of their rough breaths was the only thing she needed in the entire world. After a few minutes, she felt David press a kiss to her back, and then another and another as he kneaded her hips. "I love you so fucking much."

Smiling, she turned her head to the side, chewing on her lip as he rolled his hips against her, waking the ache of the welts and her sore ass, but it didn't hurt. Not really. Nothing really hurt at all, and *this* was what she'd wanted. This feeling. This perfect, blank bliss.

"I love you too, baby," she answered softly, and he finally braced a hand on the chair to lift himself from her, sliding out of her slowly.

"Come on, angel. Time for a shower." David helped her stand up, although her legs were still shaky, but he obviously noticed because he wrapped an arm around her waist to steady her. "You good?"

"Dazed and confused," she replied with a quiet laugh, and he chuckled.

"Good." Kissing the side of her head, he leaned her back on his chest so he could work at the belt around her wrists. As soon as her arms were free, he guided her toward the bathroom.

"Wait, what about the drive?" she asked, turning to look at him.

"I'll look at it *after* we take a shower and a nap. The files aren't going to disappear, angel. I promise." With a nudge, he pushed her into the bathroom, leaving her against the vanity while he turned on the water.

And *this* was the other side of David. The light to his darkness, the care and concern to balance out his need for pain and suffering. Her very own Jekyll and Hyde — but she loved both sides of him. He was right that she loved when he made it hurt, when he forced her to take whatever he wanted to dish out, but it wasn't just that.

It was that she trusted him to always come back to her after he indulged his dark side.

To love her, even though the world had tried its best to ruin them both.

Together, they could survive anything. Even the murder of Jean-Luc and whatever the Faure family might throw at them. They'd overcome too much already to let this destroy them.

TWENTY-ONE

David

David had set his alarm for an hour, just long enough to lie in bed with Lianna and make sure she was resting, but he'd ended up closing his eyes as well, and when the soft trill went off, he forgot for a moment what he was supposed to be doing.

Files. Search the drive.

Looking down at the mound of golden waves on his shoulder, he wished he could see Lianna's face to know how deep in sleep she was. Unfortunately, he had to move either way, because — while they'd both needed to burn off some steam when they got home — time was still ticking with the Faure family. They needed the evidence now, not whenever he decided to get out of bed, which would be *never* if he actually had the option to stay with her.

She was in danger, more than he even thought she understood, and ultimately that was the motivation he needed to carefully shift out from under her. Lianna groaned in her sleep, rolling onto her stomach where he'd just been, and he just watched her for a moment. Beautiful was an understatement, and the things she let him do to her... the things she *wanted* him to do to her... it seemed impossible. Harry had made him start thinking about the future, but even if he'd imagined the perfect future years ago, there's no way in hell he would have thought up someone as perfect as Lianna was for him.

And he'd do whatever it took to keep her safe.

Once he'd moved over to the dresser, he eased a drawer open to grab a pair of sweatpants, slipping them on in silence. Having shut the drawer just as carefully, he made it all the way to the doorway before Lianna's voice made him pause. It was her 'not wanting to wake up' grumble, but she turned over a second later to look at him. "What're you doing?"

"Just getting started on the drive. Go back to sleep, okay?" He turned into the hallway, and she called after him.

"Wait, I'm getting up too. I can help."

Sighing, David leaned back into the doorway. "No, you can't, angel. Digging through the files is going to be a one-man thing. Why don't you rest?" Grinning, he looked her over as she tossed the covers off. "I'm sure your ass is sore."

"Ha. Ha." Lianna rolled her eyes and got out of bed, giving him a solid view of her backside. The welts weren't raised anymore, but he could still see several of the marks from the belt, and bruises were already rising to the surface. "I'm not just sleeping in here while you do something this important."

"Fine." Shrugging, he gave up on arguing the point. "Why don't you pick something for us to eat and order in. I'm going to get set up." Heading into the living room, he grabbed his laptop and the drive from her purse and took them over to the couch.

It didn't take long to gather everything he needed, and the laptop was loading the drive when Lianna stepped out of the hall wearing one of his T-shirts and her pajama pants. Grabbing her phone, she dropped into the chair he'd fucked her over just an hour before, and he caught the way she bit her lip and adjusted how she was sitting.

"Told you I'd make you regret pushing my buttons," he said, opening the drive on his computer to start digging through it.

"Who says I regret it?" Lianna retorted, grinning at him before she looked at her phone again. "What do you want to eat anyway?"

"Food." Skimming through the list of folders, an overwhelming weight settled on his shoulders. There was no file structure, or if there was... it definitely didn't make sense to him. The folders just had numbers, sometimes with letters that could have been abbreviations, but he didn't know of what. He was going to have to start at the top and just work his way down.

"I think I'm going to order from that place with the soup I like," she mumbled, and he looked up at her, smiling as she stared at the screen in her hand with her brow furrowed like the decision was hard for her to make.

"Sounds good, angel. I'm getting started on the drive, so just order me whatever sounds good. And some coffee," he added, looking at the massive number of files inside the first folder. "A lot of coffee."

"Is it bad?" she asked.

He couldn't lie to her. "It's a mess, but if there's anything in here, I'll find it." With the computer on his lap, he rested the drive beside him and leaned back on the couch to get comfortable.

About ten minutes had passed when Lianna stood up and started pacing, tapping her phone on her palm, and he glanced up at her, tempted to ask her to sit down so he wasn't distracted... but the pacing seemed to help her, so he stayed quiet. Then she wandered over to the window, looking out over the city, and he was about to get back to work when he saw her put her phone against her ear.

"What are you doing?"

"I'm calling Rémi," she answered, and he sat up straight, but she held out a hand before he could argue. "Don't try to talk me out of it."

"Well, I really don't think this is a good idea, angel."

"Would you rather us find out when we land in Nice that they've put out some kind of hit on us?" she snapped, and he clenched his jaw tight. He'd been sure that their game earlier would have kept her chilled out for a little while longer, but it seemed he wasn't the only one focusing on the ticking clock.

"Fine. Just be careful," he said, pointing at the coffee table. "And put it on speakerphone."

"I won't do anything stupid," she muttered, flipping the phone to speaker as she returned to the chair, holding it in front of her. Rémi didn't answer the first time, and he silently hoped she'd let it go, but Lianna just called him right back.

This time the phone only rang twice before they heard, "Hello?"

"Hello Rémi, it's Lianna."

"What is it?" he asked, already sounding defensive and wary of the call.

Taking a deep breath, Lianna looked up at him before she spoke. "I— I just want you to know that we're looking for proof, and I promise you we're going to find it. We just need a little time."

"Proof of what, Lianna?"

"That we didn't have anything to do with this," she explained, and he had to admit she sounded steady, confident. "And... maybe something that could prove who *was* involved. I don't know, but all I can do is tell you again that we had nothing to do with your dad's death."

"I want to believe you..." Rémi began, a sigh whispering over the line. "But I can't. Uncle Marc said that my father was worried you'd retaliate and—"

"Fuck Marc," she snapped, and David groaned as she continued. "I'm talking to *you* right now. I know I left on bad terms with Jean-Luc, and while I'm still upset over what he did... I'll have to live with what happened between us for the rest of my life. I know that, deep down, he just wanted to help me, and he *did* help me in other ways. It may have been manipulative, but I'm choosing to believe he meant it when he said he cared about me, and I hate that the last words I spoke to him were in anger."

Rémi was silent for so long that David was worried he'd hung up after her rant, but when he eventually spoke, he sounded a lot calmer. "He meant it, Lianna. My dad cared about you a lot. In the days after you left... he kept bringing it up. Talking about how he should have handled things differently."

"Why would he have said something like that to you if he thought I'd do something to him?" she pressed.

"I don't know... but I can't just take your word on this, Lianna. I need actual proof, and I have my own people looking into it. I haven't made any decisions yet."

"Good, maybe they'll find something too." Lianna nodded and met David's gaze, and he could see the hope in her eyes that everything would work out. "I just wanted you to know that David and I are looking into some files we have here. Michael... I mean Joseph Blanc, helped me get them."

"You spoke to Joseph?" he asked, sounding surprised.

"Yes. I went to Rikers to see him, because I *am* going to prove that we didn't do this to Jean-Luc," Lianna said, her voice strong, confident. "I know you lost your father, and I can't imagine how horrible all of you are feeling... but I lost him too. I lost any chance of knowing him for real, of figuring out if we could ever move past what happened. And although he was a little overprotective... I have to believe that he did what he did because he thought it was right."

Clenching his teeth tight, David fought the urge to comment. Harry had already made it clear that Jean-Luc didn't act any differently than Harry would expect any family member to react, and he couldn't even deny that the man had a right to be angry. He'd done horrible things to Lianna, and that was the only thing Jean-Luc had known about him — courtesy of Michael. Still, he didn't believe that everything in that family was sunshine and roses. It wasn't possible.

Rémi let out a quiet, frustrated groan. "I don't know what scares me more in this nightmare. That you did it, or that someone else was able to get close enough to our family to do it."

"I understand that..." Lianna replied softly. "I'm just asking for more time before you make a judgment call on this. We're going to do everything we can to get you the proof you want."

"I'll see what I can do, Lianna, but I can't promise you anything. I have to think of the whole family, the Faure name, not just myself."

Of course you do. David focused on the computer screen in front of him so he wouldn't distract Lianna from the call. She was leaning forward, rubbing her forehead as she nodded.

"I guess that's all I can ask of you, Rémi. I'll be in touch as soon as I can, okay?"

"You do that," Rémi said, and a few seconds later the call ended.

Lianna groaned, dropping her phone onto the coffee table before cradling her head in her hands. "I swear to God, David... if we don't find something on that hard drive we are so fucked."

"I'm well aware," he mumbled.

"Any luck yet?" she asked, looking up at him as she angled herself to try and look at his screen.

"I just opened the drive, Lianna!" he snapped, biting down on his frustration. "Just... go open a bottle of wine, sit down, and let me focus."

"Fine." She rose and headed toward the kitchen, but he could tell that she was stressed out and probably pissed at him for being a dick. Grabbing the remote, he turned the TV on and flipped it to one of the music stations just to fill the silence.

He needed to focus, because the call with Rémi had only made it clearer that whatever connection Lianna had made with the family wouldn't be enough to keep her safe. If they couldn't prove that it was Marc, or at least cast doubt on someone else... they were definitely fucked.

His eyes were blurring, but David wasn't going to give up. He'd been looking through files for over eight hours, and as the time in the corner of his screen ticked closer to midnight, he felt like he was watching a doomsday clock. *Countdown to disaster.*

Stretching, he cracked his neck and rolled his shoulders, looking over at Lianna who was curled up, asleep, at the other end of the couch. She'd been asleep for about an hour, and judging by the deep, even breaths, she wasn't waking up anytime soon.

But that didn't mean he should do what he was thinking about.

The files he'd found earlier in the evening weren't what he should be looking at right now. He was supposed to be finding proof to save both their lives, but every time he clicked back into the main drive, the folder tempted him. Michael had saved all of it, and he should have known he'd eventually run into them on the drive. Every single video he'd sent to her father when he thought she was the key to making him break, along with hours of security footage that he never sent to anyone. Opening the folder, he scrolled through the thumbnails, tilting his screen away from Lianna just in case she woke up.

I shouldn't be doing this.

It was wrong. These videos should have been evidence in his criminal trial, not tempting him to watch them again like his own private porn server. Still, he couldn't help but wonder how many of them Michael had watched. Did he watch all the way to the end of their time together?

Swallowing, he scrolled back to the top, and tried to force his hand to click back out of it, to get back on task — but he didn't. Muting the computer, he clicked on one and it opened in a small window that he quickly maximized. It was from when she was on the floor. On the mattress. Chained wide and so vulnerable. *Perfect.* He didn't need the sound because he could remember every sound she made, knew the sounds he could pull from her even now, but there was fear then. Real, honest fear, and when his dick started to get hard, he groaned, closed the laptop, and leaned his head back on the couch.

Fuck, fuck, fuck.

He still liked it. Seeing her like that still turned him on, even though he knew the difference between the way he'd fucked her on that mattress and the way he'd fucked her earlier in the day — but both were driven by the same urges. There was something wrong with him, but it wasn't going anywhere. He knew that he liked to hear the panic and fear in her voice when he made it hurt, he liked it when she fought him just so he could take control.

But she liked it too.

Hell, even in the basement she'd surprised him by just how fucking wet she got.

Scrubbing at his eyes, he tried to get the images out of his head, because no matter how much he wanted to rewatch every one of those videos... he wanted the real thing more. He wanted her, and he wanted the way she smiled at him in the mornings, the way she laughed, the way she whispered that she loved him. Those were the kind of things he could have never forced out of her.

Moving back to the main drive, he highlighted the folder and felt the pricking of guilt as he deleted it. When the progress bar popped up, he stared at the cancel button, debating whether it was right to destroy the evidence against himself. But in the end, it wasn't about him — it was about Lianna. No one needed to see those videos again. No one should see her like that. And the videos weren't necessary anymore, no matter what Michael thought of him... Lianna wouldn't ever need them. He'd never give her a reason to. The progress bar finished, and he minimized the drive, emptying the recycle bin to erase them completely. David took a deep breath, sitting back against the couch as the reality of what he'd just done settled over him.

He was free. Not absolved, not forgiven for what he'd done, but the risk of someone like Michael using it to come after him was gone.

Looking over at Lianna, he let himself actually think about what a future with her would be like. If they made it out the other side of this Faure mess... would she marry him? Would she want a family with him? Could he ever be like Tommy and Liam, a normal husband... a father? There was a slight rush of panic that made him reach for the cup of coffee beside him, but it really wasn't as terrifying as he thought it would be. Lianna would be an amazing mother, and just the thought of getting her pregnant made his dick twitch.

Fucking focus, idiot.

Adjusting himself, he scanned through the folders, getting back on track ~~with where he'd been~~ before he let temptation detour him. It was taking him way longer than he'd ever expected, and part of the issue was that he didn't completely know what he was looking for. Proof that Marc and her father had been working together, but that could be anything he'd gathered in the last few years. Any of the surveillance he'd done on Lianna and her father could be what they needed, and that meant skimming every single goddamn file that looked like it could be from the right time frame.

Two hours later, he was debating giving up and grabbing some sleep when he clicked on a file to bring it up and his heart started racing. Sitting up straight, he maximized it, looking over it again and again.

This has to be enough proof.

Reaching over, he shook Lianna's leg. "Wake up. Angel, wake up!"

"What?" she mumbled, groggy with sleep.

"I think I found something," he said, the thrill of it impossible to contain as she shoved herself upright and leaned close. "I mean, it has to be enough. I swear, I've looked at thousands of files tonight and this... *this* has to work. Right?"

Lianna leaned in, reaching for the track pad on his laptop to control the screen for a moment, and the smile that spread slowly across her lips was completely worth every minute of his search. "We've got him."

Laughing a little, David rubbed at his face, looking up at the ceiling as he tried to accept the possibility that they might not be completely screwed anymore. There was a chance that they'd be okay, that he'd actually get to have a future with her. Then he remembered what they had to do before that future was possible and he groaned. "Does this mean we have to go back to France?"

"Yes, David," she said, patting him on the arm. "We have to go back to France."

"Fine, but we're not leaving tonight. I need sleep." Closing his laptop, he set it back on the coffee table with the hard drive, and Lianna took its place, straddling his lap.

"You sure you need to sleep?" she asked, grinding against him with that smile still plastered on her face. "Because I'd really like to say thank you."

All it took was one flashback from the videos he'd destroyed earlier in the night, and he pulled her closer, lifting his hips so she could feel the growing hard-on. "How are you going to thank me, angel?"

"Come to bed, and I'll show you." Lianna slid off his lap, walking backward toward the hall, and he had no trouble following her.

He'd follow her anywhere... even back to Provence.

TWENTY-TWO

Lianna

Two Days Later

"Are you sure you don't want to rent a room somewhere and at least take a nap?" David asked, and she knew he was tired. They both were. There had been too much to think about on the transatlantic flight, but there was no use in waiting. Waiting was just going to drag this out, and they needed to act before Rémi made a decision without all the facts.

Glancing at the passenger seat, she sighed. "Are you saying I look tired?"

"I'm not saying anything like that," he replied, clearly frustrated with her. "But we're about to confront your family with just about the worst news we could show up with... and I figured you'd like to be well-rested for that."

"No." She shook her head, focusing on the narrow road ahead as they drove away from Nice and into Provence. "I want to get this over with."

"Okay…" he said, and she was grateful he'd dropped it. Arguing now wasn't going to help either of them, and she wasn't changing her mind.

The last few miles of their drive to the Faure estate were silent, but they both tensed when the familiar wall bordering their property showed up on the side of the road. Slowing down, Lianna checked the rear-view mirror to make sure no one was behind her, and she waited for the gate to appear.

There.

Lianna turned the little car into the drive leading up to the gate. When they'd arrived before, she hadn't noticed the size of the gate, but its presence now was foreboding. How had she missed these security elements the first time? Too enamored by Jean-Luc and Cécile and the beauty of everything to pay attention to the ugly reality, to all the literal signs warning people from entering the property.

If only she'd actually listened.

She rolled down the window, leaned out, and pressed the button on the little call box. When she sat back, waiting for the house to respond, David reached over to take her hand.

"No matter what happens, I've got you," he whispered, squeezing her hand tighter, and she squeezed back.

"I love you, baby."

"I love you too, angel," he whispered, but he was cut off by a scratchy voice leaving the intercom in French.

"*Who is it?*"

"*I'm here to see Rémi Faure,*" she replied, continuing the conversation in French, even though David would have no idea what she was saying.

"*And who are you?*" the guard asked.

"*Tell him it's Lianna.*"

"*One moment,*" the man replied, and the sudden stiffness in his tone spoke volumes.

Sighing, she dropped her head against the seat and looked over at David. "He told us to wait… but I'm quite sure he remembers me."

"At least they didn't have to taze you to make you leave."

His joke made her laugh, which she wasn't sure she could actually do as high strung as she felt, but it died fast when the gate suddenly swung open. "Fuck."

"We have to go now, angel," David said gently, but it still took her a moment take her foot off the brake and get the car in motion.

"I know…" she whispered, trying to talk her heart into slowing down just a little, because it felt like it might explode inside her chest at any moment. A spontaneous heart attack wasn't going to endear her to the relatives who were convinced she'd killed the patriarch of the Faure family. The drive wasn't near long enough for her to feel better though, and as she pulled to a stop near the front door, she saw one the guards open it and step out to hold it wide.

Oh shit. Fuck, fuck, fuck. Are we really doing this?

"I'm going to be right by your side the whole time, okay?" David tugged at her hand until she finally looked at him, and the level of concern in his face told her all she needed to know about how panicked she looked.

"Good. Don't leave me." Nodding, she tried to pull it together, to calm down, or at least fake it before she walked into the house. "You have it, right?"

"Of course I have it," he answered, squeezing her hand once more before he released it and opened his door. "Let's go."

Climbing out of the car, she swallowed hard, and waited for David to join her before they ascended the steps side by side. Instead of letting them inside, the guard raised his hand to stop them, moving forward to pat them down in rough swipes of his hands. He started with David, and she thought David was going to punch him when he reached for her.

"This isn't necessary, we're not armed," she called into the house.

"*Let them in.*" The command floated out of the house in French, and she was pretty sure it came from Rémi. Whoever it was, the guard stopped instantly, moving aside to let them into the large foyer, but it didn't feel as big as usual since it was packed with all of the relatives she'd been smiling and laughing with a little over a week ago. Jean-Luc's entire family, including Amanda and the twins, and she was surprised to see Marc and his wife and kids standing off to the side as well. No one was smiling now, though. Their faces were a mix of anger and sadness, betrayal and distrust. All of it directed at her and David.

"You have a lot of nerve showing your faces here, but this just makes it easier to avenge my brother," Marc said, snapping his fingers before he pointed at them. "Phillipe, Adam, take them—

"Wait," Rémi interrupted, raising a hand, and the guards who had been in the process of drawing their weapons froze in place. For the first time since they'd found the proof, Lianna actually wondered if it would matter. Raising her hands, she let them hang in the air beside her shoulders, and she saw David do the same in her peripheral vision.

"I told you I was going to get you proof, Rémi." Lianna tried to sound calm and confident, even though she felt neither. "That's why I'm here."

"This is ridiculous!" Marc snapped. "She'd say anything to save her life."

"Please, Rémi," she begged, looking only at him as she ignored Marc's ranting. "It will only take ten minutes and you'll see that I never lied to you."

"Rémi, don't let this girl—"

"They flew here from the US, the least I can do is give her ten minutes," Rémi said, cutting his uncle off in a serious tone before he looked at her. "What do you have?"

"It's in my pocket," David answered, pointing down at his jeans without moving his hands. "Just don't shoot me. I've already taken a bullet for her once, and I really don't want to do it again."

"*Everyone put your weapons away. My children are here*," Rémi snapped in French, and the guards slid them back into their holsters, hiding them once again beneath their suit jackets. Turning to David, he nodded, continuing in English. "Go ahead, show me what you have."

"I'm going to get it out of my pocket, okay?" David said, looking around the room as he slowly lowered a hand, reaching into his pocket to pull out a small, black flash drive. "Here, Rémi."

"What is this?" he asked, approaching David to take it from him.

"It's a flash drive." Lianna answered, but judging by the look Rémi gave her, *that* was not the question he was asking. "The proof is on it. You just need to see it for yourself."

Marc huffed before raising his voice, speaking French directly to Rémi. "*You can't be taking this show seriously. They're making a fool of you in front of your family!*"

"*I will see what she brought me,*" Rémi replied sharply, glancing at his uncle before turning to the family and switching to English. "Amanda, I want you to go upstairs with the children. Emilie, take Zoé from *Maman*, and go with her."

"*I want to stay here!*" Emilie whined.

"*Now, Emilie!*" Rémi replied in kind, and his tone made it clear that she wasn't allowed to argue. It was surprising how quickly he'd stepped into the role as head of the family. No more laughing and joking — not that this was the time for it anyway — but he still looked different. Carried himself differently than he had less than two weeks before.

Amanda shifted Gabriel on her hip and beckoned Emilie. "Come with me, Em. You can help me keep them happy."

Sighing, Emilie took Zoé from Cécile and reluctantly followed Amanda up the stairs. Everyone waited in silence until they disappeared down the hall, and it was Rémi who acted first. Turning to one of the guards, he spoke in quiet French. *"Phillipe, bring my laptop from my office."*

"You don't even know this woman," Marc said, stepping closer to Rémi, and she knew he was only speaking French to keep David out of it. Or, perhaps he'd never realized just how much French she spoke. He hadn't exactly spent much time around her when she was here before. *"She's an American, and just because she shares some of our blood, doesn't make her family. We don't know what Alain taught her when he kept her away from us."*

"Stop, uncle," Rémi answered quietly. *"There is no harm in seeing what she brought before I make a decision."*

David took a half step closer to her, whispering, "What the fuck is happening?"

"Marc doesn't want Rémi to look at the drive," she explained under her breath.

"Of course not," David mumbled, and she agreed. If anything, Marc's behavior would only cause more issues for him.

A moment later, the guard returned with a laptop, setting it on a narrow table against the wall. Rémi opened it, typing in his password to unlock it before he plugged in the drive and looked over his shoulder at them. "What am I looking for?"

"It's on the top-level of the drive. An AVI file named 'Marc,'" David answered, staring at the man who was rapidly turning red in the face.

Turning back to the laptop, Rémi opened it and expanded the video on the screen. It revealed the same overhead shot of her father's penthouse that had also recorded the night David took her. As he clicked play, studying the screen as others moved closer to see it, Lianna cleared her throat.

"I told Jean-Luc before I left that Marc had been meeting with my father. I saw him at my father's home a few years ago, and they introduced him to me as someone else. I didn't even know he was my uncle until I saw him at the birthday party you all threw me. Jean-Luc swore that Marc had never worked with my father, that neither of them had, and I called him a liar... which I regret. Because those are some of the last words I said to him, and I was wrong." Glancing at Marc, she turned back to Rémi who was still watching the two men talking in the penthouse. "My father and Marc kept it from Jean-Luc, from everyone. Joseph Blanc didn't even know they were meeting."

"*Alain was my brother, why wouldn't I go see him?*" Marc asked, continuing to speak in French as he moved closer to Rémi, but he didn't respond. He was still watching the video where Marc and her father were talking, pouring drinks, and then they moved into his office and off camera.

"You can see the time and date stamp in the bottom right corner," Lianna added, pointing toward the laptop while still keeping her hands raised. "That was from two years ago. Even more recently than when I saw him myself."

"*This proves nothing,*" Marc sneered, looking her over with all the disgust she was sure he'd been hiding on her previous visit.

Turning to Marc, Rémi replied to the man in English. "I heard my father asking you about Alain on one of the voicemails he left you. What did he want to know?"

Giving up on French, Marc waved a hand dismissively. "How should I know? She had him killed before we ever had the chance to talk."

"I didn't hurt Jean-Luc, Rémi," Lianna said, keeping her voice calm and even. "I didn't have any reason to."

"Liar!" Marc shouted, pointing at her. "You resented him. You resented this entire family for excluding you!"

Staring at him, Lianna could only huff out a bitter laugh as she shook her head. "Are you insane? Jean-Luc reached out to *me*. He welcomed me here. Cécile sent me family photos. They threw me a birthday party — the nicest one I've ever had. What would I have to resent?" she asked, dropping her arms to her side just so she could wave a hand toward him. "In fact, the only person who wasn't welcoming to me was you. And you pretended like you'd never met me before, even though we both know that's not true. You went out of your way to avoid me when I was here. Jean-Luc even got upset with you the day we were all supposed to have lunch together!"

"What were you doing with Alain, Marc?" Rémi asked softly.

"Visiting him," he snapped defensively. "He's my brother, I can—"

"Why didn't you tell my father?" Rémi tilted his head as he continued. "Why didn't you go together? We both know how much my father wanted to mend the relationship between him and Alain."

"You didn't know your father as well as you think, Rémi," Marc replied, shaking his head as he looked around the room with a frustrated sigh.

"What is that supposed to mean?"

"He didn't want Alain back in the family!" Marc shouted, gesturing wildly. "Alain went to the states, took a new name, started over to create his *own* legacy. Your father hated that he managed to be successful away from his shadow, but *I* never turned my back on my little brother."

"So, you admit you went behind my father's back?" Rémi stared at him, and it seemed everyone in the room understood the dangerous ground Marc was walking on except the man himself.

"For the family! For the Faure name. Your father didn't want to listen to Alain's ideas, his successes, because they weren't *his*."

"No, he didn't want to hear about them because they weren't the direction he wanted this family to go," Rémi explained, keeping a much more controlled tone than his uncle.

"But you have a chance now to change direction. To get things back on track," Marc urged, taking another step toward Rémi before the stiff way his nephew faced him gave him pause. He didn't stop talking though, and it was like watching him put the noose around his own throat. "The things that Alain and I worked on are still lucrative, and I can help you. I can teach you how to lead this family into a successful future."

"Is that what you told Jean-Luc when he asked you about my father?" Lianna asked, and he rounded on her, rage coating his face.

"*Be quiet, whore,*" he growled in French.

"Answer the question!" Rémi shouted. It was the first time he'd raised his voice, and Marc looked surprised as he faced him again.

"Your father would have bankrupted this family in another decade, Rémi, and I know you don't want that to be your legacy. The Faure name still holds power, and it's your responsibility now. This is your chance to correct his mistakes."

"*The only mistake Jean-Luc ever made was trusting you, you bastard!*" Cécile suddenly shouted, lunging forward as Mathieu grabbed her arm and Anaelle moved forward to help, both of them looking to Rémi for direction. But Cécile kept screaming in French, tears filling her eyes. "*I can't believe you killed your own brother!*"

"*Maman, stop!*" Anaelle pleaded.

Someone screamed, and Lianna turned to see Marc pointing a gun at her. "If you're not man enough to do the right thing, then I will."

Before she could react, David grabbed her arm, yanking her toward him as he spun them around, putting himself between her and Marc just as a gunshot cracked so loudly in the room that her ears rang. It was almost exactly how he'd stopped her own father from killing her. People were screaming and crying in French and English, too fast for her to track, but she didn't care about any of that, she only cared about David. Shoving out of his grip, she ran her hands over his chest in a panic. "Are you okay?"

He looked stunned, but then he blinked, and grabbed her hands. "It's not me. I'm okay, angel. He didn't shoot me."

"What?" she asked, her heart racing so fast that she thought she might be sick, but as soon as she realized he was all right she smacked his chest, switching between fury and relief as she wrapped her arms around him. Lianna hugged him tight as she fought the tears stinging the edge of her eyes. "Don't you ever fucking do that again."

"No promises," he replied, laughing a little as he hugged her back. "But I would appreciate if we could avoid anyone pointing a gun at you for at least a year."

Wait. Who got shot then?

Twisting out of David's arms, she looked around him to see Marc lying on the floor, cussing at Rémi in French as one of the guards picked up the gun. Rémi still had a gun aimed at Marc, and he was shouting back, as was Cécile, and Marc's wife was kneeling beside him, holding her hands out toward Rémi, pleading. But everyone was too emotional, speaking too fast and talking over each other, and she had no fucking idea what they were saying.

Finally, Rémi, shouted over everyone. "*Admit it! Admit you killed my father!*"

David pulled at her arm, tugging her back from the chaos, as he quickly whispered under his breath. "What the hell is happening?"

"Rémi wants Marc to admit he did it. I'm pretty sure Marc's wife is begging him not to kill his uncle," she whispered back.

"Fuck that, he needs to die," David growled, but she shushed him so she could listen to the rapid French.

"*Please don't do this, please*," Natalie begged, keeping one hand on the bullet wound in Marc's stomach and the other held out toward her nephew.

"*I'll never forgive you for this*," Rémi said, and she could see the emotion in him even though it was clear he was trying to appear calm and in control.

Marc groaned, glaring up at him as he snarled. "*Jean-Luc was weak. He was always too weak to lead this family, and I tried to save us. But you're going to turn out just like him.*"

The sudden gunshot made Lianna jump, and David pulled her closer, but there was no need as Natalie started screaming. Rémi had pulled the trigger, shooting Marc in the chest, and there was no doubt he'd die because no one was going to call the cops or an ambulance. Not here.

Taking a step closer, Rémi stood over the man, and spoke loud enough for everyone to hear him amid the chaos. "*I'm not weak, and neither was my father.*"

Cécile broke free of her children a moment later, shoving Natalie out of the way to kick Marc before she fell to her knees, grabbing at his shirt to shake him. "*How could you do this? How could you kill him? He was your brother! He loved you!*"

"*It wasn't him!*" Natalie shouted, sobbing as she moved to the other side of Marc, and her children moved close to her, hugging each other. "*It couldn't have been him! He wouldn't!*"

David dragged her further away, and even though she wanted to keep listening, she couldn't ignore his need to protect her, or his urge to understand. Tugging at her arm, he waited for her to look at him before he asked, "What the hell just happened?"

Still dealing with the shock of watching Marc dying only a few feet away, she blinked and tried to organize her thoughts to explain. "Marc called Jean-Luc weak and said that Rémi is going to turn out just like him... which he's clearly not."

"Apparently," David agreed, and they both turned to watch the insanity unfolding around them.

TWENTY-THREE

David

The entire room had dissolved into chaos. Too many people screaming in French, crying, but he didn't give a shit about any of them — he just wanted to get Lianna away from it. Unfortunately, she wasn't budging, and he could tell by the intense look on her face that she was doing her best to listen and translate, whispering snippets of it to him when she got the chance, although how she could make out any of it in the jumble of noise he had no idea.

At least Rémi had finally lowered the gun, which made him feel slightly better, but he wouldn't feel safe from the new head of the Faure family until they were out of this house. The only good part of the day so far was getting to watch Marc bleeding out on the floor. He wasn't even conscious anymore from what David could tell, and he would no doubt be dead in minutes.

One arm wrapped around Lianna's waist, he held her against him, mostly to keep her from walking toward them in her goal of hearing more of the hysterical words.

Sooner than he expected, Marc's wife cried out, and he couldn't deny the raw pain in her voice as she sobbed, leaning over her husband's body. Their two children knelt down beside her, also crying, but he didn't even bother Lianna for the translation for whatever they were babbling about. The bastard had deserved to die. If David had gotten a vote, he would have suggested something a lot slower and a lot more painful for making Lianna his target.

The two kids helped their mother from the floor, the three of them hugging and crying and mourning a man who was apparently the same brand of evil as Lianna's father had been. Rémi was comforting his mother, but he left Cécile with his brother and sister to approach Marc's family.

Facing Marc's wife, Rémi looked between her and the two adult kids, speaking in slow, calm French, but when Lianna gasped, he nudged her and she sighed irritably, leaning in close to translate as Rémi spoke. "It's time for you to decide where your loyalty lies. I understand you're grieving the death of your husband and father. Unfortunately, I know too well how that feels. Marc killed my father. I killed him. You need to decide if our family has suffered enough loss. Where does your loyalty lie?"

Oh shit.

The wide-eyed look on the woman's face seemed more than appropriate, and he had to respect when her son stepped forward, putting himself between Rémi and his mother. As the two faced off, no one spoke, in English or French, but eventually Rémi shook his head and raised the gun again, this time pointing it at his cousin.

Tensing, David prepared to throw Lianna to the floor and cover her if some kind of shootout started, but he knew she wouldn't move an inch while the standoff was still going on... and he kind of wanted to find out what was going to happen anyway.

It seemed like it took forever for the boy to raise his hands and reply to Rémi with more French, which Lianna leaned in to translate again. "Our loss ends here, cousin. My father made mistakes. He has paid for them. My mother, sister, and I do not wish to contest your authority. Our loyalty lies with you. With Faure."

Turning to the side, Rémi set the gun down beside his laptop and turned back to his cousin to speak with him. Lianna whispered the words a few seconds after Rémi said them. "Good. I think our family has lost enough this week, cousin. Now we just need to mourn."

Watching the two men embrace didn't mean much to David except that Rémi probably wasn't going to decide to shoot him and Lianna. When they separated, they nodded at each other, and Rémi turned around to take over supporting his sobbing mother. His two siblings looked lost, stunned, as Rémi moved with Cécile toward the stairs.

"He told them that he's going to help Cécile to her room," Lianna explained, pausing when Rémi suddenly stopped before the first steps and faced everyone, raising his voice to shout something else. "Apparently no one is allowed to leave until he gets back."

"Great," David mumbled, frustrated that his plan to get Lianna safely out of this fucked-up situation was blocked. One of the goons moved to block the door, tilting his chin at David, and he realized he was one of the assholes that pulled him out of his bed. It was so tempting to deck the bastard, but nothing good would come from drawing attention to themselves. So, instead, he led Lianna to the side of the foyer, away from the dead body and the grieving family, and the temptation to break all the teeth in the goon's mouth.

Lianna sniffled, and he looked down to see she was crying, tears streaking her face. He'd been so distracted by the room's chaos that he hadn't realized when it started, but he pulled her against his chest, holding her tight. "Hey angel, why the tears? Everything is going to be okay now."

Letting out a sob, Lianna sniffed harder and shook her head as she pushed back from his chest, struggling to keep her voice hushed. "It's all my fault..."

"That's bullshit. None of this is your fault."

"It is!" she argued, wiping at her cheeks. "If I hadn't come here, if I hadn't tried to become part of the family, Jean-Luc and Marc would be alive. The family would all still be together."

"Sure, maybe, and Marc would still be plotting behind his brother's back, waiting to turn the whole family against him," David added, and she made a little pained sound as she glared up at him.

"Don't pretend you care about them."

Groaning, he pulled her back into his chest, leaning down to whisper in her ear. "As much as I usually like to watch you cry, it's not like this."

Lianna mumbled something that sounded a lot like 'asshole,' but he let it slide when she melted against him, wrapping her arms around his back. For a while there, he'd been sure that Marc was going to snap and kill them both. Kill everyone. If Rémi hadn't acted when he did, there was no way to be sure what would have happened, but it was definitely a relief just to have her in his arms again. Safe, alive, and without a target on either of their backs.

"I never thought it was you, Lianna," a woman said from beside them, and David leaned back to let Lianna look at her cousin. *Anaelle, that's her name.*

"I wouldn't have blamed you if you did," Lianna replied quietly, shrugging a shoulder. "You lost your dad."

Anaelle wiped at her cheeks, sniffling softly. "So did you, right?"

Lianna shook her head, turning to face her cousin more directly. "Not like you. My father wasn't like Jean-Luc. Your dad loved all of you so much, and he was so kind, and he didn't deserve this." Her voice cracked, and she started crying again, and David let go of her so the two women could hug.

He wasn't upset over any of their deaths, especially not Lianna's father or Marc... but it seemed like Jean-Luc might have been the only sincere Faure brother.

Admitting that he was wrong about him wouldn't mean much now, and he couldn't go back in time to change the way he'd already acted toward his family, but he could acknowledge that the man wasn't the utter bastard he'd assumed he was. All David could hope was that Rémi really was planning on following in his father's footsteps. Moving away from the more illicit criminal activities that Jean-Luc had begun, cleaning up the Faure family's image, and building a future that wouldn't be so drenched in blood.

Hours later, David was frustrated that they were still under some weird form of house arrest inside the Faure estate. Even after Rémi had returned downstairs, he'd asked everyone to stay. He'd been polite about it, but it wasn't like the goons were moving away from any of the doors, which meant it wasn't really a request at all. As the various members of the Faure family had disbursed around the house to mourn in their own way, he and Lianna had found a secluded spot in one of the smaller sitting rooms to wait out the lockdown.

She'd finally stopped crying, but he could tell she was carrying the weight of guilt when it just wasn't necessary. Whether Jean-Luc acted for the right reasons or not, he'd still crossed a line by kicking him out the way he did, and by trying to control Lianna's life when he didn't actually know a thing about her.

Berating the memory of a dead man wasn't going to help her though, and so David had just pulled Lianna into his lap and held her while she sulked in silence, both of them staring out the windows at the little flower garden. In one of her brief talkative moments, Lianna had told him that Cécile and Jean-Luc had planted the garden together. Then she'd started crying again as she explained that *he* didn't plant them, because Cécile told him he had a black thumb. Apparently, he'd shared the information on one of their days at the house before Jean-Luc had gone outside to work in the garden with his wife. It was something so normal and domestic, and it may have been the last time the two were out there.

Even if he had a long list of reasons not to like the man, David could understand the sadness in that memory. It was probably why they were the only ones in this room — none of Jean-Luc's family wanted to stare at the flowers.

A knock against the doorway had them both turning to look at it, finding Rémi hovering in the doorway. "May I come in?"

"Of course," Lianna answered him, shifting off David's lap to sit beside him on the couch. Rémi looked somber as he approached them, his gaze lingering on the windows for a moment before he took a seat in the chair closer to Lianna.

"I brought you some things," he said, holding out a bundle in his hands, which David quickly recognized as his wallet and phone. "I found them in my father's desk. I'm assuming he kept them when he sent you away."

"Ah, thanks," David replied, as Lianna passed them to him. "I was hoping my wallet hadn't been tossed in the fireplace."

Shrugging, Rémi sighed and leaned forward, bracing his elbows on his knees. He looked like he had the weight of the world on his shoulders, and even though he was only a few years older than David, he seemed like he'd aged ten years during the past week. Rubbing at his forehead, Rémi raised his gaze to meet David's. "I won't apologize for what my father did. He didn't tell me the entire story, and it's honestly none of my business, but from what my dad shared about your history... I don't know if I would've responded any differently."

Shit. David's stomach turned, and then Lianna reached over to intertwine their fingers, squeezing his hand in an unspoken move of solidarity. Rémi huffed out a quiet laugh when he saw it, shaking his head a bit as he sat up straight.

"Like I said, it's really none of my business. I do think my dad saw the error of his ways after Lianna left. Not in his opinion of your history, but in how he handled it with both of you." Rémi looked at Lianna with a sad smile. "He wanted you to come back very badly. I think you being here would make him very happy, despite the circumstances."

"I wish I'd left him differently," Lianna whispered, sniffling. "I was angry, but I could have been more... reasonable. I could have at least listened to his side of things before I left, and maybe if I'd explained what I saw with Marc I could have—"

"There's no use speaking in 'what ifs,' Lianna. You reacted with your heart, and I know my dad understood that. He was guilty of thinking with his heart often."

Nodding, she was quiet for a long moment before she squeezed his hand a little harder. "I just have to say one 'what if.' I really think my life would have been very different if I'd known someone like Jean-Luc my whole life. If I'd known all of you... grown up around you. I don't think I would have been so lonely, and maybe he could have stopped my father before he hurt so many people."

"Well, I can tell you that my father wished he'd known you longer as well. We all feel the same way about you, and your invitation here is a permanent one. You will always be welcome, and I hope you'll come back." Rémi took a deep breath, looking David in the eye for a moment before he glanced back at Lianna. "And... I am sorry for accusing you. Everything seems so clear in hindsight. However, my uncle was very convincing that you had done this, using your father's connections." Shaking his head, he leaned back in the chair. "But part of me never believed it. I should have looked at him harder."

"I'm grateful you trusted me as much as you did. You could have just reacted, and it would have made sense because you were in pain, and while I know we don't know each other well—"

"But I hope we will," Rémi interrupted, smiling a bit. "You are family, Lianna, and I hope you'll stay through the funeral. My father would be comforted to have you at his graveside, finally with your family."

Lianna glanced at David, but he knew she needed to do it. She needed the closure. So, he squeezed her hand, giving her silent permission, or at least silently promising he wouldn't be a dick about it, and she smiled at him before she turned back to Rémi. "I'd be honored to attend the funeral. We both would."

"Thank you, *both* of you," Rémi said, standing up and waving at one of the goons in the hall. "I just have one more thing that Lianna left behind."

The guard carried in the gift bag from her birthday, and David hadn't even realized Lianna had left the bracelet behind. It was just one more way she'd chosen him over everything else, but he didn't need her to choose that again.

"Thank you." David nodded, accepting the bag, and Lianna looked at him in surprise. "It's an heirloom."

"That's right," Rémi agreed. "We really did discuss what of our grandmother's jewelry would fit you, and everyone agreed on the bracelet. If you'd like, I can hold onto the stocking for Christmas?"

Lianna glanced at him again, smiling before she faced her cousin. "That sounds wonderful."

Taking the stocking back from him, Rémi held it in his hands, nodding at them both. "You can stay as long as you like, I hope you know that. You'll both always have a home here."

"We appreciate the offer, but after we lay Jean-Luc to rest… I think we need to go home to our family for a while." Looking over at him, Lianna smiled and warmth spread in his chest as she called Harry her family. "Because I want to get to know them too."

"That sounds like a good plan, angel," he replied softly, and she leaned over to press a quick kiss to his lips before she faced Rémi again.

"I still have more things to handle, but I'll have the staff prepare a room for you both." Rémi took a few steps to the door before he paused, chuckling a little. "And, David?"

"Yeah?" He looked over at the man, seeing a glimpse of the guy he'd gone four-wheeling with in the half-smile he wore.

"I've still got that suit if you need to borrow it… since you didn't bust the seams on it last time."

Laughing under his breath, David nodded. "I think I'll take you up on that."

TWENTY-FOUR

Lianna

_____

Two Weeks Later

"Dylan, take that out of your mouth!" Claire said, giving an apologetic smile before she rushed out of her seat. Lianna watched Tommy's wife chase down their two-year-old, scoop him up, and fearlessly reach into his mouth to pull out a Lego before she set him down beside his brother again and leaned down to talk to them.

"I swear, seeing how wild their kids are has me nervous about having our own." Jessica shook her head, laughing a little as she faced Lianna again and picked up her iced tea to take a sip. "So, I have to ask. How long have you and David been seeing each other?"

"Um, almost a year?" she answered, and the realization surprised her. Time had flown by with everything going on, but it was already November, and January was just around the corner, which would be a year. Not that him abducting her from her father's penthouse was really an anniversary worth celebrating.

"Well, you guys look good together," Jessica said, leaning back in her seat as she shrugged. "And he seems really happy. I've only met him a few times since Liam and I got together, but he was always so... serious. Had that whole tall, dark, and brooding thing down to a science."

Lianna laughed. "You're right about that. He's still got it down to a science, by the way."

"Who has what down to a science?" Claire asked, dropping back into her seat. "Sorry, I swear if they act up again, I'll send them to go harass their dad."

"It's okay." Toying with the strap on her purse, Lianna took a breath, because she'd known this line of conversation would happen at some point. "I was just answering some questions about me and David."

"Oh, yessss." Claire clapped her hands together, leaning forward with a big smile. "I have to hear about this, because I was pretty sure David would be a permanent bachelor."

"They've already been together a year," Jessica filled in, and Lianna felt a blush rising in her cheeks.

"Wait, how haven't we seen you before now?" Claire asked, before shaking her head and reaching over to pat Lianna's leg. "Never mind. I'm sure that wasn't your decision. He probably didn't even tell you about the guys, even though they're basically brothers."

"Yeah... I didn't really know about them until David started working for Harry, but this is the first time I've met them."

"Well, don't feel bad about it. They've got some secret cabal when it comes to David," Claire continued. "I mean, the guys have always been close to David — they practically grew up together from what I understand — but that guy doesn't let anyone into his private life. I've been with Tommy since I was twenty-one, and after *nine years* I probably still couldn't fill a page with information about him."

"That doesn't surprise me," Lianna replied, hiding her awkward smile by drinking some of the iced tea Harry's wife had made. She just... couldn't quite remember the woman's name. There were a lot more McConnells than she'd expected to be around at once... or maybe it was just having so many people in such a small space. Lianna was still trying to get everyone straight, but the two wives had been talking to her for a while now in the front room of Harry's house and so she felt solid on their names, and the names of Claire's two kids — mostly because of how often Claire had to shout them.

Now, she just needed to memorize faces and names for everyone else, including the three McConnell brothers. The family wasn't really that complicated, Lianna just felt overwhelmed by it — which had to be exactly how David felt in France, so... she didn't really have room to complain. But she was trying a lot harder to learn everyone's names and connections than David had.

So far, she'd learned that Claire was married to the oldest McConnell, Tommy, and they had the two kids currently sitting on the floor with a massive bin of Legos. Both were incredibly cute, but extremely mischievous toddlers and Claire had already missed half the conversation chasing them, changing them, bringing them back into the room, and doing a hundred other mom things that made Lianna tired just thinking about it. Jessica had kept her company though, and she was pretty hilarious, which worked out well since she was married to the middle McConnell, Liam, who was apparently a constant joker.

Not that Lianna actually knew how Liam or Tommy acted. They'd introduced themselves when she and David arrived, and then quickly dragged David into the living room to watch a football game, which was where all the guys still were — laughing and cheering and shouting at the TV, and each other, in equal measure. Today was supposed to be about her getting to know the McConnell clan, but she had no idea how she was supposed to get to know everyone if the women and men sat in separate rooms the whole time.

"So, this might be a weird question, but is this... normal? The guys in one room and us in another?" she finally asked, and the two women laughed.

"Not at all. Normally we'd be in there, and Jessica would be shouting at the TV more than any of the guys."

"I like football!" Jessica rolled her eyes. "Claire is just annoyed because Tommy never pays attention to the boys when football is on the screen."

"Did you see Dylan try to eat a freaking Lego? He's two, which means he's pretty much constantly trying to kill himself *or* following his brother around to figure out how Connor is trying to kill himself so that he can join in!" Groaning, Claire threw her hands up. "If I could tie them to him, I absolutely would."

"They do have those leashes for kids," Jessica suggested, and the visual had all three of them laughing.

"There's your Christmas idea, Jess. Get us some leashes for the boys!"

"Wait, wait, we were talking about Lianna and David," Jessica said, leaning forward. "I have to know—"

"What were you saying about me?" David asked from behind her, and Lianna twisted in her seat to look up at him as he lifted his eyebrows at them.

"Only good things, baby," she answered, winking at him.

"Actually, I was just telling Lianna that it's basically a miracle you brought her here since you've always tried to be so mysterious and private," Jessica corrected, and Lianna turned to stare at her, eyes wide before she couldn't hold back the laugh.

"Oh, really?" David said as he stepped into the room to rest his hand on the back of her neck. He slipped his fingers under her hair to squeeze the tense muscles, massaging her neck, which had her sighing in relief.

"You don't get to act surprised, David. I've been with Tommy for years, and you're always quiet if we're around!" Claire added. "But I know you and the guys mess around and talk whenever we're out of the room or not there. I'm just glad Lianna was finally able to crack open that silent mystery man thing you've had going for so long."

"I called it brooding," Jessica said, and Claire snapped her fingers.

"Yes! Brooding, that's the right word."

"Am I brooding?" David asked, leaning over her to catch her eyes, and she tried to bite back her grin, but she failed miserably.

"Well..." Lianna tilted her head a little before she nodded. "Yeah, baby, you are, but you're very handsome when you do it."

"At least I've got that going for me," he mumbled, leaning down to press a kiss to her lips before he stood up to look at the girls. "Sorry if I've been an asshole to you guys. I'm working on it."

"Language," Claire groaned, glancing over at her kids to see if they'd heard.

"And *that* is why I tend to keep my mouth shut," David replied, and Lianna looked up at him as that lopsided smile lit up his face. He looked so... relaxed. Happy. And it was strange in the very best way.

Reaching up, she pulled his hand away from her neck to hold it. "Did you come in here because you missed me?"

"The guys are busting my ba—" He caught himself, glancing over at the kids before he continued. "They're busting *me* over hiding you from them. Apparently, Sean and Tommy have a bet right now that I hired you to pretend to be my girlfriend."

"And you want me to go and convince them otherwise?" she asked, grinning.

"I'm surprised Liam didn't get in on that action." Jessica waved an arm at Lianna, laughing. "Because she's gorgeous."

Heat took over her cheeks as the blush burned higher, and David rescued her by pulling her to her feet. He slipped his arm around her waist and said, "And that is exactly why I'm going to bring her back in there, so they shut up and I get my fifty bucks."

"Tommy can be such an idiot," Claire muttered. "He only made that bet to screw with you, David, but we should head in there anyway. See if Shannon needs any help with lunch." Claire stood up, moving over to the kids, and Jessica shooed Lianna out of the room.

"Go ahead, I'm gonna help her clean up. We'll be there in a minute."

"Okay." Glancing up at David as he led her down the short hall to the living room, she whispered, "Did they really make a bet?"

"They're idiots, so yes, they did." He paused at the end of the hall, holding onto her waist. "You doing okay?"

"The girls are really nice. Everyone has been super nice. I just wish I knew more about them." Wrapping her arms around him, she let him move her back against the wall as she tried to figure out how to ask the question on her mind. "Why... didn't you tell me that you guys grew up together?"

"I told you I'd known them since we were kids."

"That's different. Claire said they're like your brothers."

David sighed, reaching up to push a hand through his dark hair. "Yeah, they've always been that way... I just didn't recognize it."

"What do you mean?" she asked, keeping her voice quiet.

"Let's talk about it later, angel." David turned toward the living room, but she pulled him back.

"Come on, you're throwing me in the deep end here, and I can see how important Harry and his family are to you." Hooking her fingers through his belt loops, she tugged him closer. "Give me a little insight, please?"

"Harry used to pick me up and bring me here when things got bad with my dad. Like if the bills didn't get paid or there wasn't food in the house." David shrugged like the confession wasn't a big deal. "I liked hanging out with the guys, but..."

"But?" she pressed, and he looked down at her, his intense gaze narrowing for a moment before he shook his head.

"I just felt like a charity case, okay? Once I got old enough to make money on my own, I pulled away from them, and Harry. Before I started working for him again, I hadn't seen them since Liam's wedding. Before that? I think I only saw them a few times after Tommy's wedding. I haven't been a good friend to them, and I definitely haven't been like a brother in a long time." David leaned his forehead against hers, his voice almost too soft to hear. "I had a lot on my mind the last few years... specifically *you*."

"Right," she mumbled back, reaching up to cup his face so she could look into his eyes again, tracing his cheekbones with her thumbs. "But you've got me now, David. And you're definitely not a charity case anymore. So... you can be whoever you want to be with them. You can get closer if you want, but if you're just doing this for me then—"

"No." Shaking his head, he blew out a breath and gripped her hips. "I've spent a lot of time talking to Harry the last year, and he's brought up a lot of things I haven't thought about in a long time. I loved my dad, I always will, and while it may not have been the best thing for him to do, the time we spent researching and figuring out all of your father's dirty secrets, trying to find his weaknesses... that was how we connected. Both of us working to avenge my mom's death. I've spent my entire life just wanting to make him proud of me, and I was so focused on our mission that I didn't really pay attention to the bad stuff. Hell, I'm pretty sure I blocked it out. But... Harry was always there. Even after my dad stopped talking to him, he watched out for me. Kept me fed and clothed and did all the stuff my dad should have been worried about."

Clenching his jaw, David closed his eyes, and Lianna stayed quiet, her arms looped around his neck so he'd know she was listening. When he opened them again, she could tell he didn't want to talk about it, but he was. For her.

"My dad did his best, and I wish I could believe Harry that he would have accepted you, maybe even liked you eventually... but he's been gone awhile, and I'll never know what he'd have to say about the shit I've done, or about us ending up like this. But Harry's still here. He's always been here when I needed him. His entire family has, and... being here feels more like coming home than anywhere else."

Oh, wow.

"Family doesn't have to share blood, David," she whispered, trying not to push him. "Based on everything I know about Harry, everything I've seen... he loves you like a son. I mean, *everyone* here seems to care about you, to love you like family — you just have to decide if you want it."

"I know." David pulled her away from the wall and into his chest, leaning down to bury his face in her hair, and she just held on, waiting for him to work through whatever was going on in his head. It seemed to take a few minutes, but eventually he spoke again, quietly, just loud enough for her to hear. "Wanting this... wanting to be a part of this family... it feels like even more of a betrayal than wanting you."

"This isn't a betrayal." Leaning back, she waited for him to look her in the eye so he could see that she meant it. "You got your revenge, David. My father's company is destroyed. He's *dead*. Marc is dead too, and even though we might never know how much of that shit he was involved in, it doesn't matter, because he's gone. And the Faures are headed in a new direction under Rémi. You didn't just fulfill your dad's plan, you exceeded it. You told me that you guys never even expected to take on the Faure family, but *we* did. We exposed the corruption that was still there. And if you don't think your dad would be proud of that, then what the fuck would he have wanted from you?"

"I don't know," David answered quietly, and she sighed, biting back her frustration.

"That's because there isn't anything else, baby. It's done. All of it." Lifting onto her toes, she kissed him, holding it for a moment so he'd understand how much she loved him, and that she wasn't going anywhere. "You made your dad proud, and he would want you to be happy. He'd want you to stay connected to the man that was his best friend for God knows how long. There's a reason Harry was in your life, and it's because your dad let him in. He let him be that close to you, he made Harry a part of the family you two had together, and your dad may be gone, but you still have Harry. And now you have a chance to make Harry proud of you too."

"Dammit, angel," he whispered, voice rough as he pulled her back into the kiss, pressing her against the wall again as he slowly took control of every movement, every careful brush of lips, every flick of tongue and nip of teeth. It wasn't rushed, wasn't possessive or dominating in the way it usually was... this was different. A whole new kind of intimate that had nothing to do with sex. It was just about the two of them, and even though every kiss from David sent a thrill through her blood, heating her skin everywhere he touched, in that moment she didn't want or need anything more.

It was perfect.

"Come on, man, my kids are here!" One of the McConnell brothers shouted, groaning just as another started laughing, and someone whistled. They broke apart, and she felt distinctly like she'd been caught doing something terribly wrong.

"Shove it, Tommy," David said, flipping him off, which only made the man laugh harder.

"Was this how you planned to win the bet?" Another McConnell asked, grinning. "Make out with her in the hallway until someone walks by to 'catch you?'" he asked, holding up air quotes before he nudged his brother.

"You didn't even join the bet, Liam," the younger one added, and she finally remembered his name was Sean.

Tommy. Liam. Sean.

"Wait, wait, we gotta settle this," Tommy said, holding his hands up to quiet his brothers. "Lianna, just tell us the truth. Did David pay you an extremely large amount of money to come here today and pretend to be with him?"

"If I didn't love him so much, there wouldn't be enough money on the planet for me to put up with his shit," she answered, and for a moment all four men had looks of surprise until they exploded with laughter, coming forward to slap David on the back as he started laughing too, giving her a look over Liam's shoulder.

When he mouthed, *'you will pay for that later,'* she just grinned and followed the men into the living room.

"I like her," Sean said.

"Finally, someone else to put David in his place. We've been handling that shit solo for a long time," Liam added, and then Jessica walked in behind him, immediately reaching up to smack the back of his head.

"Language, jackass. The kids are coming."

"You just cursed!" Liam argued, grabbing his wife by the hips to drag her back to him when she tried to move past. She started laughing, squirming in his arms, and Lianna wondered what exactly Liam had done to get that reaction.

Maybe David isn't so different from them after all.

"I am not changing the next diaper," Claire announced as she walked in behind Connor, who ran for his dad at top speed. Tommy grabbed him from the floor, immediately flipping the toddler upside down and making him squeal with delight as Claire bounced Dylan on her hip. "I swear, if you drop him, I'm going to tell him when he's older."

"I've never dropped him," Tommy argued, righting his son before he set him on the floor and nudged him toward David. "Go say hi to Uncle David."

To Lianna's surprise, David actually leaned down to talk to the toddler, which looked ridiculous and cute all at once. He was so big, so muscular, and the girls had been right that he'd always had the whole tall, dark, and brooding thing down — but the way he talked to Connor made him look anything but scary.

"You two finish your make-out session?" Claire asked under her breath, and Lianna turned to look at her, knowing she had to be bright red. "Don't worry about it. I just went upstairs to clean the boys up and give you guys some privacy."

"That... is mortifying."

"Nah. When we open the wine later, ask me to tell you about Shannon walking in on Tommy and me when we lived here for a bit." Rolling her eyes, Claire laughed quietly. "*That* was mortifying."

"Everyone needs to wash up!" Shannon called from the kitchen, and Lianna waited for her turn to wash her hands in the sink before returning to sit next to David on the couch so she could pretend to watch the football game.

The way the McConnells, and David, reacted to the game was way more entertaining. They argued over the ref's calls, made stupid bets about different plays or who would catch the ball, and Jessica was right there next to Liam shouting at different players. During a lull, David leaned over and whispered, "I love you, angel."

She smiled, leaning down to kiss him, but the second their lips touched the brothers started shouting.

"Ohhhh! Look at that!"

"My kid is sitting over there!"

"Get it, David!"

Rolling her eyes, she sat up straight and called back, "If you're jealous, go kiss your wives!"

"I can do that," Liam said, grabbing Jessica and kissing her hard even though she started laughing.

"Who is Sean gonna kiss though?" Tommy asked. "Oh, wait, I know. *Mom!*"

"Shut up!" Sean growled, shoving his brother.

"Leave Sean alone," Shannon called from the kitchen table where she was enjoying a glass of wine. "He's going to find the perfect girl for him when the time is right."

"Aww, Mommy to the rescue," Liam said, and Sean flipped him off.

Everyone's laughter morphed into cheers as Harry finally came inside holding a tray of steaks along with a few hot dogs for the kids. Raising it high, Harry tilted his head to the table. "Come on, better get it while it's hot!"

Shannon directed everyone to their seats while Jessica helped her get the dishes out of the oven and onto the table. Beers were distributed, and Lianna was grateful for her glass of wine.

Just as everyone got settled, Harry stood up, holding his beer in the air. "I know we're all hungry, but I want to welcome David and Lianna to the first of *many* Sunday lunches that they'll be joining us for." Glancing at David, Harry lowered his voice. "Not getting out of it now, boy."

"Cheers!" everyone shouted, clinking glasses and bottles, and Lianna felt like she was glowing when Shannon winked at her just before their wine glasses touched.

"Okay, now——"

"Wait, wait," Liam said, standing up as he cut his dad off. "I've got an announcement as well."

"Go on then, we're hungry!" Sean yelled.

"Shut up, Sean." Grabbing his wife's hand, Liam raised his beer with a wide grin and said, "Since we're all here this weekend, Jess and I wanted to announce that we are expecting another little McConnell in May!"

"About time you start catching up. I'm already two ahead!" Tommy called out.

"This is *not* a competition," Jessica shouted, shaking her head, and Claire burst out laughing.

"I am so happy for you both!" Shannon covered her mouth, standing up to come around the table and hug Jessica. "I just want a girl. *Please* have a girl!"

"Mom! You'll love the baby no matter what," Liam replied, and Shannon waved a hand at him.

"Of course I will, but please give me a girl. I've been outnumbered by you boys my entire life!" Laughing, she turned to hug Liam, and Harry stepped in to hug them as well, a round of congratulations flooding across the table before everyone returned to their seats.

Tommy reached across his wife to shove David's shoulder, his grin wide. "What about you two? When are you getting married and having some kids?"

Flipping him off, David laughed and gave a quick shrug. "We'll get around to it."

"We will?" Lianna asked, stunned, and he turned to look at her. Still so hot. Still tall, with his tawny brown eyes and his dark hair... but he wasn't brooding. He almost looked bright, like he was glowing from the inside out, that inner light showing in his grin even as it turned wicked.

"Eventually," he answered. "I'm having more fun practicing right now." Leaning over, he pulled her into a kiss, and she couldn't hide the smile as the boys started whistling, harassing them both for the public display of affection and for David's dirty comment, but mostly... everyone was just overjoyed for them. For each other. For the whole family.

And they were a part of it. She didn't know the McConnells very well yet, but she could feel the love. It was the same kind of love she'd felt when her cousins had accepted her, when Jean-Luc and Cécile had welcomed her into their home — and, blood or not, the McConnells were her family now too, because they were David's.

When they finally separated, he reached over to squeeze her thigh, and she knew there'd be plenty of fun to be had that night. For now, they returned their focus to filling their plates and listening to everyone catching up, sharing stories, teasing each other like a real family.

As Lianna watched them, she was overwhelmed by how completely whole she suddenly felt. There was still sadness mixed in with all the joy, but she felt *loved*. Not just by David, but by the McConnells here, and by her cousins in France. In less than a year, she'd lost everything, reached the lowest and darkest point in her life, suffered and struggled... and somehow, by some kind of miracle, she'd managed to come out the other side of tragedy with a life more full than she'd ever expected.

Not just one family that cared about her, but two.

And a man that would happily burn down the world for her, as long as he got to fuck her until it hurt amid the ashes.

She'd always said that she and David were two sides of the same coin, one dark and one light, but she didn't think that was true anymore. They still had their dark side, but they weren't on opposite sides of the coin anymore.

Now they were both in the light, both loved, both discovering their place in the world... and their future had never looked brighter.

THE END

Keep reading for a note from Jennifer Bene.

Hello lovelies,

It's taken a long time (much longer than I ever meant) for us to get to the end of David and Lianna's story. I'm sorry for making you wait so long, but I do hope you loved getting to walk the path of redemption with them, and all of the other characters.

There was one scene in this book that I wanted to include, but it wasn't possible to fit it in with the flow of the actual story, so I've included it as a bonus after this note.

So, if you want to know what happened with Jean-Luc… all you have to do is turn the page.

- Jennifer Bene

Jean-Luc

Shifting the SUV into park, Jean-Luc reached into the cup holder to check his phone again. It seemed to be all he did, but whenever his mind went quiet, it always returned to Lianna's anger, the things she'd shouted at him before she left — and her continuous silence since.

He shouldn't have been surprised that there were no missed calls, Marc's home was only a twenty-minute drive from his own, and he'd checked the phone before he left. Still, there was that ever-present tug at the back of his mind that once she'd calmed down, she would take the time to listen to his apologies. He just had to be patient, give her space, and hope that in time she would see why he'd taken action against David. All he'd wanted to do was keep her safe, but he'd crossed a line. It didn't matter that her decisions made no sense to him, or that the bastard didn't deserve to touch her again... she'd chosen him.

Smiling bitterly, Jean-Luc turned off the car and got out, tucking the phone in his pocket as he looked out over the vineyard on his brother's property. The view was beautiful, but in his mind all he could see was David standing in front of his desk, so full of rage as he'd whispered, '*She's going to hate you if you do this.*' To his surprise, the monster had been right, and the error had cost him all of the trust he'd worked so hard to earn from his lost niece.

However, there was plenty of blame to go around for the situation he found himself in.

Of course, David bore the brunt of it for his vile, abhorrent actions against Lianna... but he wasn't alone. Alain had spent years isolating her out of some kind of petty spite, refusing to even acknowledge the family waiting for them both. Joseph Blanc had failed to be honest with him about Alain's business dealings on more than one occasion and had almost failed to protect Lianna — it was David who blocked Alain's bullet — but Joseph had put Alain down when it was clear he was too far gone.

And then there was him.

He could have pushed harder, could have insisted that Alain bring Lianna home... but he'd been more concerned with pushing Alain away than pulling Lianna closer. If he'd reached out earlier, if he'd welcomed her into the family despite her father's arguments, perhaps David would have never got his hands on her.

So many things could have been different if he had only acted.

And he wasn't going to make that mistake again.

One of the last things Lianna had said to him was about seeing Marc at her father's home in New York. She had felt so betrayed, had called him a liar, and he'd seen Alain's rage in her then. The walls had come down between them just like they had when he'd refused Alain's requests when they were both so much younger. But if he could get her answers, if he could explain why Marc had visited Alain... there was a chance he could repair with Lianna what he was never able to mend with his youngest brother.

"Jean-Luc!" Marc called out, raising a hand as he walked across the gravel drive. "I apologize that I've been so busy, I know you've wanted to talk."

"Yes. I wanted to speak with you about Lianna, but you've been surprisingly difficult to reach."

Shrugging a shoulder, Marc laid a hand on his back and turned him toward the vineyard. "I am sorry for that, but you're here now. Let's talk about our niece's behavior."

"So, you have heard that she left?" Jean-Luc asked, turning to watch his brother's face as they moved down one of the paths between the vines.

"Our children text at the speed of light," Marc replied, chuckling softly. "It seems our American niece left in quite a dramatic way?"

"She was upset with me because I sent David home." Tucking his hands into his slacks, he debated sharing the reasoning behind it, but decided that would only damage his relationship with her further in the future. He'd already mentioned too much of it to Rémi.

"Should I ask why?"

"It's unimportant now. I upset her though, betrayed her trust, and so… when she left, she was very upset with me." Shading his eyes, he scanned the vineyard, taking in the rolling hills that led to the lavender planted in the distance.

"That is unfortunate, Jean-Luc. It would have been nice to have her join the family."

"Do you really think so?" he asked, pausing their walk to face his brother. "She was here for several days, and despite countless calls... you couldn't be bothered to even arrive to her birthday party on time. Then when I planned a family lunch for you to get to know her better, you sent your family ahead alone. Without you."

"I was busy, Jean-Luc, and—"

"I don't want to hear your excuses," Jean-Luc cut him off calmly, waving a hand as he continued the walk, needing to burn off the building frustration.

"What do you want me to say, Jean-Luc?"

"The truth, Marc," he answered, stopping once more. "I would prefer if you were honest with me about your opinion of our niece. Can you do that?"

Sighing, Marc planted his hands on his hips and looked across the vines before eventually bringing his gaze back. "I think that if you weren't carrying so much guilt for abandoning Alain, that you would have never looked for her. That girl wasn't raised in this family. She didn't even know we existed, and you went and fetched her like an abandoned pet. Did you really think she would understand our world? That she could somehow become a Faure?"

"She *is* a Faure. Our blood runs in her veins, and—"

"She is not a Faure!" Marc snapped, pulling a breath in through his nose before blowing it out slowly, speaking much more calmly when he continued, even though his words were anything but comforting. "I mean that she's not like our children, she doesn't know this family, or its history, and she doesn't belong here."

Jean-Luc had known there was something off with Marc during Lianna's visit, but he had wanted it to be anything else. Another affair, another gambling debt that he would have to clean up so that Marc's wife remained ignorant of her husband's failings. He'd wanted his brother's avoidance of Lianna to be anything but this. Disliking her for Alain's mistakes, for being born away from their home, under a different name — none of which the girl could have controlled.

"Why, Marc?" he asked, shaking his head slowly. "Why would it matter what name she carries, or what our brother's decisions changed about where she was born and what she knew?"

"It means everything, Jean-Luc. Our family cannot take in every stray you find, every by-blow that carries a shred of our blood."

"So, it's about money?" His disappointment only grew the more his brother spoke, and he hesitated to push any further, but stepping cautiously around his brothers' feelings had only failed him in the past. "You pushed her away, ignored her, insulted her with your absence... because you didn't want her to receive a share of whatever inheritance comes after we're both dead and gone?"

"You have four children. Two grandchildren already. Do you really want to risk their futures over this accidental Faure?" Marc was saying such terrible things with more sincerity than he'd heard him speak in a long time, and he felt it like a pain in his chest.

"You think Alain's only child, the only bit of him we have left to us... was an accident?"

"Be rational, Jean-Luc. If Alain had seen her as his child, he would have brought her home. This isn't my opinion, it is our brother's, and you're just refusing to honor it." Marc scoffed, turning away from him to walk a few steps ahead.

"And how do you know that, Marc? I could barely get our brother to return a phone call when we needed to move money around, but you're confident that you know what Alain thought of his only daughter?"

"He made it clear with his actions."

"With his actions or his words, Marc?" Jean-Luc tried to control his anger, but it was difficult as he wrapped his fingers into a tight fist at his side. "Did you go see Alain in New York, Marc? Did you visit him and discuss his opinions of Lianna, or were you discussing other things?"

"You know that Alain refused to see either of us after——"

"Do not lie to me, Marc. I have kept you out of harm's way too many times for you to lie to me. Lianna said she saw you in her father's home, and yet when you arrived at the party you pretended you'd never seen her before. Then you did nothing but avoid her while she was here, and while at first I thought she was mistaken... it seems more likely that you didn't want to risk her remembering the first time you met."

"You're being ridiculous." Marc didn't seem offended by the accusation... which told Jean-Luc all he needed to know.

Closing the space between them, he grabbed onto his brother's arm to shake him. "It's true, isn't it? You were there with Alain. How many times did you go to see him, Marc? How many of your trips to the states were actually trips to visit our brother?"

"Let go of me, Jean-Luc," Marc growled, ripping his arm free. "You want the truth, brother? You're an *idiot*. You've always been an idiot. Too naïve, too weak. Our own father saw the failure in you, but he was too tied to tradition to make the *right* choice for this family. He let you take over, knowing you would lead us to disaster with your idealistic beliefs, and you would have already brought us to the brink of disaster without my help."

"What help is that? The debts we've had to cover for your gambling habits? The payoffs we've had to make to your mistresses? Which of your contributions to this family have pulled us back from disaster?"

"You are driving the Faure name into the ground! Letting profitable lines of business go to satisfy your moral code is pointless, there will always be someone waiting in our shadow to take our place. You're not improving the world with your crusade. You're only destroying your family. Your *blood*." Shaking his head, Marc stepped back from him, a look of disgust on his face. "We couldn't let you do that. The Faure name carried power when we were young, it was enough to make anyone who tried to step into our path fear our retribution, but you've done everything you could to ruin that. We had to protect the family, the Faure name, by not giving up what our family has worked for generations to accomplish. *That* is what Alain and I met about, because he felt the same way."

"So, this is the truth. You are a traitor." Jean-Luc felt sick as he realized his brothers had worked against him every step of the way. "You call me naïve, Marc, but it's you and

Alain who have been naïve. Do you really think that this life is sustainable? The police, the governments, everyone is moving forward, advancing, and it's only a matter of time until they track things back to us, to our children. You're accusing me of putting our family at risk when everything I've done, every choice I've made, has been to save this family. To protect our future. Leaving those things behind, no matter the profit we could make in the short term, no matter who takes it over, *that* is what will keep our family together. We have plenty of business in more legitimate lanes, less targeted lanes. We will be fine."

"No, we won't!" Marc shouted. "Alain was right. We should have stopped you when we were young. You never should have taken over this family, and now you're trying so hard to create this idyllic family life, gathering the abandoned and lost from across the world just so you can feel good as you sit across from them at the dinner table — but soon enough there will be nothing left. You'll drain this family dry with your ridiculous crusade."

The words were a slap in the face. His brother, *both* of his brothers hated him. Marc had never supported his moves to change the family, he'd merely taken the information to Alain so they could subvert every decision. Swallowing the betrayal and the hurt and the anger, he tugged his suit jacket down and looked Marc in the eye. "Well, Alain is gone, and whatever network you built died with him. So, it seems it's a good thing I'm in charge, and that I'm teaching Rémi how to lead this family in the right direction."

"You've always been weak," Marc shouted at him, but he turned away from the man he'd called brother for over fifty years.

Lianna was right, about more than she even knew, and he'd make sure she knew the truth, she deserved that.

"You never deserved to carry our father's name, never deserved to be called Faure!" Marc continued to shout, his rage clear. "You are a weak, pathetic fool, but your son doesn't have to be."

"What?" He stopped, spinning to face his brother, not believing that Marc would threaten his son — and then he saw the gun and pain punched him in the chest, knocking him back and down. When he hit the ground he was confused, trying to get up, but there was a ringing in his ears, and he couldn't get a full breath. There was something in his mouth, choking him, making him cough as Marc stepped up beside him. Wiping at his mouth, his hand came away red, and he dropped his palm onto his chest, patting until he found wet and a stab of pain forced him to cough out more blood.

He'd shot him.

Marc shot him. His own brother.

Ignoring the pain, he pulled air in anyway, just so he could look into Marc's eyes and ask, "Why?"

"Because you're weak, and I won't let you tear down what our family has spent generations building. You won't destroy us, and I'll make sure Rémi does the right thing for all of us." Crouching down, Marc touched him on the shoulder. "Don't worry about him, Jean-Luc, I'll guide him. I'll take care of all our children."

No. He tried to say the word, but it wouldn't come out. It was getting harder to breathe, and the pain was too much. Black was starting to splotch his vision and he knew that wouldn't be getting up from the ground. Marc wouldn't let him, even if he could figure out how to draw another breath.

When Marc stood, he could see the sky, and it seemed too beautiful to die under. Days like this didn't end in tragedy, they ended with a meal on the terrace, with his children laughing and talking, with Cécile's hand in his while they watched the sun go down together.

But he wouldn't be on the terrace with them this evening.

He wouldn't be able to hold his grandchildren again or wrap his arms around his children that had grown so tall and so independent as they became their own unique people.

He'd never get to bring Lianna back to them, to make sure she wasn't alone, to make sure she felt loved.

Worst of all, he'd never again get to listen to Cécile fall asleep in his arms, or slip into sleep listening to her soft, even breaths... and she'd never kiss him awake again.

Another gunshot pushed back the black for a moment and he forced his eyes open to see Marc holding onto his arm, face a mask of pain. His brother had betrayed him, and everyone he loved was in danger... and he couldn't do a thing about it.

He just had to trust that Rémi would see what he had been blind to, that his son would stand strong, that he would rise and take his place, following the lessons he'd taught him — even though there was so much more he'd hoped to teach him. He'd wanted to give him advice on dealing with teenagers, he'd wanted to walk his daughters down the aisle, to see his future grandchildren, to see his own children's faces reflected in the next generation.

He'd wanted to grow old digging holes for Cécile to plant her flowers in, and then he'd wanted to go before she did, so he'd never have to spend a day without her. But he wasn't ready yet.

Not now.

There was still so much life left to live.

About the Author

Jennifer Bene is a *USA Today* bestselling author of dangerously sexy and deviously dark romance. From BDSM, to Suspense, Dark Romance, and Thrillers—she writes it all. Always delivering a twisty, spine-tingling journey with the promise of a happily-ever-after.

Don't miss a release! Sign up for the newsletter to get new book alerts (and a free welcome book) at: http://jenniferbene.com/newsletter

You can find her online throughout social media with username @jbeneauthor and on her website: www.jenniferbene.com

Also by Jennifer Bene

The Thalia Series (Dark Romance)

Security Binds Her *(Thalia Book 1)*

Striking a Balance *(Thalia Book 2)*

Salvaged by Love *(Thalia Book 3)*

Tying the Knot *(Thalia Book 4)*

The Thalia Series: The Complete Collection

The Beth Series (Dark Romance)

Breaking Beth *(Beth Book 1)*

Fragile Ties Series (Dark Romance)

Destruction *(Fragile Ties Book 1)*

Inheritance *(Fragile Ties Book 2)*

Redemption *(Fragile Ties Book 3)*

Dangerous Games Series (Dark Mafia Romance)

Early Sins *(A Dangerous Games Prequel)*

Lethal Sin *(Dangerous Games Book 1)*

Standalone Dark Romance

Imperfect Monster

Corrupt Desires

Deviant Attraction: A Dark and Dirty Collection

Reign of Ruin

Mesmer

Jasmine

Crazy Broken Love

Standalone BDSM Ménage Romance

The Invitation

Reunited

Standalone Suspense / Horror

Burned: An Inferno World Novella

Scorched: A New Beginning

Appearances in the Black Light Series (BDSM Romance)

Black Light: Exposed *(Black Light Series Book 2)*

Black Light: Valentine Roulette *(Black Light Series Book 3)*

Black Light: Roulette Redux *(Black Light Series Book 7)*

Black Light: Celebrity Roulette *(Black Light Series Book 12)*

Black Light: Charmed *(Black Light Series Book 15)*

Black Light: Roulette War *(Black Light Series Book 16)*

Black Light: The Beginning *(Black Light Series Book 17.5)*

BOOKS RELEASED AS CASSANDRA FAYE

Daughters of Eltera Series (Dark Fantasy Romance)

Fae *(Daughters of Eltera Book 1)*

Tara *(Daughters of Eltera Book 2)*

Standalone Paranormal Romance

Hunted *(The Dirty Heroes Collection Book 13)*

One Crazy Bite

Dangerous Magic

Made in the USA
Monee, IL
26 July 2020

37063027R00192